## It was a kiss to die for...

Teri's eyes fluttered shut as Jack groaned and stood up, pulling her with him. He was sure he'd died and gone to heaven.

It took Jack a moment to realize Teri had gone absolutely limp in his arms. He pulled back and stared at her still face, her kiss-swollen lips slightly parted.

He grinned and kissed her lightly on the nose. "Hey, my kisses aren't that lethal. Or did you just doze off?" he teased.

There was no response. Jack's smile fell away. "You really did pass out," he muttered, lowering her carefully to the floor. "I guess that's what happens when frail little beauties like yourself skip meals to chase deals."

Just looking at her, he could tell something was terribly wrong. Trying not to panic, Jack checked for a pulse at the base of her throat. Nothing. Desperate, he pressed his ear against her chest. Absolutely nothing!

Reality hit him full force and he jumped into action. It had been his kiss that had taken her breath away. Surely he could give it back to her now....

Dear Reader,

Have you ever wished you had a second chance at a once-in-a-lifetime opportunity? A chance to make another decision, to take a different path?

No doubt we all have. And now American Romance introduces you to four women who actually get that unique opportunity—whether it's to marry the one that got away or to have children or to follow an exciting career—in MAYBE THIS TIME.

Emily Dalton continues this original quartet with a story of a special woman who gets a second chance at life itself and of the man and boy who are her destiny.

Don't miss any of the MAYBE THIS TIME books— for stories that will touch a spot in every woman's heart!

Regards,

Debra Matteucci
Senior Editor & Editorial Coordinator
Harlequin Books
300 East 42nd Street
New York, NY 10017

# Emily Dalton

## HEAVEN CAN WAIT

## *Harlequin Books*

TORONTO • NEW YORK • LONDON
AMSTERDAM • PARIS • SYDNEY • HAMBURG
STOCKHOLM • ATHENS • TOKYO • MILAN
MADRID • WARSAW • BUDAPEST • AUCKLAND

To two of my favorite parents,
Guy and Deloris Johnson.
Thanks for a golden year in Sunny
California and my own bedroom.

ISBN 0-373-16650-8

HEAVEN CAN WAIT

Copyright © 1996 Danice Jo Allen.

# Chapter One

It was raining cats and dogs. Or in this part of southern Louisiana, on a rural road somewhere between the Mighty Mississippi and acres of cypress swamps, with the wind gusting to seventy miles an hour, it could even be raining snakes and alligators. But despite the storm and the fact that it was already nearing ten o'clock at night and was pitch-black outside, Teri was determined to get to Oak Meadows.

Once she got the old gentleman, Beauregard Tremain, to sign the final papers, Teri would make one of the fattest sales commissions that year, ensuring her place in the New Orleans Five-Million-Dollar Club for Realtors. And it was only October 28! She had two months left in the year to make more sales and firmly establish herself as top agent at Sugarbaker Realtors.

There was a flash of lightning, and a deafening clap of thunder sounded directly overhead. A rush of wind pelted the windshield with huge drops of muddy rainwater, and Teri's Lincoln Continental veered to the right, edging the shoulder and coming dangerously close to the rail that separated swamp from road.

"I'm going to be just fine," Teri told herself with forced calmness as she gripped the steering wheel. It was a good thing she drove this tank to cart around clients. A sports car would have been blown off the road by now, she thought smugly. Besides, she was almost there. This sale was much too important to put off signing the papers till tomorrow.

And Beauregard Tremain might change his mind again. He'd been vacillating for two weeks and Teri had finally gotten a firm promise from him that he'd made up his mind for good. He'd put off making the decision because he'd been hoping to hear from his photojournalist son, who was assigned to the latest political hot spot in Eastern Europe. He wanted to confer with him about the sale of Oak Meadows, a stately mansion that had been in the Tremain family since before the Civil War.

But Teri was frankly glad Mr. Tremain had been unable to reach his son for a phone conference. She doubted that Jackson Tremain, nicknamed Stonewall, had changed any since high school, and he might throw a wrench in the machinery just to spite her.

Both graduates of Riverbend High ten years ago, Teri and Jack had always been on opposite sides of everything—from debate teams to school politics to who should be voted prom queen. He'd wanted his steady girlfriend to win. Not only had they both been as stubborn as mules about their opinions, but they'd also been highly competitive.

Rivalry aside, Jack might feel a genuine attachment to Oak Meadows, though you'd never guess it by the amount of time he spent there. But he still might think the estate ought to remain in the family, as it had for nearly a century and a half. Jack could be very persuasive and he just might spout some sentimental claptrap and talk his dad out of selling, thereby causing Teri to lose her hefty commission.

What right did Jack have to argue against his dad's decision anyway? He was never around to help out. In fact, since his wife's death nearly two years ago, he'd even added to his seventy-year-old father's responsibilities by leaving his four-year-old son at Oak Meadows while he made a name for himself in the world of journalism. He'd even won a Pulitzer prize.

Teri was relieved when she finally saw the signpost that indicated the private road leading to the fancy wrought-iron gates of the Oak Meadows estate. She turned right between two massive, moss-covered oak trees and crossed a wooden bridge that seemed to sway in the wind. Teri was uncomfortably aware that the old bridge traversed a stretch of bayou that was infested with all sorts of creepy-crawlies.

Five minutes later, she stopped the car on the circular drive in front of the house, as close to the porch steps as possible. She sat there for a minute as the wind rocked the car and rain pummeled the windshield and streamed down the glass.

She was surprised to note that her hands were shaking, but the drive had been pretty hairy and she hadn't taken the time to eat since an eight o'clock breakfast with a client, consisting of half a sweet roll and three cups of coffee. And all the coffee she'd drank since then probably didn't help matters.

Her doctor had warned her that her frequent bouts with an irregular heart rhythm had to do with her poor dietary habits and stressful life-style. He'd told her that if she didn't change her ways, she might have to be put on medication temporarily, but Teri didn't think she *could* change. Type A personalities ran in the family. Besides, she was too busy to even try.

Teri got out of the car and made a dash for the large, sheltered porch. She rang the doorbell, managing to get only slightly blasted by the driving rain. Mr. Tremain didn't know she was coming because she'd been at an Open House when she'd received word that he was ready to sign, and when she'd tried to call him on her cellular phone, interference from the storm kept the call from going through.

When the door finally opened, Mr. Tremain stood there in his robe with his mouth gaping for a few moments, then his ingrained Southern hospitality kicked in.

"Miss Taylor! What are you doing out on a night like this? Come in! Come in!"

Mr. Tremain ushered Teri inside and straight to a cozy library off the main hall. Teri had been afraid he'd lead her into this particular room, which, unfortunately, seemed to be his favorite. Every time she entered the antique-filled room, she was faced with a huge oval painting of the original owners of the mansion that hung over the ornate marble mantel.

Although Teri wasn't the slightest bit superstitious and certainly didn't believe in ghosts, somehow she always felt that this room belonged to the past . . . and to the people in the portrait—Stephen, Caroline and their son, five-year-old Samuel Tremain.

That she was selling the house away from the Tremain line didn't make Teri any more eager to face that formal family portrait showing a dark, broodingly handsome man in a Confederate uniform, standing behind his seated wife—her gown full and fluffed around her, her blond hair shining like a halo—their little boy on a velvet stool at her feet, wearing short pants and with a satin bow at his throat, leaning on her knee and clutching a stuffed bear.

To make matters worse, the portrait had been painted outside, with Oak Meadows as the backdrop. The stately white mansion with its classic Doric columns seemed as much an integral part of the family as any of the human subjects in the painting.

Whenever she showed the house, people who noticed the portrait would almost always comment to her or to Mr. Tremain that the founding family appeared blissfully happy, but Teri's impression of them was quite different. She always got the creepiest feeling that the lifelike painted eyes watched her with suspicion and disapproval.

Tonight there was a fire burning and the room was softly lit by Victorian-style hurricane lamps, one by a chair near the fire and the other at the end of a Queen Anne sofa. The portrait was partially obscured by shadows, which made it a little easier to avoid staring at. But not much.

"Take my seat, Miss Taylor," her kindly old host insisted, gently urging her along toward the overstuffed chair. "It's the snuggest place in the house right now. Sit down and warm yourself while I change into something more appropriate for company."

"No, Mr. Tremain, please don't bother," Teri protested, but she knew he wouldn't listen. A Southern gentleman simply didn't entertain females in his robe and pajamas.

"I'll be back in a jiffy," he assured her with a smile, then disappeared into the hall.

Teri eased back into the chair, absorbing the warmth Mr. Tremain had left behind in the cushions. Her eyes drifted shut in an involuntary reaction to the security and comfort suddenly surrounding her after such a dreadful drive up from the city. But her eyes abruptly flew open when an earsplitting clap of thunder shook the house.

The lamps blinked off and on and the fire danced maniacally as the wind whooshed down the flue. The house creaked and groaned and a loose shutter banged with an uneven rhythm against an outside wall. She could almost feel the painted eyes of the Tremains staring down at her, but she determinedly refused to stare back.

Despite everything, Teri was still glad she'd come. Nothing was more important to her than a big sale. Her career was everything.

"Sorry to keep you waiting, Miss Taylor," Mr. Tremain apologized as he reentered the room, fully decked out in slacks, string tie and sport coat. "But I thought I'd better check on little Samuel, just in case the thunder disturbed him. But he's sleeping like an angel."

Mr. Tremain was a handsome man, with a full head of silver hair he wore in a fifties-style pompadour with long sideburns. Everything else about him implied conservatism and Southern gentility, but his hair screamed Elvis.

"Tea, Miss Taylor?" he offered. "Or perhaps a bit of sherry?"

"No, thank you, Mr. Tremain," Teri said, briskly snapping open her briefcase and pulling out a manila folder full of papers. "I'd better head back to town as soon as possible."

Mr. Tremain sat down on the sofa and frowned at her. "Don't tell me you came all the way out here just so I could sign those papers? I planned to drive into the office tomorrow."

"Well, I saved you the trip, didn't I?" Teri replied.

"And risked your neck doing it," he scolded, his eyebrows lowering over his pale green eyes. "No real-estate deal is worth putting yourself in danger."

Another clap of thunder and the flickering of lights punctuated his words, but Teri didn't agree. This real-estate deal—and a lot of others she could recall off-hand—was worth any amount of discomfort and danger it took to get it finalized. "I wasn't in any real danger, Mr. Tremain," she insisted.

"Your family will be worried about your being out on a night like this," he added, continuing to pursue the subject despite Teri's attempt to shrug off his concern.

"There's no one to worry about me," she assured him with a bright but perfunctory smile. "My folks live in California and I'm not married. I don't even have a cat waiting up for me." She forced a laugh. "Any pet I'd have would starve to death because I'd never be home to feed it. I even kill houseplants."

Mr. Tremain just scowled at her. "I believe you were afraid I'd back out on the deal," he finally observed with a keen look. "But I gave my word, Miss Taylor, and an honorable man's word is as good as gold."

"I'm glad to hear that, sir," Teri replied, but she wouldn't stop feeling edgy until he put pen to paper and the ink was dry. "But since I'm here, you might as well sign the contract tonight. Then I can call Mr. Schofield's broker and tell him it's a positive go. As you know, Schofield's already put down the earnest money and made you an extremely lucrative offer in writing. He's very eager to hear your decision."

Mr. Tremain stood up and began pacing the braided rug in front of the fire. "He's offering a hell of a lot of money, all right, but I'd feel better if I could meet this Schofield fellow in person. He hasn't even seen the house. He does everything through that mealymouthed broker of his."

Teri shrugged. "Schofield's a busy man, and he apparently has implicit faith in his broker."

"The broker mentioned that Schofield wasn't planning to live here, but was going to turn Oak Meadows into a 'commercial venture.' I suppose he means a bed and breakfast. Bah! The blasted things are turning up all over the place," he grumbled. "Oak Meadows has always been a home, not a hotel."

Teri inwardly groaned. She'd hoped he wouldn't get all sentimental again, lamenting the fact that his home wasn't being sold to a family but to a businessman. It was a good thing he didn't know Schofield's real plans for Oak Meadows, which were far more crass and commercial than a bed and breakfast. If Mr. Tremain knew the truth, Teri doubted that he could be induced to sell Oak Meadows to Schofield even at three times the money offered. *Well,* Teri rationalized as she suppressed a twinge of guilt, *I'm certainly not obligated to reveal a buyer's plans for property he's purchasing.*

"Haven't you occasionally taken in overnight guests, Mr. Tremain?" she countered.

"Only once in a while, when there's been a need either on my side or theirs. But I'm mighty particular about whom I offer hospitality to."

"That's wise," Teri murmured politely as she stood to place the papers on a coffee table in front of the sofa. Then she uncapped her ballpoint pen and boldly offered it to Mr. Tremain.

Mr. Tremain stopped pacing and stared distastefully at the proffered pen. "Once I sign those papers, there's no turning back, is there?"

"As the buyer, Schofield can change his mind, give up his earnest money and back out. But as the seller, you could possibly be sued if you renege, Mr. Tremain." Teri was legally bound to explain this, but she was hoping desperately that he wouldn't let the finality of what he was about to do discourage him from signing. The sale of Oak Meadows would be a huge feather in her professional cap.

"Well, I see no other solution to my problem," Mr. Tremain said resignedly, more to himself than Teri. "I wanted to talk to Jack first, explain why this is necessary, but it's harder to get ahold of that boy than it is to get an audience with the Pope." He sighed deeply and took the pen, stooped over the table and signed his name with a flourish.

Just as he dotted the last *i,* there was a long, blinding flash of lightning that lit up the room as brightly as midday. Under those circumstances, Teri couldn't ignore the portrait any longer. Sure enough, when she looked up at *them,* she couldn't help but imagine them glaring down at *her* . . . looking none too pleased.

What followed was the loudest roar of thunder Teri had ever heard . . . then the lights went out.

"Hell's bells," Mr. Tremain muttered under his breath. "I hope that's not some kind of sign that I've made a big mistake," he joked weakly.

By the orange glow of the fire, Teri glanced briefly at the treasured signature, then stashed the papers in her briefcase with a sigh of relief and triumph.

Mr. Tremain walked to the mantel and reached for two thick candles. He lit both and handed one of them to Teri. "I'd better make sure Sam's got a flashlight in case he wakes up and things look a little too dark to 'im."

Teri nodded. "And I'd better go." She had turned away from the portrait, but the hairs on the back of her neck were standing up like porcupine quills . . . as if *they* were still watching.

"No, don't go. Not yet," Mr. Tremain urged her. "I'll be back in a minute."

Teri nodded again, but now that the papers were signed, she was anxious to get the heck out of there. She felt like a criminal trying to escape the scene of the crime. She'd rather face the fury of the storm than the imagined contempt of three long-dead Tremain ancestors.

As soon as Mr. Tremain left the room and went upstairs to check on his grandson—ironically named after the little boy in the portrait—Teri crept into the hall and used her cellular phone to call Ken Jacobs, Schofield's broker. There was a lot of interference, but she got through and was able to explain over the static that Schofield's offer had been officially accepted. Set to get a big commission out of the deal, Jacobs was naturally very pleased.

After Teri hung up and dropped her phone into an open pocket of her large purse, there was another blinding flash of lightning and an accompanying peal of foundation-jarring thunder. The house seemed to tremble, and loose shutters banged harder than ever against the house. But then Teri realized that she wasn't hearing shutters. Someone was pounding on the front door!

Teri got goose bumps all over. Who would be visiting Mr. Tremain at this time of night and during such a storm? Well...who besides a workaholic Realtor?

Holding the candle aloft, she peered up the dark stairs. "Mr. Tremain?" she called. "There's someone at the door."

There was no answer and the pounding became more and more insistent. Teri was at a loss to know what to do until she heard a muffled voice through the thick door, shouting, "Dad! Dad! For crying out loud, let me in, will ya?"

Teri couldn't believe it. Was it possible? Could Jackson Tremain be on the other side of the door, showing up exactly two minutes too late to stop his father from signing the contract?

Obviously, it had been an incredible stroke of luck that she'd decided to drive to Oak Meadows that night, although she wished fervently she was headed home and wouldn't have to face Jack Tremain when he found out that his father had sold the ancestral estate.

But she couldn't leave him standing outside on the drafty porch, so she unlocked and opened the door, admitting a staggering, dripping figure in a soaked trench coat with rain streaming in rivulets off his face and hair. Glancing quickly outside, she saw a Ford Explorer parked next to her Lincoln.

Teri hadn't seen Jack since his wedding. He and his high school sweetheart—the prom queen—were married a year after graduation. Jack's bride had been the quintessential sweet Southern belle. She'd been soft, simpering, sensual, sensational-looking and submissive. In fact, Pamela Devereaux had been everything Teri wasn't and could never be . . . and Jackson had adored her. She remembered his look of heartfelt sincerity at the wedding as he'd said, "I do."

It had come as quite a shock to the alumni of Riverbend High when two years ago word got out that Pamela had cancer. She'd died a mere four months later, leaving behind a two-year-old toddler and a grief-stricken husband. Teri had been too busy to go to the funeral, but she'd heard it had been a highly emotional one. From one of their famous debates in high school, Teri remembered that Jack didn't believe in an afterlife, and that must have made Pam's death even more devastating.

Perhaps because of the pain of losing his young wife, or maybe because of the work he did—photographing and writing about war and famine and political strife—Jackson Tremain only vaguely resembled that fresh-faced bridegroom she remembered so vividly.

Teri lifted the candle so the light fell fully on his face. Accentuated by the way his dark, collar-length wet hair clung close to his scalp, his features were much stronger now, more chiseled, more angular, more rugged. And the beard stubble and the jaded, jet-lagged look about his piercing green eyes only added to his world-weary, utterly masculine aura.

Teri got goose bumps again, but this time it was because she had a vivid, all-too-stirring image of Jackson Tremain swooping her into his arms and carrying her up the staircase "Tara" style. Then she realized why. Since he'd lost that bland look of extreme youth, he bore a strong resemblance to the guy in the portrait . . . Stephen Tremain.

Now her goose bumps were getting goose bumps and her heart was skipping beats.

"Stonewall," she uttered, transfixed. "You've changed."

Jack ran his fingers through his wet hair and flashed a lazy grin. "From what I can see of you, Teri the Terror," he said in a raspy voice, taunting her with the nickname he'd given her in high school, "you haven't changed a bit." He eyed her short, shag-cut blond hair and her slender figure in a navy blue blazer and straight skirt. "You still look like a pixie in a power suit."

"I like short hair," she said defensively. "It's easy to take care of."

"And it gives you the extra time you need to run the world, eh, Teri?" he teased sardonically, his eyes snapping with good-natured malice.

"Well, someone has to," she retorted, fighting a smile. But all the while, she was edging toward the door. Any minute now, things were going to get pretty explosive, and she had no desire to stick around and feel the blast. Besides, suddenly she wasn't feeling too well.

"Jackson? Jack, is that you?" Mr. Tremain's disbelieving voice came from halfway down the stairs. "My God, son, you're home!"

Teri had never seen Mr. Tremain move so fast. He set the candle he was carrying on a table, then the two men collided in the middle of the hall like a couple of bull moose, hugging and slapping each other on the back till Teri was afraid they'd beat each other to death. They murmured manly endearments, then Mr. Tremain grabbed his son by the shoulders and held him back so he could give him a thorough once-over.

Teri picked up the second candle and obligingly moved closer so Mr. Tremain could get a good look. Thankfully, the men were so wrapped up in each other, they didn't notice how much her hands were shaking, making the candle flames flicker and dance.

"You look like hell, son."

"Thanks, Dad." Jack shrugged sheepishly. "I feel even worse. I haven't slept, shaved or bathed in two days."

"And you haven't cut your hair for two months. Want the name of a barber?"

"As long as he's not yours."

Mr. Tremain humphed and chuckled at the same time. "Still a wise guy, I see." His smile wavered and his next words were touchingly halting. "When I couldn't reach you and I hadn't heard from you for over three months, I got worried, Jack.''

Jack squeezed his father's shoulder. "I know, Dad. Things got crazy for a while," he admitted. There was a pause, then in a tentative voice, "How's Sam?"

"He's in bed, son. It'd probably be best if you let him sleep through the storm, then surprise him in the morning."

"You two have a lot of catching up to do," Teri said, handing each of the men a candle and moving nervously toward the door. Watching their reunion seemed inappropriate, and it brought out feelings in Teri she'd just as soon forgo…feelings like envy. How would it be to have someone to come home to? Besides, any minute now, Jack would wonder what she was doing there. "I'll leave you two alone," she said, reaching for the doorknob.

"Not so fast, Teri," Jack growled. "What are you doing here anyway?"

*Whoops. Too late.*

"Didn't you go into some kind of sales profession?" He glanced down at her large briefcase. "You're not trying to sell my dad a set of Ginsu knives or something, are you?" he teased.

This rush of questions was followed by dead silence. Beauregard Tremain looked at the ceiling and Teri looked at the floor. Neither of them wanted to spill the beans.

"What's going on, Dad?" Jack asked, darting a suspicious glance back and forth between his father and Teri.

"This is something the two of you should discuss alone," Teri muttered, trying to turn the slick doorknob with a sweaty palm. Then she jumped back when there was another unexpected knock at the door.

"I never have this much company," Mr. Tremain said, more wonder in his voice than irritation. "Not even when the sun's shining."

He opened the door and the three of them stared out at two sopping wet, sixtyish women in matching pink sweatshirts with the single word *Hollywood* emblazoned across their amble bosoms with bright red glitter paint. Sunshades personalized with their names had slid down and were resting low and lopsided just above their penciled-on eyebrows. The same glittery lettering boldly spelled out, respectively, *Viv* and *Ginger*.

The rain had plastered their iron gray hair to their scalps, soaked through their stark white polyester pants and splotched the leather of their neon pink sneakers.

They were each holding bright yellow umbrellas. Ginger's was open and the movie title, *Singing in the Rain,* was printed across its shiny vinyl canopy. Viv had apparently used her umbrella handle to rap on the door. She still clutched it in front of her like a scepter. There were two small suitcases sitting on the porch at their feet.

The only discernible physical difference between the two women was that Ginger was wearing tortoiseshell glasses that magnified her blue eyes to unnaturally large proportions...and those Bambi-size eyes were fixed adoringly on Beauregard Tremain.

"Oh my," Ginger murmured, blinked, then stared, then blinked again. "Oh *my!* You remind me of Rory Calhoun. He was such a handsome man in his heyday, and he's *still* handsome...the Silver Fox. Say, did you catch him in *Red Sundown* back in 1956? I never saw a man sit a horse better than Rory Calhoun!"

Now it was Mr. Tremain's turn to blink. "Er...I...that is, I don't remember when I last saw a Rory Calhoun movie, but even if I did..." His voice trailed off in confusion. "Do I know you ladies?" he demanded, obviously stunned by the appearance of two female senior citizens on his porch during a raging storm, women who looked like they'd had a head-on collision with a souvenir store on Sunset Boulevard and were comparing him to a star of dozens of "B" Westerns in the forties and fifties.

"No, Mr. Tremain, you don't know us," Viv said. She was the one without the glasses who appeared to be able to meet his gaze without suffering heart palpitations. "The clerk at the Grab and Go convenience store five miles up the road said you sometimes take in overnight guests."

Mr. Tremain's brows knitted in a frown. "There's a motel right next door to the store. Why didn't you just stop there for the night?"

Ginger's chin plopped onto her chest and she stared at the ground. Viv glanced at her companion and shook her head dolefully. "My sister hasn't been able to stay at a motel since . . . *the murder.*"

"What murder?" Jack demanded, peering around his father's head.

"You know . . . the one at the Bates Motel." She clutched her throat. "That shower scene was terrifying. I *do* hope you have tubs in the house."

"Are you talking about the movie, *Psycho?*" Teri inquired incredulously.

"The very one," Viv admitted with an approving nod and smile. "If I keep my eyes closed most of the time, I can tolerate a shower now and then, but Ginger hasn't showered in thirty-five years. That is, unless you can count the soaking we got just now walking up to the house!"

Not stopping to inquire exactly where they'd parked their car—Teri could only see her vehicle and Jack's from where she stood near the door—Mr. Tremain suddenly seemed to notice the ladies' drenched condition and his compassionate nature took over.

"Hell's bells, ladies," he exclaimed with a look of contrition. "What am I thinking, letting you stand out there in the wind and cold while I gab away like an old hen?" He gave his candle to Teri and caught each woman by the hand, drawing them inside.

Teri watched Jack rub his jaw in a gesture of frustration. She knew he was anxious to find out what she and his dad had been up to, and the arrival of Viv and Ginger was going to delay hearing the desired explanation. But Teri was relieved to know she'd be able to get away before the fur flew.

"Come and warm yourselves by the fire," Mr. Tremain fussed on. "My stars and bars, ladies, you're as wet as a couple of tadpoles and your hands are as cold as Mississippi mud pies." He turned to Jack. "Grab those suitcases and shut the door, son," he ordered. "Then escort Miss Taylor to the library, will you?"

Teri watched as Mr. Tremain cupped the ladies' elbows and, in his most courtly manner, led them down the hall to the library, their umbrellas dripping and the thick treads of their sneakers making loud, squishy noises on the parquet floor. But despite their drowned-rat appearances, their faces were wreathed in smiles.

Teri turned to leave, but the door was shut again, and Jack was leaning against it with his arms crossed over his broad chest.

"Excuse me, Jack," Teri said, refusing to meet his gaze and all too aware of what an attractive, substantial hunk of male he was as he blocked her way. "Stonewall" seemed a fitting nickname for him even now...*especially* now. "I'm sure your father will understand that I have to go. It's late and I—"

"You're not going anywhere." His uncompromising reply was delivered in a low, rough tone. "Not before I get some answers."

Teri crossed her own arms and lifted her gaze to his. Just as it had in high school, his stubborn behavior brought out a corresponding stubbornness in her. "Who or what's going to stop me, Jackson Tremain?" she demanded.

Jack was about to reply when his attention was diverted by his father's showing up again. "So, Dad," he said with a grim smile, "did you come in here to tell me what's going on? I don't think I can let my *old friend,* Teri, leave until I know what you two are up to."

Mr. Tremain sighed. "You're quite right," he said gravely. "We can't let Miss Taylor leave."

"I've lived in Louisiana all my life, Mr. Tremain," Teri protested, exasperated. "I know how to drive in a storm. I'll be fine."

"Does your car float?"

"What?"

Mr. Tremain sighed again and offered an apologetic smile. "The bridge is damaged, Miss Taylor. As Miss Vivien and Miss Ginger were crossing it, parts of the foundation gave way and the front tires of their car dropped through the wood. But those plucky ladies stayed calm despite the fact that they didn't know whether or not the bridge would hold till they got out of the car and onto land. They even had the presence of mind to grab their overnight cases and umbrellas. So,

Miss Taylor... I'm afraid you're going to have to spend the night, too."

Jack looked grim but triumphant. "I don't suppose you've got a nightie in that giant briefcase?" he said with a raised brow.

## Chapter Two

Spending the night at Oak Meadows was the last thing Teri wanted to do. She had no desire to be around when Mr. Tremain told his son about selling the house. She didn't really know what Jack's reaction would be, but judging by Mr. Tremain's reluctance to find a private moment to break the news about the sale, Teri feared the worst. And Jack would blame the whole thing on her.

But she had no choice. The bridge was damaged, and even if she had the foolish urge to cross it anyway, it was blocked, too. And, call her a coward, but she'd rather cross the English Channel in an inner tube than brave the murky depths of the bayou in a boat during such a storm.

And what would she do on the other side without a car? Hitch a ride and end up with an ax murderer? Who else would be out on such a night? Well…except, as she'd conceded before, an overzealous Realtor.

Mr. Tremain had maneuvered them all around the library fire for a little friendly chitchat and, more practically, to "dry out" before bed. Teri sat in the overstuffed chair as before, Jack was stretched out on the floor by the fire, Viv and Ginger were perched perkily on the sofa, and Mr. Tremain had pulled a wing chair forward to sit directly across from the sisters.

The electricity was still out, but several candles lit the room in a cozy glow. Trouble was, Teri didn't feel the least bit cozy. She kept her briefcase close at hand, as if ready to fight for the signed papers should Jack try to wrestle them away from her, although she knew she'd never resort to such desperate measures to make sure the sale of Oak Meadows went through...or at least she hoped she wouldn't.

Mr. Tremain had brought out sandwiches, cookies and tea, but Teri couldn't eat. She knew she should eat a little something just to get her blood sugar up, but she was too wired and anxious to swallow a single morsel of food.

Her mouth was really dry, so she drank some tea, even though the caffeine was making her hands tremble harder than ever. Her heart seemed to be skipping every other beat, then throwing in an extra beat now and then to make up the difference.

Although her doctor had expressed concern about her "irritable heart," Teri considered it more of a nuisance than anything. In fact, she'd missed her last doctor's appointment to show a house to some eager buyers. But since there was no pain in her chest to accompany the palpitations, no shortness of breath, and since her heart always settled back to its normal rhythm eventually, what was the big deal? she reasoned.

She hadn't dropped dead yet, had she?

But if Jack kept looking at her the way he was, she'd never get her heartbeat back to normal. He'd taken off his trench coat and was lounging in front of the fire in a close-fitting black turtleneck tucked into a pair of well-worn, stonewashed jeans. The hankie-soft material hugged his slim hips and every lean muscle of his long legs.

He rested his arm on one up-drawn knee and just *stared* at her. There was irritation and suspicion in his gaze, but there was something else, too.... His eyes appraised her frankly, seeming to travel over her body with a sexual curiosity, leaving Teri feeling seared by the heat.

Somehow, it was ten times worse being stared at by Jack than by the painted eyes of the portrait, because the chills that shimmied up and down her spine were generated by someone very much alive ... someone warm and breathing and too sexy for words. Her heart revved into a faster and more erratic beat.

"Our mother named us after movie stars of the thirties," Ginger was saying as she reached for another cookie, then she stopped suddenly to coyly cover her mouth with her hand and bat her lashes at Mr. Tremain. "Oops! I've just given away our ages, haven't I, Viv? Well, anyway, Mother loved the movies and her favorite stars were Vivien Leigh and Ginger Rogers."

"Now if only we'd had their looks and talent," Viv remarked matter-of-factly, "we could have pursued a movie career, too."

Mr. Tremain chuckled, and the twinkle in his eyes seemed to indicate that he found Viv and Ginger vastly entertaining. Beauregard Tremain—better known as Beau by his friends and family—was always kind and polite, but Teri could tell that he was truly interested in his unexpected houseguests. She fervently hoped they'd talk so long and stay up so late that Jack would give up and go to bed without confronting his father tonight. But by the stubborn set of Jack's jaw, Teri didn't think that was going to happen.

"What did you pursue as careers?" Mr. Tremain asked Viv and Ginger. "Or are you ladies of leisure?"

"Oh, no," Viv responded firmly. "Ginger and I are, er, affiliated with a potato chip factory in Boise, Idaho. That's where we live... Boise."

Then, for reasons Teri thought were blatantly obvious, Ginger added, "Viv's a widow and I... Well, *I've* just never found the right man."

Teri saw Jack roll his eyes. Mr. Tremain blushed to the roots of his silver pompadour, cleared his throat and quickly moved the conversation along by inquiring, "Er, what brings you lovely ladies to the South?"

"The plantations," Viv answered promptly. "*Gone with the Wind* was our favorite movie... until Indiana Jones came along, of course."

"But even Harrison Ford can't sit a horse like Rory Calhoun," Ginger interjected emphatically, beaming at Mr. Tremain as if she'd given him a personal compliment.

"I'm surprised you ladies didn't tell us about the accident the minute you arrived at our door," Jack remarked. "It must have been pretty scary, and there's still a chance the bridge could give way and the car and the rest of your luggage will get a bayou baptism. In the face of all that, you seem in remarkably good spirits."

"The accident was no biggy," Viv scoffed, airily waving a hand. "And the only luggage I'm really concerned about is the case that holds our potato chip collection."

"We have chips resembling several of our favorite stars," Ginger piped in.

"We have excellent insurance on the car," Viv continued. "Besides, Ginger and I don't let little things like storms and collapsing bridges upset us. We actually enjoy a bit of a scare now and then." She leaned slightly forward and lowered her voice. "And what scares us most are ghosts. We've been told that there are ghosts aplenty in these wonderful old plantation houses." Now they both leaned eagerly forward. "Surely Oak Meadows has a ghost, Mr. Tremain?"

By the way his dad's face lit up, Jack knew it was time to step in. Oak Meadows definitely didn't have any real ghosts—in Jack's opinion there were no such things as disembodied spirits—but there were lots of supernatural yarns about the place that had been handed down through the generations. These women would keep his father up all night telling ghost stories and Jack didn't have the patience to wait till morning to find out what business Teri had at Oak Meadows.

"Dad, it's getting late and there's still that little matter we need to discuss," Jack tactfully interrupted, pushing to a sitting position, then standing up.

Jack's dad looked up at him with a guilty, wary expression on his face. He definitely liked the potato chip sisters, but he'd probably been encouraging them to talk and linger downstairs partly as a delaying tactic. This reluctance on his dad's part to talk privately really spooked Jack. His business with Teri must be pretty serious. Damn it, if he could only remember what Teri did for a living, he'd have a clue about what she was doing here on such a night!

"I'll show you ladies to your rooms and make sure you have plenty of matches and candles and a flashlight with a strong battery," his dad said with a note of resignation in his voice as he rose slowly to his feet. "My son is a photojournalist and he just got back from a long and dangerous assignment in Eastern Europe. I'm sure you understand that we have a lot to talk about."

"Oh, how exciting," Ginger exclaimed, smiling approvingly on Jack. "You're a photojournalist just like the man in *The Bridges of Madison County!* I was one of the minority who never read the book, but I *loved* the movie. So few men can look macho in their sixties, but Clint Eastwood still rings *my* chimes. Paul Newman's another senior sexpot, and if you don't mind my saying so, Mr. Tremain, you're quite the silver fox yourself."

Jack watched his father bask in the glow of Ginger's blatant flattery, wondering for the first time if he'd been lonely for female companionship since his mother died five years ago.

"You ladies are going to turn my head," his dad joked, flustered but obviously pleased. "But if you want me to call you Viv and Ginger, I must insist that you call me Beau."

The potato chip ladies tittered and smiled and followed "Beau" out of the room. Teri was about to sneak out behind them when Jack stopped her by grabbing her free hand. As if she were carrying secret documents for the government, she still clutched her briefcase in the other hand and hadn't let it out of her sight since he'd arrived.

Teri turned around reluctantly and faced Jack in front of the fire. "Not so fast, kiddo," he said. "You still haven't fessed up about your business with my dad."

Teri sighed and pulled free of Jack's grasp. Although her features were still as cover-girl pretty as in high school, her face looked drawn and pale, as if she'd been under a lot of strain lately. "I still think this is something you should be discussing with your father, not me. I'm an innocent third party, just carrying out your father's wishes."

Jack's brow furrowed. "What the hell wishes are you talking about? You didn't get a law degree in your spare time, did you, and now you're writing up last wills and testaments? Or are you a funeral director selling my father a swampy plot next to the freeway?''

"Certainly not," she replied stiffly.

"Then what are you? What could you possibly be selling that my dad needs?''

"I'm not selling anything."

"Then what's *he* selling *you?*"

Her eyes shifted away. "He's not selling *me* anything, but..."

As her voice trailed off and her gaze darted up to the portrait above the mantel, then quickly down to her shoes, the truth hit Jack like a brick between the eyes. It was so obvious he didn't know why he hadn't seen the writing on the wall the minute he'd walked in the door. He must be more jet-lagged than he thought. "Oh, my God. You're a *real-estate agent.*"

"You make it sound like a dirty word," she mumbled defensively.

"It is if you're trying to talk Dad into selling Oak Meadows."

Teri lifted her chin. Her blue eyes flashed just like they used to in high school. "*He* called *me,* not the other way around. And I haven't talked him into anything. He told me he was ready to sign the papers, so I—"

Jack grabbed Teri's arm, effectively silencing her. "So you hightailed it over here before he could change his mind. Please don't tell me he's already signed the papers?"

For the second time, Teri shrugged out of Jack's grasp. "I wish you'd quit manhandling me, Jack. Yes, he's signed the papers."

Jack closed his eyes and shook his head. "Damn it, Teri."

"I don't know why you're so surprised or so upset. The taxes alone on Oak Meadows are budget busting. Repairs are needed throughout the house and grounds—take the bridge, for example—and as for the upkeep around here, there're far too many flower beds and rosebushes for any one person to maintain, much less a man going on seventy. Why should it be such a big surprise to you that your dad wants to sell this albatross and move into a place that's more convenient and cheaper?"

"We discussed it once when—" He cut himself off, unwilling to bring up Pam's death. "Dad mentioned the idea before, but I was dead set against it. He thinks he'll save *me* money by selling the house because I'm the one who's been paying the taxes and maintenance. He loves Oak Meadows. This is where he belongs, not in some sterile condo with a hanky-size yard." Jack raked his fingers through his hair, which had dried in a haphazard tumble of long waves as he sat in front of the fire. "Besides, this is a great place for Sam to grow up. It's safe and there's room to run around and play. And—damn it!—Oak Meadows is *home!*"

"But not to you anymore, Jack," Beau Tremain admonished from the doorway. Teri watched as a flash of lightning and a peal of thunder accompanied Jack's dad into the room. His expression was deadly serious. "You come here to visit your boy and your old pa now and then, but Oak Meadows is not your home. A home is where you spend your time, son, and you're gone ten months out of the year."

"I don't have a choice, Dad," Jack protested. "It's my job."

"Don't give me that bull," Mr. Tremain said sternly. "You volunteer for these long, risky assignments. You're running away, son, and you're counting on me to keep the home fires burning till you decide you're finally ready to mosey on down to old Lou'siana. I can't do it anymore, Jack."

"Don't I give you enough money, Dad?" Jack asked, his concern evident.

"I *could* use a little more money to make some repairs around here, but that's not—"

"So why didn't you say so?" Jack exclaimed, clearly frustrated. "*I* certainly don't know what needs to be done around here."

"No, you wouldn't," Jack's father flatly agreed. "But money's not the issue."

"What is the issue, then?"

Teri watched the ongoing drama with interest, but she was feeling increasingly light-headed, so she backed away to a chair and slowly sat down. When she reached for a pitcher of water on a nearby table to pour herself a drink, her hands were shaking so badly she gave up the idea and just sat there, hoping she'd feel better soon. The storm raged on, inside and out.

"The issue is this, Jack," Mr. Tremain continued, easing himself into the wing chair and staring up at his glowering son. "I'm lonely. Sam's lonely. All we've got is each other and this big old house. It isn't enough, Jack. If you were here to play with the boy, or if he had a mom and brothers and sisters, it'd be different. This house used to be a home, but now it's just an empty shell. It'd be better to sell the place and fill it with people, even if they have to pay for the pleasure of staying here."

"So now you're telling me that I need to get married so you and Sam will have company?" Jack asked incredulously, throwing his hands in the air.

"You don't even keep company with females, Jack," Mr. Tremain stated, then added quietly, "At least not the marryin' kind. You just cut women out of your life after Pam died, and your son's suffering for it." As if on cue, a little boy's plaintive wail could be heard coming from upstairs. Mr. Tremain immediately stood up. "The storm's finally got to him, I guess. He's probably having a nightmare."

"I'll go," Jack said, turning toward the door.

"No," Mr. Tremain countered, stepping in front of Jack. "He hasn't seen you for four months. He won't recognize you—"

"Come on, Dad, that's just not true!" Jack protested.

"It's dark and he's half-asleep, Jack. Either he won't recognize you or he'll wake up completely, and we won't get him calmed down again for hours. I'd better go."

Jack stood with a stubborn expression on his face for a minute, then sighed and gave a nod of resignation. "You're right. You'd better go."

"We'll finish this conversation in the morning, Jack. But you might as well understand that even if by some miracle you managed to convince me that Sam and I ought to stay on at Oak Meadows, it's already too late. I've signed the papers and I've given my word to Miss Taylor." His chin lifted proudly. "I'm a man who keeps his word." Then he squared his shoulders and left, headed for his grandson's room.

Teri licked her lips and swallowed against a throat as dry as the Sahara. Her hands were still shaking too hard to hold the water pitcher, and she was too proud to ask Jack to pour her a drink. She breathed deeply, trying to slow the beating of her heart by sheer force of will, but it wasn't working. She was too dizzy to beat a hasty retreat, so she just sat there, waiting for Jack to pounce.

It didn't take long. He stood in the middle of the room, his head hanging, his hands on his hips, for a couple of minutes after his dad left, then he lifted his head and glared at Teri. "This is all your fault."

Teri jutted out her chin. "How do you figure?"

"You should have insisted that he talk to me before allowing him to sign the papers."

"I don't have the right or the power to tell your father what to do. And for that matter, neither do you. Besides, it doesn't sound like it would have made any difference. He only wanted to talk to you so he could tell you what he'd already decided."

"You could throw the papers in the fire...right now," he suggested.

"Not on your life, Jackson Tremain," Teri informed him frostily. "What happens to these papers will be determined by your father, and your father alone." She paused, averting her eyes. "Besides, I've already notified the buyer."

Jack shook his head and moved languidly in Teri's direction. His slow approach was deceptive. She knew the fight was far from over and she wished desperately that she could leave, but her hands and feet felt like blocks of ice and such a condition would surely impede a quick and dignified exit.

Jack stood over Teri's chair and crossed his arms. Her eyes slid up his six-foot-plus physique. She knew he was really ticked off at her, but she still couldn't ignore his raw animal magnetism.

"When I said earlier that you hadn't changed a bit since high school, I was basically talking about your looks, Teri. You're still damned attractive. But now, after spending less than an hour with you, I can see other changes. You've gotten more single-minded, more ruthless. You still want to win, win, win. In high school, you had a conscience, but now you don't care who you hurt.''

Jack's words were harsh and unfair, but Teri felt strangely removed from the situation and uninterested in defending herself. Her most pressing concern was trying to control the trembling that was invading all her limbs, and hoping that Jack hadn't noticed. She was starting to get scared. Her bouts with an irregular heart rhythm had never been this bad or lasted this long. Her pulse was racing.

To make matters worse, Jack was suddenly leaning over, his hands clamped down on the chair arms and his face thrust within inches of hers. She stared into moss green eyes that churned with anger and other strong, but otherwise mysterious, emotions.

"What, Teri? No snappy comeback? No excuses?"

"This place is too much for your dad," she managed to whisper in a hoarse voice. "He's lonely, and so is Sam—"

"But that's not why you want him to sell the house. Admit it, Teri. You want the commission and the prestige of finagling a deal other Realtors would barter their souls for. You're in it for you, and only you."

"So what if I am?" Teri snapped back. "My career means everything to me."

"Because it's all you have," Jack stated bluntly. He laughed, the sound harsh and humorless. "Believe me, I know what I'm talking about. You're substituting your work for real life. You're still driven to achieve, just like in high school...only worse. And, just like in high school, you're missing out on all the good stuff, sweetheart." He raised a brow. "As I recall, you didn't even go to the prom."

"It was a silly dance I didn't have time for." Teri defended herself, ignoring the way the room suddenly started to spin like a dish on the end of a stick. "I *could* have gone. I was asked to go, but I didn't have time to—"

"To enjoy yourself, Teri? You didn't take time then, and you obviously don't take time now, either. Do you realize how much you're missing? All the small but infinitely satisfying pleasures—"

He broke off and stared at Teri's parted lips. Her gaze was drawn to his lips, too. She watched, mesmerized, as he leaned even closer...so close his breath fanned her cheek and made her mouth tingle with expectation.

"You were so busy editing the school paper, heading the debate team and organizing fund-raisers to get money for computers in the library, you never kissed a boy behind the bleachers at a football game, did you, Teri?" he whispered seductively. "And you never necked in the back seat of a souped-up Camaro at make-out point in Bogart Park. But I can assure you that lots of guys wished you'd made the time, Teri. And one of those guys was me."

By now, Teri's heart was nothing more than a remote, flickering rhythm. She was cold and clammy and ready to pass out...and probably would have keeled over already if Jack hadn't suddenly got so darned interesting! The only warmth she felt was Jack's breath as his mouth captured hers in a teasing, tender kiss that would have curled her toes...if only she could feel them!

Another flash of lightning followed by a clap of thunder imbued the already charged atmosphere with enough electricity to light up Rice Stadium. The kiss deepened into a long, sweet exploration by tongue and teeth;

thrusts and nibbles and erotic dips. It was a kiss to die for....

Teri's eyes fluttered shut as Jack groaned and stood up, pulling her with him till she was stretched full-length against his rock-hard body.

She enjoyed ten blissful seconds in Jack's arms before a darkness fell over her consciousness like a black velvet curtain at the end of a tragic play.

The saying went, "It ain't over till the fat lady sings." Well, somewhere in the distance Teri heard a soprano trill the sweetest, truest aria she'd ever heard....

It took Jack a moment to realize that Teri had gone absolutely limp in his arms. He pulled back and stared at her still face, her thick lashes stark and black against her pale cheeks, her kiss-swollen lips slightly parted.

He grinned and kissed her lightly on the nose. "Hey, my kisses aren't that lethal. Or did you just doze off?" he teased.

There was no response. Jack's smile fell away and his brow furrowed with concern.

"You really did pass out," he muttered to himself, lowering her carefully to the floor. "I guess that's what happens when frail little beauties like yourself skip meals to chase deals."

But once he got her stretched out on the floor and a pillow under her head, he realized something was terribly wrong. She looked too pale, too motionless. Trying not to panic, he reached down and caught her hand, checking her wrist for a pulse. He couldn't find one.

Almost completely panic-stricken, Jack checked for a pulse at the base of her throat. Nothing. Desperate now, he pressed his ear against her chest. Nothing. Absolutely nothing!

"Oh, my God!" he whispered hoarsely, staring incredulously for half a second before throwing his head back and yelling at the top of his lungs. "Dad! Dad! Get in here, quick!" Then he bent down and immediately began administering CPR.

Not only did Jack's dad scramble down the stairs, but so did Viv and Ginger. They each gasped with astonishment and horror as they entered the room, then stood around Jack and threw a million questions at him at once.

"What happened?"

"Did she hit her head?"

"Is she breathing?"

"Is she *bleeding?*"

"What did you *do* to her?"

Between mouth-to-mouth resuscitation and heart thumps, he only made time to heave out, "Call 9-1-1!"

"It won't do any good, Jack!" his dad said. "They can't get over the bridge…remember? And in this storm, they'd never get here in time!"

"Call them anyway!" Jack bellowed between breaths. "Someone could meet them with the boat!"

Beau rushed away to do as he was told, and the potato chip sisters wrung their hands and mumbled fervent prayers.

"The phone is dead," his father revealed, dashing back into the room seconds later. "There's no one else to help, Jack. It's up to you, son."

With the sweat dripping off his face and his own heart slamming against his ribs, Jack kept blowing air into Teri's lungs and pressing the heel of his hand into her chest, hoping against hope for some response. One min-

ute, two minutes, three minutes ticked by...but still there
was no discernible heartbeat.

*My God!* thought Jack. *She's dead! She's dead and
I'm the one who killed her!*

## Chapter Three

Teri had the strangest feeling. One minute she was overcome with darkness and too weak to even open her eyes. The next minute she was as light as air....

It sounded insane, but by all appearances she was watching her own...*death!*

It was a bird's-eye view, looking down from where she floated above the chaotic scene like a weightless astronaut in a space shuttle. She watched and she hovered and she felt very much *there,* but no one seemed to notice her.

She could see everything and everyone, including herself. Peering critically down at her pale, lifeless face, her first thought was that she was in dire need of a little blush. She was definitely no Camille...gorgeous to the last breath.

It was fascinating, and very moving, too. Jack was trying desperately to save her life. Any regular guy would have thrown in the towel by now, but Jack was too stubborn to give up. Sweat dripped off his brow and down his beard-stubbled jaw. She found it interesting to note that even though she was obviously somewhere outside her body—hopefully on her way to Heaven—she could still think Jack looked sinfully sexy.

Mr. Tremain—bless his heart—appeared very distraught. His usually immaculately groomed silver hair was mussed by nervous fingers, and his string tie was askew.

The potato chip sisters had obviously been roused from bed by the emergency, because they were dressed in loose-fitting "movie-star" pajamas. Viv was in aqua blue and had a pouting Marilyn Monroe splashed in a provocative pose on the front of her pajama top. Ginger, in mint green, had James Dean as a front-and-center decoration. They both had their hair wrapped in bubble-gum pink sponge curlers, and their wrinkled faces were greasy from recent generous applications of night cream.

Teri was flattered to see that, despite having just met her, Viv and Ginger were still inspired to pray that Jack's resuscitation attempts would be successful. With their eyes rolled heavenward in a reverent pose, sometimes it appeared that they were looking right at her...or *through* her.

But as Teri noted these details, she seemed to be floating farther and farther away. There were feelings of regret, particularly about Jack. The kiss they'd just shared—which, she thought with a chuckle, could very appropriately be called the "kiss of death"—had been a real eye-opener. She'd felt strongly drawn to her old high school nemesis, and could see that there were possibilities for something special between them.

Knowing herself as she did, however, Teri realized that she'd probably never have made time to explore those possibilities, no matter how tantalizing. She seldom dated. And when she did, any relationship that appeared to have a chance of blossoming eventually died of neglect. *Her* neglect. She was always too busy proving herself.

And now it was too late.

Suddenly, Teri found herself in a tunnel. Normally rather claustrophobic, she didn't seem to mind being where she was. The tunnel was cool and dark, and she was very relaxed. There was a feeling of expectation— that Christmas-Eve feeling—that something wonderful was about to happen.

Then she saw the light. It started small, like a distant star, then grew larger and brighter till Teri was blinded by it. Soon she was surrounded, engulfed, *consumed* by the light. She felt warmed, loved, accepted. The feeling was *better* than Christmas, better than anything Teri had ever experienced.

Then, while she squinted and blinked, shadowy shapes began to materialize beyond the brightness. The shapes solidified into people and they began approaching her. Eventually, the light receded and settled around her like gentle sunshine, and the people's faces came into view.

She recognized them. There was a man, a woman and a small boy. They were the people in the portrait—Stephen, Caroline and Samuel Tremain! But the little boy was minus his teddy bear. Caroline looked almost regal in her magnificent Victorian gown, and Stephen was especially dashing in his Confederate uniform.

Standing before them in the blue, off-the-rack suit she'd died in, Teri felt a little gauche. And considering how uncomfortable the portrait had always made her, and in light of her recent part in selling Oak Meadow away from the family line, Teri was understandably nervous.

But as they lined up and trained their gazes on her, Teri felt no disapproval, no prickly sensation at the back of her neck and no desire to flee. And why should she flee, she reasoned. She'd just arrived . . . and she was home.

So she was stunned when Stephen said, "Teri, you have to go back."

As Teri's mouth fell open in disbelief, Caroline smiled and patted her hand, saying in a sweet Southern drawl, "How can you even think of dyin', my dear, when you haven't yet learned how to live?"

Then little Samuel tugged on her sleeve and entreated, "Say hello to Bartholomew for me."

"Say please, Samuel," his mother gently instructed.

"Please, ma'am?" he added with an appropriately angelic smile.

Teri had no time to reply, no time to ask who Bartholomew was. The change was immediate. Her new friends disappeared and she felt herself literally being sucked back through the dark tunnel, but not at the same pleasant, leisurely pace as before.

Suddenly, she was flat on her back again, weighted down by the flesh and bones of mortality. She hurt all over and it took every ounce of effort she could dredge up just to take that first breath....

"SHE'S BREATHING! Oh, my God, she's breathing again!" Jack shouted at the others, hardly able to believe it himself.

"Praise the Lord," Jack's dad murmured fervently.

"It's a miracle!" Viv and Ginger exclaimed, dancing for joy, their bouncing bosoms making ripples in the faces of the movie stars on their pajamas.

Jack quickly felt for Teri's pulse and was relieved to find it strong, although still a little too fast. She moaned and turned her head from side to side, apparently trying to regain consciousness.

"Put her on the couch, Jack," his father suggested eagerly. "She'll be more comfortable there."

Jack thought so, too, and he gathered her into his arms. She weighed next to nothing. His father hurried over to place a pillow where her head would rest.

Jack laid her down, then sat on the edge of the sofa, bracing an arm on either side of her. "Teri?" he whispered softly, urgently. "Can you hear me?"

Teri's eyes fluttered open. Jack was never so happy to see those sassy blue eyes of hers, though at the moment they appeared slightly unfocused.

"Do you know who I am, Teri?" he asked, testing her.

A small smile curved her lips. "Sure I do," she answered groggily. "You're Jack. You look like Stephen, but your voice is deeper."

Jack and his dad exchanged a puzzled glance at this enigmatic statement, but after all she'd been through, they were just glad she was talking again, even though she wasn't yet making sense.

Since no doctor or paramedics were available, Jack used his own first-aid training—which had come in handy in the war-torn areas he frequented—and spent the next few minutes making sure Teri was stable and comfortable. Since people didn't routinely keel over dead simply because they'd been kissed, Jack knew Teri had a serious medical problem that needed attention. But when he asked her if she was taking medication, she shook her head.

"I have an irritable heart," Teri explained after Mr. Tremain had fixed her a bowl of soup and she'd managed to sip a few spoonfuls and drink some milk. Then she immediately lay back down again and looked up at Jack from under droopy eyelids.

"I'd say 'irritable' is an understatement," Jack remarked grimly, covering her with an afghan he'd pulled from the back of the sofa. "I'd say your heart is downright bad tempered. Has anything like this ever happened before?''

Jack watched Teri anxiously as her eyes closed and she turned sideways and snuggled against the pillow, her hands tucked under her cheek, her hip making a curvaceous mound under the afghan. "Nothing this bad," she mumbled. "But let's talk about it tomorrow, Jack. I'm so..."

Her voice trailed off and Jack immediately reached for her wrist to check her pulse. It was strong and steady, chugging along as if it had never stopped.

Jack felt someone's hand on his shoulder and he looked up into Vivien's cold-creamed face. "She's just sleeping, Jack, and that's probably exactly what she needs right now."

"What she needs is a doctor," Jack said gruffly.

"As soon as we can get across the bayou without drowning, we'll take her to the hospital in Franklin," his dad said soothingly, his hand on Jack's other shoulder. "That'll be the closest."

"Doesn't she look like an angel?" Ginger crooned, her bifocal-magnified eyes teary as she stared at Teri from the foot of the sofa.

"She nearly *was* one," Jack grumbled. "And how do we know her heart won't get 'irritable' again before we can get her to the hospital?"

"We'll just have to watch her closely through the night," Beau said. "And I think she'll be more comfortable upstairs in one of the bedrooms. We can take turns sitting up with her."

"I'll put her in my room, and you folks can go to bed. I'll sit up with her," Jack said decisively.

"Jack, you're already dead on your feet," his father argued worriedly.

Jack scowled at him.

"Bad choice of words," his father admitted sheepishly. "At least let me sit with her for the first couple of hours while you take a nap."

"You can sit with her while I take a cold, five-minute shower, but that's the longest I want to be away from her. I wouldn't be able to sleep anyway, Dad. Not when there's a chance she could try to buy the farm again." When he realized that his "buy the farm" euphemism for death also more or less described what Teri had been up to at Oak Meadows that night, he exchanged a wry look with his dad and said, "Enough talking. I'm going to carry her upstairs now."

All the others cleared away from the sofa as Jack bent over and lifted Teri in his arms. As before, he noticed how light she was and decided she needed a little fattening up. That was probably a major part of her problem, he thought grimly. She didn't eat right and she worked too hard. And the hell of it was, this experience probably wouldn't change her a bit.

Jack stared down at her as he walked into the hall. She was so pretty, her features so delicate and feminine. And she looked so peaceful at the moment. Who would ever know by looking at her that she had the stubborn temperament of a mule, the tenacity of a pit bull with a bone and the craftiness of a fox? She looked just the way Ginger had described her... like an angel.

And despite her too-trim figure, she still had enough curves to feel quite enticing pressed against his chest.

At the bottom of the steps, she shifted and opened her eyes for a moment. "Wh-what are you doing, Jack?"

"I'm carrying you up the stairs," he replied, unable to repress a roguish grin, "to my bedroom, Scarlett."

She smiled back, shut her eyes and nestled trustingly closer. "Whatever you say, Rhett," she sighed, seeming to fall immediately to sleep again.

Jack's chest swelled and his heart thumped a little harder. He carried her up to his room, his father following just behind with a candle, while Viv and Ginger watched from below.

"What are you thinking, Ginger?" Viv inquired as her sister continued to look up the stairs long after the others had disappeared down the dark, second-story hall.

"I'm thinking that Beau Tremain has a good butt," Ginger replied with a gleam in her eyes. "Yes, that man's just my cup of tea, Viv. Why? What are *you* thinking?"

"Well, while I will admit that Beau Tremain does have a Mel Gibson derriere, I was thinking that watching Jack carry Teri up the stairs was just like watching that scene in *Gone with the Wind* when Rhett carried Scarlett up the staircase. Of course, Teri doesn't have Vivien Leigh's long hair, but it was still quite romantic."

"I think Teri looks like Meg Ryan."

Viv nodded judiciously, training her flashlight on the bottom stair. "I think you're right. Now watch your step, Ginger. We'd better hit the hay, 'cause I think things are going to be pretty exciting around here tomorrow, and I want to be up bright and early so I don't miss anything."

"Do you think Teri will be all right?" Ginger asked her.

"Oh, heavens, yes," Viv replied bracingly. "In fact, now that she's come back from the dead, I think she's going to be more than all right."

TERI WOKE UP to the spicy scent of after-shave and the feel of someone's arm draped over her hip. She blinked open her eyes and stared into the face of Stonewall Jackson Tremain. She was lying on her side under the covers, and he was on top of them, fully clothed in a pair of navy blue sweatpants and a matching top. A quick peek under the sheet revealed the fact that *she*, however, was wearing only her panties and bra.

*Interesting*, she thought wryly. *I remember dying, but I don't remember taking off my clothes.*

Teri shrugged, then glanced eagerly about her. The room was drenched in early-morning sunshine, and the fresh smell of wet earth drifted in through the window, which was cracked open about two inches. The filmy curtains wafted in the cool breeze.

If she'd been alone in bed, she would have thrown off the covers and padded barefoot to the window to look outside. She felt so good, so glad to be alive! But she couldn't bring herself to disturb Jack, who was sleeping peacefully. And it was really a toss-up which would be more fun and more life-affirming—enjoying the view from the window, or enjoying the view from right where she was.

Jack had shaved since last night, but it looked like he'd done a hasty job because Teri counted two small nicks on his chin. His dark hair was a tumble of waves, as if he'd showered then lain down beside her without combing or drying it. She marveled again at how masculine and handsome he looked even—or should she say especially?—at such close proximity.

But what was even more marvelous and amazing was the fact that Teri had no desire to dress hurriedly and start making calls on her cellular—to the office to check in, to her tons of clients, or to the mortgage companies she constantly dealt with. In fact, she felt quite content to stay precisely where she was for an indefinite period, just staring at Jack. But then she amended that thought, knowing she wouldn't be able to look much longer without touching, too. She lifted her hand, thinking how pleasant it would feel to trace the shape of his lips with her fingers.

Suddenly, Jack opened his eyes. He blinked confusedly. Teri dropped her hand to the bed, smiled and said, "Hi, Stonewall. Sleep well?"

Jack immediately sat up and stared back at her. His eyes still had a hazy quality, as if he'd just gotten off the bus from dreamland. There was a pillow crease on his cheek, and with his long hair all tousled around his face, he looked adorable.

"Teri," he said in a husky voice, the kind one has in the morning before the first sip of coffee or orange juice, "how are you feeling?"

Teri couldn't resist a languid stretch. "I feel *wonderful!* I haven't slept so well since I was a baby."

Jack just stared. He couldn't help it. This girl didn't seem like the Teri he'd gone to school with, or the woman he'd argued with in the library. And she definitely didn't look like the near corpse he'd been breathing air into like a madman last night.

Her cheeks were flushed with color and her short, wispy hair was splayed on the pillow, looking like gilded brush strokes on a white canvas. Her slim arms were raised above her head in a luxurious stretch, making the sheet fall provocatively over the swell of her small breasts peeking above a little scrap of a white lace bra. And she was smiling as if she didn't have a care in the world.

Why wasn't she calling her office to check in? Why wasn't she calling her clients in a blind panic, trying to reschedule meetings she was going to miss today? Specifically, why wasn't she calling the buyer's mortgage company to arrange for a meeting to close the deal with his dad?

The only reason he could come up with for Teri's calmness was that she was planning to claim a complete recovery, then skip out before Jack had a chance to take her to the doctor.

No way, José.

"Give me your wrist," he ordered, expecting an argument. Surprisingly, she complied. He checked her pulse and was pleased to discover that it was a strong, steady ninety. A little fast, but certainly not racing. "Still too fast," he murmured, not willing to be too optimistic, thereby giving her an argument to use against going to the hospital. "You'll let me know if it gets irregular or starts racing again, won't you?"

"Of course I will," she answered, much too cooperatively.

He eyed her suspiciously.

"I trust you, Jack," she added matter-of-factly. "You saved my life."

He stood up and raked a hand through his disordered hair. "I take it you remember what happened last night?"

Teri nestled into the blankets, laying her hands in a relaxed pose over her flat stomach. He could see every line of her figure under the thin bedding, and despite her slenderness, there were some nice curves evident ... curves he'd uncovered last night when he'd undressed her and put her to bed.

"Sure I remember what happened," she answered lightly. "And you were great, Jack. You just didn't give up. I've never seen anybody work so hard to save someone's life."

"*Seen?* How could you have seen anything?"

"Not that I see that sort of thing on a daily basis, of course. But I'm endlessly grateful. I was too young to die." She paused and smiled, then said, "Say, I'm famished. Do you think you could rustle up some breakfast for me?"

Jack gave her a baffled look and started pacing. "How can you be so matter-of-fact about what happened? My God, Teri, you nearly..."

She raised a brow and smiled even more broadly. "Croaked? Kicked the bucket? Went west to the last roundup? Turned up my toes?"

Jack stopped in his tracks, paralyzed by disbelief. "It's nothing to joke about. You nearly *died!*"

She nodded, her smile falling away to be replaced by a thoughtful—but not the least bit distressed or unhappy—frown. "Actually, I *did* die. It was an interesting experience."

Jack could feel his hackles rising. "Not for me, it wasn't. You scared the hell out of me."

Teri's meditative gaze wandered to the window and the drifting curtains. "I don't believe in hell anymore, Jack. At least not the fire-and-brimstone variety."

He propped his fists on his hips and glared. "Oh? And does this insight into the mythical afterlife have something to do with your nearly dying last night?"

She laughed softly. "Oh, Jack! How many times do I have to tell you? I *did* die. And yes, of course my experience last night has influenced the way I think about the afterlife."

He gave a beleaguered sigh. "I was being sarcastic," he clarified.

"Well, *I'm* being sincere," she replied with unruffled calm.

Jack frowned. "Are you saying you had an NDE during your cardiac arrest?"

"An NDE?" she repeated, puzzled.

"It's an abbreviation for 'near-death experience.'"

She nodded, her puzzled expression disappearing and another stunning smile spreading over her face. "Well, yeah, I guess I did have an NDE. And, boy, was it ever mind-blowing. Really incredible."

Jack just shook his head. Why didn't people understand that when their bodies were in the process of dying, their brains did weird things? There was nothing mystical or otherworldly about it. The brain released chemicals that brought on strange dreams. The whole thing was simply a universal physiological process, which doctors and scientists had never been able to document adequately simply because most of the people who experienced this phenomenon weren't around to be interviewed. They were dead!

But he decided to humor Teri. He was so glad she wasn't really dead—that she hadn't literally died in his arms as Pam had—that he was willing to listen to her describe her so-called near-death experience and let her get it off her chest and then forget it. Besides, he didn't want to get her excited or riled up, risking her heart going into overdrive again...which was also the reason why he didn't dare bring up the subject of the sale of Oak Meadows, though it was never far from his thoughts.

"You want to tell me about this, er, near-death experience?" he offered, valiantly trying to hide his lack of enthusiasm.

Teri gave him a keen look. "I may have nearly lost my life last night, but I didn't lose my ability to know when I'm being placated," she said dryly. "You know how I hate being placated."

"So that hasn't changed about you," he observed grimly.

She raised her chin a notch. "I know you're a skeptic, so I'll keep my revelations to myself. Besides, I'm starving to death ... not literally, of course. So, unless you've got some scrambled eggs stashed in the closet, I'm going to get dressed and go downstairs and—"

"You're not leaving that bed till you've been examined by a doctor, or until we can get you safely to a hospital for a thorough checkup," he said, his tone building in intensity and volume with each word, just waiting for Teri to start arguing. "If it happened once, it could happen again."

"That's fine, Jack," Teri said soothingly, giving Jack the distinct impression that now *he* was being placated. "I know I need to take care of myself—and I've already been told how to do that by my regular doctor—but if it makes you feel better, I'll allow myself to be examined. But not on an empty stomach. If you won't let me get out of bed, you're going to have to bring breakfast up here." Suddenly, her face lit up as if a light bulb had been switched on inside her head. "Say, that's a great idea! You know, I've never had breakfast in bed before. And everyone should enjoy breakfast in bed at least once in their lives, don't you think? It sounds like fun!"

Jack stared at her again. As long as he'd known her, Teri had never expressed the desire to enjoy much of anything. It was always work, work, work. She was driven to achieve, not to have fun. Just before she'd collapsed last night, he'd been lecturing her about taking time for the small, everyday pleasures ... although he himself had done precious little of that since Pamela died. Was it possible that he'd gotten through to her? But even if he had, he didn't think the change would last.

"What do you want for breakfast, Teri?" he asked her. "I'm sure Dad's kitchen is well stocked with everything you could possibly want."

Teri cocked her head to the side and considered, then said, "Oh, just surprise me, Jack."

Now this was a real shocker. Teri, the control freak, was allowing *him* to decide what *she'd* eat for breakfast? Now he *knew* this new carefree attitude couldn't last. Maybe the lack of oxygen to her brain during the cardiac arrest had affected her personality.

Oh, how he wished there was a doctor in the house!

"Okay," he said, playing along. "But you stay put while I get someone in here to sit with you while I rustle up breakfast."

Teri shrugged, and Jack left, returning in less than five minutes with Viv and Ginger. He'd stopped first at his dad's room, then Sam's, but they were both empty, leading him to suppose they'd taken a walk to the bridge together to check out the damage. Jack had then knocked on the potato chip sisters' bedroom doors and had been relieved to find them still upstairs. They'd been eager to help and seemed to be just waiting to be asked, but Jack was still nervous about leaving Teri alone with them. Or, rather, he was nervous about letting anyone but himself watch over her and make sure she didn't perform another death-defying trick like last night's.

In the kitchen, Jack was relieved to find the power back on. But when he picked up the phone, it was still dead. He wouldn't be able to call a doctor any time soon, and if there was another emergency, he wouldn't be able to get through to 9-1-1, either. After breakfast, he'd have to take Teri across the bayou in a motorboat and hitch a ride to the hospital once they got to the other side. Such a plan certainly wasn't ideal, but he didn't want to wait too long to get her some medical attention.

Working quickly, he made scrambled eggs, toasted and buttered an English muffin, then found a jar of homemade peach preserves in the fridge and put it on the tray with a glass of milk. There was no way he was going to give Teri anything that might overstimulate her heart, like coffee or tea.

On an impulse, he rushed outside to the small greenhouse adjacent to the garage and cut a bud from one of his father's prizewinning rosebushes. He figured Teri deserved her first breakfast in bed to be special.

Just as he'd instructed when he left, the door to her room was open when he arrived with the breakfast tray. But, contrary to his orders, Teri was out of bed...*and doing the bunny hop!*

Dressed in nothing more than one of his plain white dress shirts, which she'd evidently borrowed from his open suitcase, Teri was leading the line, humming the usual melody for such silliness, then giggling like a teenager.

"Teri, what the hell are you doing?" he demanded.

Teri and the potato chip sisters started when they heard Jack's gruff tone. The line immediately broke up, but they were still laughing and poking good-naturedly at each other as if they were old friends.

"I don't think dancing is the wisest thing to be doing after what happened last night," Jack lectured, stalking into the room with the tray. "And I'm really surprised you ladies allowed this sort of recklessness," he added, throwing Viv and Ginger a reprimanding look.

As Teri climbed back into the bed, Jack tried to ignore the way his own heart skipped beats as he watched her pull her long, bare legs up and under the covers. He set the tray on a nearby table, unceremoniously grabbed Teri's wrist and took her pulse. It was fine. Despite her recent exercise, he counted just eight-five beats per minute.

"Don't be angry with Viv and Ginger, Jack," Teri said. "It was my idea. I was telling them how wonderful I feel this morning just to be alive. I said I felt like dancing a jig."

"And I said, 'Well, why don't you?'" Ginger admitted sheepishly. "And she said there wasn't any music, and *I* said you don't need music to bunny hop. And *she* said *you* said to stay in bed, but Viv took her pulse and then *she* said—"

"In short," Viv interrupted, "we didn't think it would hurt her to have a little fun. Laughter helps a person relax, you know. In fact, a good laugh actually measurably lowers your blood pressure. *You* should try it some time," she added with a cheeky grin.

Jack just crossed his arms and scowled.

"George Bush had an irregular heart rhythm once while he was in office," Ginger went on. "He was in the hospital for a couple of days, but all he had to do was give up caffeine and de-stress his life a little, and now he's as fit as a fiddle and jogging all the time." She nodded with conviction, then added, "Our potato chip likeness of George Bush is excellent. He's not a movie star, of course, but we found a chip that looked so much like him, we couldn't throw it out. Remind us to show you our collection once we rescue it from the car."

"None of us has a medical degree," Jack objected, ignoring Ginger's meandering reference to her potato chip collection. He picked up the tray and set it on the bed over Teri's lap. "We need to talk to a doctor before we really know what Teri can and can't do."

Out of the corner of his eye, Jack saw Viv and Ginger exchange knowing looks, as if he were being overly cautious. But there was no way he was going to allow what happened last night to be repeated. He hadn't been able to control the cancer that raged like a wildfire through his wife's body and took her life, but, as far as he knew, Teri's condition was manageable. As a friend, and also the culprit who had brought on her latest, most devastating attack, he'd make sure she was well cared for.

"One thing I don't need a doctor to tell me is how hungry I am," Teri announced, lifting her fork. "I could eat a horse."

Jack sat down on a chair by the bed, while the potato chip sisters hovered cautiously in the background, apparently a bit intimidated by his gruff manner. But, hell, how else was he going to make sure Teri did what she was supposed to do?

He was prepared to urge Teri to eat because he was certain that no matter how hungry she professed to be, she'd quit eating after the first two or three bites. He remembered her whatever-was-quick-and-easy diet in high school. She'd never taken the time to eat properly, and after observing her last night, he didn't think her dietary habits had improved. She just didn't seem to enjoy eating.

After three minutes, Jack was forced to admit he was dead wrong.

He sat forward in his chair, flabbergasted, mesmerized and... aroused. He'd never seen anyone eat with more pure sensual delight than—the new and improved?—Teri the Terror.

"Umm... These eggs are so delicious, Jack," she crooned, sliding her fork slowly under another bite-size mound of eggs. "They're cooked just right. Firm, yet melt-in-your-mouth soft.'' She took a bite, closed her eyes and chewed with measured, erotic deliberation. "And these peach preserves..." she enthused, piling a heaping spoonful on top of one half of the English muffin. Following the same titillating routine, she took a bite, closed her eyes, then chewed slowly while she savored the taste. "Heaven," she announced once she'd swallowed. "Sweet, but tart. And just the right texture."

"Thanks for noticing," Jack mumbled.

A dollop of preserves had stuck to Teri's pinky finger, and she slipped it into her mouth to suck off the sweet, sticky concoction. Jack watched like a starved dog. He could just imagine the feel of her slick little finger in his own mouth. And he recalled only too well how tasty her lips were when he'd kissed her. They'd been as ripe and sweet as peach preserves.

Then he remembered that he'd been kissing her when she went into cardiac arrest, the horrific memory effectively dampening his ardor. Well, almost.

Teri polished off the entire modestly portioned breakfast, then leaned back against her pillows and sighed with contentment. She picked up the rose, took a long whiff of its fragrance, then rested the petals against her cheek. "I've never enjoyed a meal more," she confessed.

Neither had Jack, and he hadn't had a single bite of food. His enjoyment had been in watching Teri...and his enjoyment had been considerable. Maybe for lunch he'd find her some double fudge ice cream....

"Daddy?"

Jack turned and saw Sam standing at the door to the bedroom, clutching his stuffed bear.

# Chapter Four

Teri stared at Jack's four-year-old son. Once or twice, while doing business at Oak Meadows with Mr. Tremain, Teri had been vaguely aware of Sam hanging around his grandfather, but she'd been too preoccupied with wheeling and dealing to really "see" him. Today she noticed everything around her and she was struck by how much Sam resembled his father. He had the same thick brown hair, the same long-lashed green eyes and the same firm, destined-to-be-stubborn jaw.

And she seemed uncharacteristically tuned in to his feelings, too. By the uncertain way he stood at the door and the struggle he made to control his facial expression, she could tell he wasn't sure what to do or what sort of greeting his father expected.

*They're strangers!* Teri thought.

Jack turned and locked eyes with his son. There was an awkward pause, then Jack muttered disbelievingly, "Sam...you've grown a foot."

Sam's alarm was evident. He stared down at his red sneakers, fully expecting to find that he'd somehow grown...a third foot!

"No, I meant you've grown *taller*, Sam," Jack clarified, suppressing a chuckle.

Teri grinned. There it was. There was the love hidden behind the awkwardness of a four-month separation between father and son. Jack loved Sam, and Sam loved Jack, but time had taken its toll.

"Come here, son, and give me a hug," Jack ordered, probably not meaning to, but sounding gruff. He extended his arms in a stiff invitation.

Sam immediately obeyed. He didn't run like kids usually do, but he did walk willingly enough toward his dad, still clutching some sort of stuffed toy. He stopped just shy of his dad's outstretched arms and stood at attention like a dutiful little soldier, his eyes fixed on his dad's face, his expression sober.

Jack stooped and hugged Sam, and Sam hugged him back... sort of. It wasn't as if he didn't want to hug his dad, it just seemed as if he was afraid to make the first move, then didn't know exactly how hard to squeeze.

Teri found herself sympathizing with Jack and Sam, and then marveled that she was so engrossed in the tender scene. Before the NDE, the abbreviated name Jack had given her brief foray into phantomland, she'd coped with real life by subduing her own feelings and pretty much tuning out the feelings of others. She'd always thought emotions were like static on your TV—they made an otherwise clear picture cloudy. It was easier to attend to life—business, in other words—when you were untroubled by that sort of interference.

"Daddy," said Sam, seeming a little more relaxed now that the first greetings were over, lifted what Teri finally recognized was a stuffed bear. "You dint hug Bartholomew."

"Bartholomew? *That's* Bartholomew?" Teri exclaimed. When everyone in the room turned and gaped at her, she apologized, saying, "Oh, I'm sorry. I didn't mean to interrupt, but I was just surprised to hear that your bear's name is Bartholomew, Sam.''

"Well, I was goin' to name 'im Chester, but Gran'pa said his name has al'ays been Bartholomew, and that we'd better keep callin' 'im that or else he'll get confused," Sam explained seriously and with a disarming little pucker between his brows.

"Isn't that the bear in the portrait over the library mantel?" Viv piped up, moving nearer as she examined the antique bear with interest.

"I'm not sure—" Jack began.

"It sure is," came Beauregard Tremain's deep voice from the doorway. "Last Christmas, I dug it out of a cedar chest in the attic and gave it to Sam. The boy he was named after was the first and only owner of the bear, so I figured it was appropriate for Sam to be the second owner. Sam and Bartholomew have been best friends ever since." Beau walked into the room, smiling and nodding at Viv and Ginger, then at Teri. "And just how are you feeling this morning, Miss Taylor?"

"Like a new woman," she replied with a chagrined smile. She felt silly and sappy admitting such a fact, but it was the truth. As each moment passed, she realized more and more what a miracle it was that she was alive... and what a unique opportunity she had to basically restart her life.

She was sure Jack thought she'd hallucinated her NDE, but finding out that Sam's stuffed bear was the identical one from the portrait and that it was named Bartholomew, just reaffirmed her belief in what happened—and quadrupled her responsibility to see that she did things right this time. She realized, too, that if she dwelt on what had happened to her, she could get mired in the sheer enormity and profundity of it. She felt it was a much better idea to simply enjoy the fact that she still had a life to live and get on with it.

"I'd like to say hi to Bartholomew, too," Teri said, smiling at the child. "After your daddy's done hugging your little buddy, could you bring him over here?"

Sam smiled and nodded shyly, obviously pleased Bartholomew was enjoying such sudden popularity. While Jack sheepishly hugged the stuffed toy, Mr. Tremain moved close to the bed and said, "We need to get you to the nearest hospital to be examined, Miss Taylor. The weather's beautiful this morning, and it should be perfectly safe to transport you across the bayou in our motorboat."

"But what about when we get to the other side?" Jack wanted to know as he and Sam moved close to the bed, too.

By now, the number of people surrounding Teri's bed could easily constitute a crowd. It was like a human fence. They meant well, and Teri felt very much cared for, but she couldn't wait to get outside in the sunshine and the wide open spaces. And she couldn't wait to get the examination over with and prove to them all that she'd learned her lesson and knew how to take care of herself. She had no intention of dying again. At least not for a long, long time.

"When I picked your purse up off the floor this morning, Miss Taylor, I couldn't help but notice you had a cellular phone," Mr. Tremain began.

"Please call me Teri," she interrupted with a smile.

"If you'll call me Beau," he countered, smiling back.

"We had access to a phone all this time?" Jack exclaimed. "I wish we'd known that last night."

"I hope you don't mind that I used your phone to make a few calls," Beau continued, ignoring Jack's frustrated outburst. "The first thing I did, of course, was to call my good neighbor, Fred Bradshaw, who lives five miles down the road. He's tickled pink to loan us a car till we can drive ours over the bridge. It's an ancient Land Cruiser, but it oughtta do. He said it would be parked just outside the gate on the other side of the bayou in about fifteen minutes. Do you think you can be ready to go to the hospital in Franklin by then?"

"Sure," she replied.

Beau smiled his approval, then addressed Viv and Ginger. "I've also got people coming out to tow your car off the bridge, ladies. It looks like you've got a couple of flat tires in front and a couple broken headlights. With your permission, I'll have the guys at the station take care of those repairs for you. Meanwhile you're welcome to stay on at Oak Meadows till you're of a disposition to move on."

Viv and Ginger nodded enthusiastically and murmured their thanks.

Beau turned to Jack. "A crew will start repairs on the bridge first thing tomorrow morning. It's not as bad as I'd originally feared, and I expect they'll get it done within the day. Meanwhile we'll have to use the boat to get to the highway. I'm sorry, Teri, that your car won't be immediately accessible to you. In your profession I know a vehicle is indispensable."

"Don't worry about it, Beau," Teri replied. "I'll work something out."

Jack stared at her as if she'd grown another eye in the middle of her forehead.

"This isn't like you, Teri," he muttered. "You're far too pleasant and accommodating. We're talking about putting a snag in your *work schedule* here. Are you sure alien body snatchers didn't come during the night and replace the old Teri with someone new they'd grown in a pod?''

"Those humanoid duplicates were duds," Ginger scoffed. "They walked around like zombies! A closer comparison for Teri would be those perpetually blissful suburban housewives in *The Stepford Wives,* circa 1975." She smiled fondly at Teri. "But I'm sure she hasn't been altered by science. It was just her NDE that's made her so happy-go-lucky."

"You told them, too, Teri?" Jack said, shaking his head incredulously. "Everyone's going to think you're a basket case."

"Actually, Teri's new lease on life reminds me more of the 1970 musical version of Charles Dickens's charming book, *A Christmas Carol,"* Viv stated, getting her two cents in. "Albert Finney played the old miser, Scrooge—"

"I believe that was also the name of the film," Ginger interjected. *"Scrooge."*

Teri noticed Jack's growing impatience with the potato chip sisters' frequent meanderings into filmdom. It was as if he wanted them all out of the room so he could have a monopoly on fussing. But that crack about the body snatchers was what got them going, so it was really his fault this time.

"Yes indeed, it *was* titled *Scrooge,"* Viv went on. "And after Ebeneezer was visited by three ghosts..."

*Just like I was!* Teri thought. She'd only given the potato chip sisters a brief, not too descriptive, account of her NDE. She hadn't told a soul about running into the original owners of the house because she wasn't sure if anyone who hadn't died would really understand. Like Jack said, they'd probably think she was a basket case.

"...he quit worrying about making money all the time and really kicked up his heels . . . literally!"

"He expended so much energy in the last half hour of the show," Ginger said, "I was afraid he was going to have a heart attack."

"I was afraid the old fool would give away *all* his money," Viv added in a more practical vein. "Then he'd be in a fix, wouldn't he?"

"Teri's going to be in a fix if she doesn't get to the hospital pretty soon," Jack broke in irritably. "Everybody needs to clear out so she can get dressed."

Jack stood there with his fists propped on his hips, looking like the king of Siam.

"Everyone but you, Jack?" his father inquired with amusement, while the potato chip sisters giggled appreciatively.

"Dad, are you gonna help Miss Taylor get dressed?" Sam asked. "She looks big enough to dress herself. *I've* been dressin' myself for two years!"

"I usually dress myself, too," Teri admitted, winking at Sam. "But your daddy's a little worried about me because I got sick last night."

Sam nodded solemnly. "Oh. Daddy was worried when my mommy got sick, too. But she died. You're not gonna die, are you, Miss Taylor?"

"No way, no how," Teri assured him, her heart going out to the little boy. . . and his father. "I'm definitely going to stick around for a long time. Now, are you going to let me say hi to Bartholomew?" she said, changing the subject. "And please call me Teri."

Jack watched with envy as Sam actually climbed up on the bed to share his bear with what amounted to a virtual stranger. But he was just as surprised at the way Teri was disregarding that precious commodity called time to spend several minutes talking kid talk with his son. And the way she'd diverted his thoughts from his mother's death was truly quick thinking. Sam still remembered his mom even though he hadn't yet turned three when she passed away.

Eventually, Jack left the room with his father and Sam, leaving Viv and Ginger to help Teri dress, although the idea of *him* helping her dress had definite possibilities.

Then he reminded himself—again!—that she'd just about died when they shared that steamy kiss, and he didn't even want to consider what might have happened if things had progressed any further.

Why was he thinking about things going further anyway? He wasn't even sure why he'd kissed her in the first place. He might be physically attracted to her, but Teri wasn't his type... even in her new and improved form. Besides, he was sure she'd change back to her old workaholic persona once the impact of her NDE wore off.

Which brought him to the matter of the sale of Oak Meadows. She hadn't mentioned it, and he didn't dare. But there would come a time when the issue would have to be discussed... and soon.

"I'M READY, DADDY!" shouted Sam from the top of the stairs. "I changed my clothes and ever'thing ... just like you did!"

Jack and Teri had just reached the bottom of the stairs when Sam's excited shout made them turn and look up. Sam had changed from a pair of shorts and a T-shirt that matched to a pair of shorts and a T-shirt that didn't.

"Ready for what, Sam?" Jack inquired.

"T'go to the hospital with you and Teri," he announced, bouncing down the stairs in his bright red-striped top and his yellow-and-blue-checked bottoms.

"I invited him," Teri whispered before Jack could say anything.

Jack was speechless. It had never occurred to him to ask Sam to go to the hospital with them. It had never occurred to him that a child would *want* to go to the hospital. Personally, he hated hospitals, but since Sam had been too little to visit Pam during her frequent admissions during the four months she was treated for cancer, thankfully he didn't have the same sad associations his father did. But Jack was still hesitant.

"I'm not sure that's such a good idea, Teri," he said under his breath.

"I thought you'd want to spend some time with him. You just got back from a long trip, and here you are, off to the hospital for who knows how long."

"Sam and I will have plenty of time to spend together before my next assignment," Jack said.

"They're not young and adoring for very long, Jack," Teri reminded him.

"And this you know from personal experience?"

She made a face at him, but went on undaunted. "From what I've *heard,* there comes a time when kids don't want to spend time with their parents anymore. Enjoy it while you can."

"But to the hospital?" he continued to argue, unconvinced.

Teri smiled. "You'll be in the waiting room. Besides, you guys ought to spend ordinary time together, not just special times set aside, like going to the amusement park. Trust me. This is the way to really get to know each other, and it just might be fun."

Jack was dubious, and he wasn't sure he liked Teri's implying that he and his son didn't really "know" each other. But there was no use arguing about it because Sam was already standing at his feet, his big green eyes staring up at him with happy expectation, his stuffed bear—still smelling like a mix of cedar chest and mothballs after all these months—clutched under his arm.

"Me and Bartholomew are ready," Sam announced again. He turned his head and looked up at his grandfather, who was standing on the landing, peering over the balustrade at them. "I already tol' Gran'pa we were goin' with ya. He says that's fine, 'cause he's goin' to be playing cheesy with the ladies."

"Cheesy?" Jack inquired, throwing his father a suspicious glance.

"Parcheesi," Beau clarified with a grin. "And maybe a little poker, too."

Jack was about to teasingly warn him not to play the strip version of the game and not to gamble away the family estate when it hit him that, technically, his father had already sold it. This reminder just made Jack grumpier.

"Can we ride in the front of the boat?" Sam inquired. "Bartholomew doesn't like to ride in the back. It makes him barf."

"Yeah, this is going to be loads of fun," Jack grumbled into Teri's ear as they followed a skipping Sam through the door and onto the porch. She just laughed.

The minute Teri stepped outside into the sunshine, she was spellbound. Was the sky always so blue, the grass so green? Did it always smell this sweet and fresh after a storm? When they stepped off the porch, she stooped to run her hand over the grass, loving the way the feathery tips tickled her palms.

Jack looked impatient. "What are you doing, Teri?"

"I'm enjoying the small but infinitely satisfying pleasures you mentioned last night," she told him, smiling mischievously. She noticed that he looked quite handsome and sporty today in his khaki pants and white polo shirt.

She also noticed that her teasing allusion to the fatal kiss made him very uncomfortable, but he only said, "Fine, but not until the doctor says it's okay...okay?"

"I'm seriously considering rolling down that hill over there..." This suggestion quite obviously horrified Jack. She laughed. "I won't do it till the doctor says it's okay," she assured him. "Besides, I'd probably better not do it in a skirt. It's just that there're lots of things I need to do for the first time."

"Didn't you do *anything* before last night?" he groused, taking her elbow and urging her toward the edge of the lawn where a deep gully sloped down to the bayou and the boat dock. A chain-link fence kept the occasional wandering alligator from crawling up the hill and into the yard. Sam hurried along beside them, pointing out items of interest to Bartholomew.

Dressed in the blue suit she'd died in—an outfit she planned to burn at the first opportunity—Teri had a little difficulty finding a modest way to board and then sit in the boat. But once inside and crossing the stretch of vegetation-thick bayou, she was bending over the side and oohing and aahing over the abundance of minuscule life teeming in the water. She'd always hated the bayou, but now she found it fascinating.

"Besides the small stuff, there's big stuff that bites in there, too," Jack cautioned. "Don't dangle your hand in the water, Teri. Not unless you want to sacrifice your fingers for some gator's lunch. You, too, Sam."

"Gran'pa already taught me not to dangle my hand," Sam said proudly. "Didn't no one ever teach you nothin', Teri?" he asked her.

"None of the important stuff," she acknowledged, ruffling his hair. "But now I'm going to teach myself."

"That's the scary part," Jack observed dryly.

AT THE HOSPITAL, Jack and Sam found lots of things to do in the waiting room while Teri was examined and tested for two hours. They watched "Sesame Street" on a TV that was suspended from the ceiling; they watched fish in the aquarium dipping in and out of a pint-size pirate's cave, complete with buried treasure and skull and bones; they played tic-tac-toe on the back of an empty tissue box; they visited the water fountain three times and the rest room twice; and they bought and drank two cans of soda pop from the vending machine.

And Jack answered lots of questions.

"Why do they hang the TV from the ceilin', Daddy?"

"So kids won't play with the buttons, and so everyone can see."

"Why's Cookie Monster blue?"

"I don't know...maybe because blue is his favorite color."

"How come fish never close their eyes, Daddy?"

"They do. It's just that their eyelids are so thin, you can see right through them."

"How come the boys and girls have dif'rent bathrooms, Daddy?"

"For privacy."

"What's privacy?"

"It's being alone when you want to be."

"Why does soda pop have bubbles, Daddy?"

"Because the people who make it want to have carbonation in it."

"What's carb'nation?"

Jack acknowledged that Teri had been right about getting to know Sam by spending some "ordinary" time together...but it was exhausting! He was about to launch into another explanation, when a young, blond, good-looking doctor walked up to them. Viv and Ginger would no doubt have immediately found a resemblance between him and Dr. Kildare.

"Mr. Tremain?"

"Yes?" Jack stood up. He didn't know why, but suddenly his hands were clammy. Maybe it was because this whole scenario reminded him of the time he'd first taken Pam to the hospital and was led into a small, sterile room and given the devastating news that his wife had cancer.

"I'm Dr. Benson. Could you come into the examining room for a minute so we can talk?"

"I just transported Miss Taylor to the hospital," Jack nervously told him. "We're not related. Are you sure you should be telling me personal stuff?"

The doctor's eyebrows lifted. "You're a friend, aren't you?"

"Sure. Yes. We're friends."

The doctor smiled. "Well, she needs a friend right now. Please come into my office."

"I've, uh, got my little boy with me," Jack said, hesitating.

"That's okay. Don't worry, Mr. Tremain. Nothing will be said that might upset him. Really, all I've got is basically good news to tell you."

Jack was marginally reassured by this cheerful announcement, but he was still nervous. He took Sam's hand and they followed the doctor down a hall and into a small examining room. Teri was inside, sitting on the edge of a gurney, swinging her legs.

"Hi, guys," she said with a smile. "Sorry it took so long."

"No problem," Jack said stiffly, unable to return her smile and made uncomfortable just by looking at her. She looked so perfect, it was hard to believe she could have something seriously wrong with her.

He sat down and pulled Sam onto his lap. Sam held Bartholomew high on his chest, right under Jack's nose. But Jack didn't mind the proximity of Sam's musty-smelling bear. He preferred the smell of mothballs to the disinfectant odor of the hospital.

"As you know, last night Teri had a serious bout with heart arrhythmia."

"To say the least," Jack commented dryly.

"It's my opinion that although you may have thought her heart had quit beating entirely, it was probably in fibrillation."

"Fib'lation?" Sam repeated. "Is that like carb'nation, Daddy?"

"I'll explain later, Sam," Jack whispered. Although he had not been able to detect even a fluttering in Teri's chest last night, Jack was only too ready to believe that her condition hadn't been as bad as he'd thought.

"We put her on the treadmill and monitored her heart with an EKG and did some other tests. I've consulted with her regular doctor—who will do a follow-up exam in his office next Tuesday—and we don't think there's anything pathologically wrong with Teri's heart that would require surgery or anything so drastic. A change of life-style and strict avoidance of caffeine and other stimulating substances should keep her heart beating normally... for the most part."

"For the most part?" Jack repeated suspiciously.

"Since she has a sensitive nervous system, there will be occasional heart flutters and short-term bouts with arrhythmia, but nothing serious—certainly nothing as serious as the occurrence last night—as long as she minds her p's and q's. That's where you come in, Mr. Tremain."

Jack didn't like the sound of that. He flicked a glance at Teri and found her watching him with that strange Stepford-wife docility plastered on her face. "What do you mean . . . that's where I come in?"

"Teri tells me . . ."

Jack noticed that the doctor called him Mr. Tremain, but he called her Teri. Hmm.

". . . that she lives alone. For the next couple of days, I don't think that would be a good idea. I offered to let her move in with me for a while . . ."

He threw Teri a flirtatious glance and laughed, but when he turned back to find Jack scowling, he sobered quickly.

He cleared his throat. "Teri doesn't want to stay in the hospital for observation, and I'm not sure that's really necessary. She's agreed to take a week off work, but she doesn't really need to curtail her usual physical activities."

"Usual physical activities?" Jack repeated. "What does that mean?"

Dr. Benson smiled at Teri again as if they had a secret understanding. "Marathons are definitely out, but rolling down a hill and doing the bunny hop should pose no problems whatsoever." He turned back to Jack, the teasing grin he wore while speaking to Teri abruptly disappearing into polite professionalism. "However, I would feel much better if she had constant company, at least for a while. She tells me that your father sometimes takes in short-term boarders, and since she's already a friend of the family..."

*A friend of the family?* Jack thought grimly, giving Teri a look of wry disbelief and getting an innocent shrug in reply. A friend of the family wouldn't help a confused old man sign away his dearest possession.

"...it seems like an ideal solution to our problem."

*Our* problem? Jack thought. He hadn't seen Teri since his wedding nine years ago. How had he gotten in so deep, so fast?

"So, what do you think, Mr. Tremain? Since you knew what to do last night when she collapsed, I feel that you're the perfect guy to have around should it happen again...although I'm almost certain it never will, as long as Teri takes care of herself. In this case, I think there were a number of extenuating circumstances that came together to cause this collapse."

Extenuating circumstances...like a kiss? Jack had the urge to excuse himself, go into the hall and bash his head against the wall several times as a means of preparing himself for the inevitable. Because he knew what he would do, what he *had* to do. He'd say yes because he felt partly responsible for what had happened last night.

True, with all the caffeine she'd drank during the day and all the late nights and lack of food leading up to her frazzled, weakened condition, Teri might have keeled over without the help of their kiss...that wonderful, spine-tingling kiss. But then again...

Dr. Benson was looking at Jack as if he was crazy. *Who wouldn't want to take care of this babe for a few days?* he seemed to be asking silently. But the good doctor didn't know Teri from way back like Jack did. While she was certainly a perfect patient today, ready to submit to the doctor's orders about changing her life-style,

Jack didn't believe it would last. She'd end up killing herself.

Jack sighed. But he could at least prevent that from happening for a while. And maybe, just maybe, by helping her for a couple of days, she'd get the idea that work wasn't everything, that you had to stop and smell the roses and so on and so forth.

Jack frowned. It sounded like a lecture he could give himself. But it was different in his case. His heart wasn't irritable; it was... broken. And once was enough.

"Is Teri goin' to stay at our house, Daddy?" Sam inquired, twisting around on his lap and staring up at Jack with big, hopeful eyes.

"Yes, Sam," Jack answered mournfully. "Yes, she certainly is."

"Thank you, Jack," Teri said. Jack looked up and Teri was smiling like an angel. Heaven help him.

# *Chapter Five*

"Okay, Jack, let's talk about the sale of Oak Meadows."

Jack nearly slammed on the brakes. He couldn't believe Teri was bringing up the very subject they'd argued about last night, the subject he'd been avoiding for fear of upsetting her.

"I'm not sure that's such a good idea," he said carefully, taking his eyes off the highway to glance briefly at Teri to gauge her mood. She looked as composed and radiant as she had since waking up that morning. But did he also detect a flicker of her old assertiveness behind that soft beam in her blue eyes? The docile Stepford-wife persona was already fading. Obviously, she had made up her mind that they were going to talk about Oak Meadows.

"Sam's fast asleep in his car seat, so we won't be upsetting him by talking about it," she countered decisively. "We've got a half-hour drive ahead of us, so we might as well put it to good use. Why shouldn't we talk about it? I'm sure it's been uppermost in your mind since last night."

She was not quite right about that. It was uppermost in his mind...just behind his concern for her. And he still didn't intend to jeopardize her recovery by engaging in a heated argument. He wasn't so much worried about upsetting Sam as he was about upsetting *her*. He was still angry about her part in the sale of Oak Meadows, and they were bound to butt heads.

"Jack, I'm not going to keel over again just because we talk about Oak Meadows," she assured him as if she'd been reading his mind. "I'm well fed, well rested, and I'm not feeling a single heart flutter. Besides, I'm approaching the problem with a different attitude this time."

"What do you mean?" he asked, throwing her a suspicious glance.

"I don't just want another sale under my belt. I want to do what's best for your dad and Sam."

She sounded sincere. She probably *was* sincere, feeling only kind and unselfish thoughts toward the world in general. After all, she'd just been plucked from the jaws of death. But Jack still didn't believe for half a minute that this halcyon mood would last. All this selfless generosity was only a temporary condition. Was it right to take advantage of her while she was feeling so magnanimous?

Jack glanced in the rearview mirror at Sam in his car seat. Oak Meadows was his son's inheritance, and Jack was sure Sam would grow to love it over the years as much as his grandfather did. A feeling of protectiveness swelled in Jack's chest, and he determined at that moment that he would do whatever it took to stop the sale of Oak Meadows.

*Even if it means taking advantage of Teri's temporary incarnation into a benevolent being?* he asked himself.

*Hell, yes!* came the heartfelt reply. A few days from now, she'd be kicking herself for losing the sale, but that was her problem, not his.

"I've already told you what I think is best for my father and for Sam," Jack said. "Oak Meadows is their home. Dad has always lived there and he loves it."

"Your dad said he was lonely," Teri reminded him...as if he needed reminding. Jack felt a pang of remorse every time he thought about his dad feeling lonely in his twilight years. "And he said Sam doesn't have anyone to play with," she added.

Jack gave a huff of exasperation. Since he considered it more of a real problem, he addressed his father's situation first. "There are other solutions to loneliness besides selling your home. Dad could get out more, spend more time with friends."

"You put him in the situation he's in," Teri observed. "He's Sam's sole caretaker while you're gone...which is most of the time, I gather."

Jack bristled. "He could hire a baby-sitter."

"Baby-sitters are probably pretty hard to come by out here in the country."

He ignored this comment and added, "And as for my being gone most of the time, with my job I have no choice."

"Everyone has choices, Jack," Teri replied with the superior air she used to assume when they argued in high school. "Now, back to Sam. He needs company, too."

Fast forgetting his intention to avoid contention for the sake of Teri's heart, Jack heatedly replied, "He's not some ragged little orphan locked away in a cold, bare room, Teri. He's got friends. In fact, he has a best friend, Mikey, from our old neighborhood in New Orleans, and he gets together with him every couple of weeks, either here or there."

"Every two weeks? Come on, Jack!"

"Sam will be going to kindergarten next fall. In school he'll be surrounded by other kids."

"That's nearly a year away. What's he supposed to do till then?"

"He could make friends with kids around Oak Meadows and invite them over."

"How? I doubt your father knows many young couples with children who live in the boonies," Teri said dryly.

"My point is this, Teri," Jack persisted, forcing himself to appear calm even though he felt anything but. "The present situation at Oak Meadows is temporary. If my dad sells the house to solve these so-called overwhelming problems, he'll regret it till his dying day."

Teri was silent, and Jack was hoping he'd gotten through to her. He strongly believed everything he'd just said.

Finally, Teri spoke. "Even if you can convince me that what you've said is true," she responded seriously, "I'm not sure if I'd be able to get your father out of the contract."

"Why the hell not?" Jack rasped, keeping down the volume but unable to keep the anger out of his voice.

"Because, as I told you last night, the buyer, a Mr. Schofield, knows your father signed the contract. He wants Oak Meadows as a business venture. He's bought other mansions for the same purpose, and he's making money hand over fist."

Jack laughed incredulously. "How lucrative can the bed-and-breakfast business be?"

Teri turned and looked out the window. She must have considered his question rhetorical, because she ignored it. "He'll fight for what he wants, Jack, and he wants Oak Meadows. If your dad tries to back out, he'll sue."

"So what if he does? I'll pay the damages."

"Don't talk nonsense. That could prove to be a considerable sum of money. Schofield can afford the best lawyers."

"You have a better idea?"

"The best solution to this problem—"

"A problem you caused," Jack couldn't help mumbling.

"Don't delude yourself," she cautioned composedly. "As I was saying before you interrupted, the best solution to this dilemma would be to convince Schofield to back out of the contract willingly."

"And just how do you propose I do that?"

Teri turned and faced Jack with a faint smile. "I have some ideas up my sleeve. Some pretty great ideas, I might add."

"They'd have to be," Jack said sarcastically. "So, tell me what these great ideas are."

Her eyes glinted. "First you have to convince *me* that sabotaging the sale is what's best for your dad and Sam—"

"No problem."

She raised a disbelieving brow. "Then together we'll have to convince your dad."

"You'll help me?" Jack asked wryly.

"I'm quite sure you couldn't do it without me," she replied with a sniff.

Jack bit the inside of his mouth. She was just too damned sure of herself and he was sorely tempted to come back with a taunting or a snide remark, but since he really did need her cooperation, he kept his mouth shut.

"Your dad's really big on this honor thing, Jack," Teri presently continued. "He gave his word. He won't go along with any plan we come up with unless he's convinced it's absolutely the right thing to do."

She had a point, Jack admitted to himself. His dad could be so damned stubborn. Thank God *he* hadn't inherited that streak of mulishness.

"With or without your help, Teri, I'll take care of my dad," he said with a determined jut of his chin.

"First you have to take care of me, Jack."

Jack felt a thrill go through him at Teri's unintentionally seductive words. He'd like to take care of her all right, but that wasn't such a good idea . . . was it?

He swallowed hard and gave her a nervous glance. "What do you mean?"

She laughed and smiled coyly. "I mean you have to convince *me* before you have to even consider convincing your father to thwart Schofield's plans for Oak Meadows. What did you think I meant?"

Jack grunted and trained his eyes on the road. She was deliberately baiting him. Stepford wives never baited their husbands. Was the profound effects of the supposed NDE already wearing off? She was showing her feisty side again. Only now her feistiness was even more attractive because she had an underlying serenity . . . a sort of good-natured nonchalance that was more intimidating than anger. But it wouldn't last.

She laughed again, which was something she'd done a lot of since last night. Her laugh was rich and throaty and wonderfully satisfying to listen to. But while Teri's laughter might be lowering *her* blood pressure, as Viv had suggested, it was only making Jack's skyrocket. The attraction he'd felt for her in high school, despite her abrasive ways, had blossomed again last night when he'd kissed her. Today, the attraction was stronger than ever, and growing.

Jack gritted his teeth. Even though he sensed the feeling was mutual, he had to resist the temptation to find out.

He didn't want to get involved.

She wasn't his type.

Besides, she was self-destructive and would eventually end up killing herself with overwork and stress—if he didn't kill her first... with a kiss.

"Jack! Jack! Pull over! Pull over *right now!*"

In a panic, Jack sped into a J-Mart parking lot, one of the last retail stores on the outskirts of town before they hit the swamps and fields.

"What's the matter?" he asked her as he screeched to a stop and turned to her without bothering to kill the engine. "Aren't you feeling well?"

"Jack, I'm—"

He grabbed her wrist and began taking her pulse. "Shhh. Don't talk now." Fifteen seconds later, he dropped her wrist and looked searchingly into her face. "Your pulse is fine. It's slower and stronger than mine. And you look... well... *wonderful.*"

"I *feel* wonderful," Teri assured him with a touch of impatience in her voice. "You're fussing too much over me, you know. I only wanted you to pull over so I could do a little shopping."

"Shopping?" he repeated blankly.

"I don't have a stitch to wear except what I've got on. Unless you want to drive into the city to my apartment today and end up driving back to Oak Meadows during rush hour, I really ought to pick up a few items of clothing. I've never shopped at J-Mart before, but they're bound to have lots of casual stuff like jeans and tops. You don't mind, do you?''

Jack was so relieved she was feeling okay, he was prepared to tolerate just about anything. Besides, she was already getting out of the car. Talk about choices...what choice was she giving him? He sighed, resigned to the inevitable. But he knew women and shopping, so he hoped he could speed things up by offering to stay in the car with Sam. If she knew they were waiting outside for her, maybe she wouldn't take all day to try on a few—

*"Toys!"* Jack turned around to observe Sam pointing a chubby index finger at J-Mart and rubbing his just barely awake eyes with his free fist. ''J-Mart gots toys, Daddy,'' Sam said excitedly. ''They got Power Rangers and ever'thing! I saw them on telebision! Can we go in, Daddy? Can we?''

''Sure, Sam,'' Jack said, smiling weakly. ''Why not? Hang on a second while I park.''

Sam didn't get out to stores like J-Mart very often, so he was bug-eyed as they went down the aisles in the toy section. He didn't actually ask for a single thing, but he eagerly pointed at the toys he liked and jabbered away about their virtues.

Jack hadn't been back in the States long enough to stock up on cash, and he never used a credit card, so he kept promising Sam he'd get this or that toy for Christmas.

''Are you sure you're going to be around at Christmas?'' Teri asked him in a whisper, then gave him a measured look.

She had a point. Admittedly, his work schedule was unpredictable, and there was no guarantee he'd be home for the holidays. But he didn't like being reminded that he was too much of an absentee parent. It made him feel guilty, which made him angry at himself . . . which made him angry with *her*. "I'll bring him back tomorrow after I've been to the bank," Jack said gruffly.

"I've got money on me. I'll lend you some," Teri offered.

"That's not necessary—"

"Don't be silly, Jack. I know you're good for it," she insisted briskly.

"For crying out loud, Teri, it's not like there's a rush. It's not his birthday or Christmas."

"Why does it have to be? If you're worried about spoiling him, don't. He's a good kid. And who said gifts only had to be given on fixed holidays?"

Jack felt cornered. It wasn't just the idea of borrowing money that bothered him, but the whole implication that he didn't know what was best for his own son. But, once again, she had a point. Sam never whined for anything and he never threw tantrums to get his way. Toys were never used as a bribe, either.

And what she'd said made him think. Why shouldn't gifts be given just for the pleasure of it? he admitted grudgingly. Did there always have to be a specific occasion to justify giving? Life was too short to wait for a date on the calendar to show affection and caring . . . whether through the buying of gifts or by expressing your love through words.

Jack shook his head to clear it. Where was this saccharine-sweet, greeting-card philosophy coming from? Maybe he should use his journalistic talents to write for Hallmark, he groused to himself.

Jack bent down and looked into Sam's animated face. "How would you like to pick out a few toys today?" he asked him.

Sam's eyes grew to the size of a Frisbee. "Really, Daddy? But it's not Christmas yet!"

"Why should it have to be?" Jack said, astounded to find himself repeating Teri's argument.

Ecstatic, Sam clapped his hands and said, "How many can I have?"

Jack laughed. "How about three big things and three small things. Does that sound okay?"

Sam nodded happily and Jack let him loose. He watched his son run up and down the aisles, excitedly picking up and setting down toys, running over with some of them to show him and Teri, trying to make up his mind which three big things and which three small things he wanted. Jack had to admit that it was a lot of fun and wondered why he'd never done it before. But he knew why. No one had ever given him the push he needed.

He slid a look toward Teri. She was watching Sam, too, her eyes glowing, a huge smile on her lips. She was enjoying Sam's rapturous shopping spree as much as he was. Seeming to sense his scrutiny, she turned, and Jack caught a flash of "I told you so" in those bright blue eyes of hers.

"Don't look so smug," he advised her, edging near to whisper. "Since you've had your alleged NDE, I suppose you're going to be even more sure you're always right . . . right?"

"When you're right, you're right," she flung back tartly, then threw him a sweet smile. "Since my *alleged* NDE, my priorities have changed. And I'm willing to impart my acquired wisdom at no additional charge. You could take a lesson from what I've learned, and all without ever once leaving your mortal body."

He gave her a crooked smile. "Thanks, but if I want to hallucinate, I can always take drugs."

Teri shook her head at him. "Disbeliever," she branded him. "You're as stubborn as you always were."

Despite the fun, Jack was relieved when Sam finally settled on six toys and they were able to turn in the direction of women's attire. Soon they'd be done and he could take Teri back to the house and distance himself from her. Well, sort of. He'd still have to keep a sharp eye on her to monitor her heart rate.

Unfortunately, before they were out of the toy section, Teri was diverted by the aisle that was lined with cellophane-fronted boxes of dolls. She stared down the row, seemingly mesmerized.

Teri wasn't sure why she'd stopped. Even as a little girl, she'd never really been into dolls. But then maybe that was why she couldn't take her eyes off them now....

"Oh... Look at all these dolls!" she whispered in a reverent tone. "They're beautiful!" she enthused, pivoting to take them all in, walking backward while she stared.

After a while, when neither Jack nor Sam had said a word, Teri wrenched her eyes away from the frilly skirts and porcelain-perfect faces and looked at her male companions. It wasn't just that they were men and not interested in dolls, they seemed surprised that she—a mature adult—was acting so gaga over a bunch of dolls. She felt herself blush.

"Don't tell me... let me guess. You didn't play with dolls when you were a little girl and now you've decided it's one of your new priorities?" Jack suggested dryly.

Teri turned away and self-consciously ran her finger along the smooth cardboard of a box containing a doll that looked just like a newborn infant, dressed in a frilly white christening gown. She lifted the box and stared at the baby doll inside with what she knew was an almost childlike awe. Why were these dolls suddenly so fascinating to her?

"You're making fun of me, Stonewall," she whispered. "But you're partly right. I didn't play with dolls when I was a kid. I was always too busy studying for a spelling bee, or running a lemonade stand," she confessed, never taking her eyes off the doll. To herself, she added, *What was I thinking?* Then, despite Jack's continued scrutiny, she impulsively opened the box and took out the doll, experimentally cradling it in her arms as if it were a real infant. "Its eyes open and shut," she observed wonderingly. "And the box says it eats, burps and wets its diapers."

"I used to do that," Sam piped up, seemingly enthralled at seeing a grown-up so worked up about a toy. "I used to wear diapers, but I'm a big boy now and I go potty standin' up... just like Daddy!"

Jack grimaced and Teri chuckled. "Yes, you're a big boy now, Sam." Reluctantly, she put the doll back in the box, saying, "And I'm a big girl, too. Much too big to play with dolls." She'd missed that particular treat and it was impossible to revert to childhood and start over. Hiding her regret and embarrassment behind a bright facade, Teri turned back to Jack and said, "So, what are we waiting for? Let's go find some fun duds."

Jack pushed the cart behind Teri as they left the toy section. He was ashamed of himself for having made fun of her fascination with the dolls. Obviously, Teri the Terror hadn't had a normal, fun-filled childhood. She'd been driven to succeed even then. And now, suddenly, she had changed? Could a brush with death really alter a person's outlook so drastically? He wasn't sure what to believe.

But he couldn't control the urge to stop short before they were too far away from the Barbie and the Madame Alexander and the Tiny Tears dolls to say, "Aren't you allowed to buy a toy for yourself, Teri?"

She turned, surprised and more embarrassed than ever. "Oh, well, what would I do with it except look at it?" she asked, shrugging off the question and hurrying on to the clothing department.

Jack grimly followed with Sam and the cart full of toys. He knew she wanted a doll, but he also knew that people frequently denied themselves things they really wanted. *That was a fact,* he heartily could endorse, slavishly watching Teri's curvy hips as they moved through the store.

Their twenty minutes in the women's section was short but torturous. Teri tried on jeans and modeled them for him, standing in front of the mirror with her hands on her hips, peering over her shoulder at Jack in an unintentionally sexy pose.

Then she picked out playful tube tops and T-shirts and bright, colorful, *clingy* sweaters. Everything she bought was so different from her conservative navy blue suit, she could have been buying them for a totally different person. Jack was confused. Who was this woman anyway? She still might be Teri the Terror at heart, but she'd taken on a whole new attitude.

Just when Jack was mopping his brow and hoping to get out of there before he threw her to the ground for carnal purposes, she decided to buy...lingerie.

Jack kept an eye on Sam as he played with his new Power Ranger toy on the carpet near the dressing room, the child completely engrossed in an imaginary world. But he also surreptitiously kept an eye on Teri as she picked out insubstantial scraps of black lace, red satin, pristine white cotton and hot pink nylon. The tantalizing colors flashed before his eyes in a never-ending, nerve-tingling parade.

By the time she'd finally paid for all the purchases and they were headed for the car with a shopping cart full of bulging plastic bags, Jack was numb. He was sure his inability to react to his surroundings was a defense mechanism, but he'd have to snap out of it if he was going to drive them the rest of the way home.

"How about a hot dog?" Teri suggested as they piled the bags of toys and clothes into the back of the Land Cruiser. "There's a vendor right over there and some picnic tables under those trees. It might be our last chance for food before we get home, and I don't know about you guys, but I don't think I can wait that long. I'm starving!"

"Yeah, Daddy," Sam said, hugging his father's leg and peering hopefully up at him. "I'm hungry, too. Are you hungry?"

Jack couldn't think of one good reason not to go along with such a plan, even though he had a sinking feeling that watching Teri eat again might be a disaster. But maybe he'd reached his limit. Maybe it wasn't possible to be any more attracted to her than he already was.

Boy, was he ever wrong.

After they locked up the Cruiser, the three of them walked to the small trailer that was dispensing hot dogs. Teri had the vendor pile her footlong with spicy relish and mustard. And sure enough, while sitting under the trees in broad daylight, even with his son chattering away on one side of him, Jack still managed to become painfully aroused while watching Teri eat.

She just did it with such *relish!* He nearly groaned aloud at his own ridiculous pun.

She was tidy, dabbing her mouth frequently with a napkin, but she just enjoyed the whole process so damned much it made you want to—

Well, it made Jack want to run away to Eastern Europe, or some other place a little less dangerous than the hot spot he found himself sitting smack-dab in the middle of today.

"TERI, YOU DIDN'T TAKE your phone," Beau commented when Teri and Jack and Sam bustled into the hall with all their bags of loot.

"I thought you might need it," Teri explained, smiling.

"That's very kind of you," Beau responded, returning her smile. "Our phone service was finally restored about ten o'clock, which is also about the time your cellular phone started ringing. I wasn't sure whether to answer for you or not, but then I decided you might appreciate it if I took messages." He handed her a whole slew of them. "You're much in demand, m'dear."

Teri could feel Jack watching her, no doubt waiting to see how she reacted to her phone messages. He probably expected her to make some excuse to call everyone back, subsequently finding herself knee-deep in work again and unable to keep her promise to take a week off. But she was going to prove him wrong.

"I'm only going to make *one* phone call, Jack," Teri informed him, meeting his suspicious gaze with a challenging one of her own. "I have to call the office and let them know what's going on. I'll instruct them to take care of my clients this week and cover all my calls."

"*All* your calls?" Beau inquired quietly. "There's three messages from Schofield's broker, Ken Jacobs, in that

pile of messages, Teri. I'm sure they're itching to se
closing date."

"Well, I'm afraid I'm going to have to treat Schofield
and Jacobs like all my clients, Beau," she told him.
"They're going to have to wait till I've taken a much-de-
served vacation before I can talk business with them.
Besides, it's doctor's orders."

Teri couldn't miss the look of relief that flickered over
Beau's features at news that would dismay most buyers—a postponement in scheduling the closing date. She
supposed she could take his reaction as partial proof that
he was in no hurry to move out of his beloved home. Jack
certainly thought so, as he was giving her a smug I-told-
you-so look.

"What did the doctor say, Teri?" Beau asked. "It
must have been good news because it looks like you
stopped on the way home and bought out a store or two,"
he added, watching Sam pull toy after toy out of plastic
bags.

"I'll fill you in on all the details, Dad," Jack said.
"Teri's going upstairs to relax for a while."

Just to irritate him, Teri raised her brows at Jack and
said, "Oh, I am, am I?" She got the hoped-for dark look
in return and laughed, saying, "Actually, I *am* dying for
a bath." She moved toward the stairs. "Then I'm going
to put on one of my new outfits. See you later, Sam," she
called to the little boy.

Sam dragged his attention away from his toys and
stood up to wave vigorously. "See ya, Teri," he called
back. "Thanks for makin' Daddy stop at J-Mart! Me and
Bartholomew like our new toys a whole bunch!"

"Don't mention it, Sam," Teri sang out as she headed
up to Jack's room.

"Remember, Teri..." Jack said, standing at the foot of the stairs. He lifted his index finger and lowered his brows in a warning. "Just one call, that's all."

"What's the matter, Jack? Don't you trust me?" she taunted.

"What do you think?" he retorted with mock severity. "And take a quick bath, 'cause I'm going to be checking on you in a few minutes."

She made a face at him, then disappeared down the hallway. Despite the way she took pleasure in irritating him, Jack was already worrying about her and considering how much time he should give her before knocking on her door—actually *his* door—when his father caught his attention by loudly clearing his throat.

"What's going on, Jack?" his dad asked with a speculative glint in his eye. "Is Teri staying with us for a while?"

"Just for a few days. That's okay, isn't it?"

"Fine with me," Beau replied readily. There was a pause while Jack's gaze wandered back up the stairs. Beau moved close and whispered so Sam wouldn't hear, "You movin' out of the bedroom, son, or are you two sharin' it?"

Jack turned and gave his father a glowering look, then realized the sly old fox was teasing. He threw his arm around his dad's shoulders and the two of them headed toward the library. "Dad," he began, "if I shared a room with that one, I'd just be asking for trouble."

"What's wrong with a little trouble, son?" Beau inquired. "Hell, you only live once."

"Or twice...if we can believe Teri," Jack muttered.

# Chapter Six

Jack walked rapidly down the hall, past the open door of his bedroom to the main bathroom with the big, claw-footed tub. "I can't believe she's still in there," he grumbled to himself. "What does a person do in a tub for thirty minutes, for crying out loud?"

Jack's irritable mutterings were only a front to hide his fear. He had expected to find Teri dressed and resting in his bedroom, not still in the bathroom doing who knew what. Drowning, maybe?

He hated having one more person to worry about. Before last night, only his father and Sam had the ability to make his heart beat fast with anxiety at the thought of something happening to them. Then Teri had to come along, crumple, nearly die, then revive in his arms, win over his son with a snap of her fingers, hold a doll with the wistful appreciation of a child, and try on a few pairs of hip-hugging jeans at J-Mart and...whammo! Suddenly, he's added her to his list of adrenaline triggers.

His first instinct was to rush in and make sure she was all right, but he controlled himself with an effort, paused outside and listened. She had the radio on, and the soft-rock tune was all he could hear coming from the other side of the thick, old-fashioned paneled door. There were no sounds of water dripping and splashing the way one would expect to hear from someone who was supposed to be taking a bath.

"Teri?" he called softly, knocking on the door. "You all right?"

He waited three seconds, every second more torturous than the last. He was about to employ SWAT team tactics, kick down the door and storm into the room, when Teri answered. "That you, Jack? Come in. The door's open."

His first reaction at hearing her cheerful voice was relief. Then a kind of nervous confusion took over. Why was she inviting him into the bathroom with her? The room was large by modern standards, with plenty of space to dress in, so maybe she was done with her bath and just needed a zipper done up or help with a button, he reasoned. But even such a small gesture of intimacy would sorely test his powers of resistance. Did he dare go in?

"What are you waiting for, Jack? I *need* you!"

She needed him. That settled the matter. She might sound normal—just as she had before her collapse last night—but that could be far from the case. Quickly, he turned the cut-glass knob, swung open the door... and stopped in his tracks.

Teri didn't need artificial resuscitation... but *he* might.

She was still bathing and half reclined in the huge tub, her chin just about level with the curved rim. The ends of her shag-cut hair were wet and curled against her slender neck like the tails of sea horses. Her cheeks were all pink and dewy. She grinned at him from a mountain of bubbles that covered her from the shoulders down and said, "Shut the door, will you? There's a draft from the hall."

Teri was thoroughly enjoying herself. A sudden mischievous impulse had made her invite Jack into the bathroom just so she could watch him squirm. She was perfectly proper, covered from neck to toe in foam and bubbles, but he obviously wasn't sure what to do, where to look. His gaze drifted from one bathroom fixture to another, then finally rested uncomfortably on her again. Tersely, he asked, "Why did you tell me to come in if you were still in the tub?"

"I'm decent," she said with a shrug that sent the frothy water lapping around her shoulders. She felt a thrill as his eyes were immediately riveted to that part of her anatomy. Okay, so maybe she also wanted to flirt with him a little.... It was a new experience for her and she couldn't think of a worthier object of flirtation than handsome Jackson Tremain. She raised an eyebrow and gave him a coy look. "You saw more of me when you undressed me last night."

"What do you want?" he inquired gruffly, looking at his shoes, the sink, the towel rail. She watched his color rise. Damn, he was a handsome man. That dark hair and those green eyes, that chiseled face and those broad shoulders. It made her wish there was room in the tub for two and she were brave enough to reach out and . . .

She shivered, making the bubbles jiggle. He immediately looked concerned. "Are you cold? The last thing you need is to catch your death . . . I mean—"

"Are you going to close the door or not, Stonewall?"

He shut the door, then crossed his arms and scowled down at her. "I thought you said you needed me," he prompted.

Thinking fast, Teri said, "I do need you. Listen to that song on the radio and tell me what the name of it is. It sounds like an instrumental version of 'Benny and the Jets,' but I'm not absolutely—"

"You called me in here to ask me *that?*" he said, raising his voice. "I thought you weren't feeling well!"

"Jack, you've become far too excitable," Teri lectured him teasingly. "You need to find a relaxing hobby. Like golf . . . or bubble baths, for instance."

Teri lifted one arm in a graceful, balletic pose and Jack watched the little scuds of bubbles slip slowly down her pale, smooth skin. He swallowed hard. The air was steamy and seductively cloying . . . filled with the intoxicating scent of lavender.

Teri sighed luxuriously, her eyes half-closed as she lifted her other arm, sensuously gliding a pink washcloth from elbow to shoulder. If Jack didn't know better, he could swear that Teri was purposely tempting him.

"I never knew I liked bubble baths till today," she said. "I was always a shower kind of girl, you know, in and out of the stall in the time it took to make drip coffee in the kitchen. But Ginger thought I might enjoy soaking for a while and she gave me a bottle of bubble bath she bought in England last year. Wasn't that nice of her?"

Jack watched as Teri scooped a handful of bubbles and held them close to her face.

"Have you ever looked at soap bubbles, Jack?" she asked him in a reflective voice after a long pause.

Suddenly he knew that she was no longer teasing. She was serious.

"I mean *really* looked at them? I never had before today. They're fascinating . . . all slick and smooth and perfectly round with tiny, shiny patches of blue. . . ."

Jack wanted desperately to say something, to make his excuses and hightail it out of there as fast as he could. But the words stuck in his throat, strangled by a huge lump of longing. Watching Teri was mesmerizing. She was enchanting....

Or enchanted.

Or maybe *he* was enchanted. Voodoo might explain the spell she'd woven over him since last night. All he knew for sure was that tearing his eyes away from her would be as painful as it sounded.

When Teri turned from her contemplation of bubbles and found Jack staring at her, she felt a rush of embarrassment. One minute she'd been flirting with him and the next minute she was rhapsodizing about bubbles. But impulses like that had come over her frequently since last night's NDE. She couldn't seem to help herself.

"You think I'm bonkers, don't you?" she said, throwing him a sheepish look. "And I can't say I blame you. It's just that since I died last night, then was lucky enough to come back, my senses have been...well...*on fire.* I feel everything more keenly. Everything I look at is brighter, more vivid. And maybe you haven't noticed, but I even enjoy food more. It's crazy, I guess, but I can't seem to help it." She paused, then admitted for the first time out loud, "It scares me a little."

Jack stared at her with a sober expression for so long, Teri was sure he was debating whether or not to send for the men in white coats to take her away. But he finally cleared his throat and said, "Don't worry, Teri. I'm sure it won't last. You'll be your old self again in no time."

Teri scowled. "I'm not so sure I want to be *exactly* like my *old self* again. You didn't like me that way, did you?"

"Well, it wasn't healthy," he hedged. "Look at it this way. Maybe this new you is a good thing...as long as you don't go too far with it."

Actually, he wasn't at all worried that she'd go too far with it. Jack's biggest fear was that in a matter of days the whole impression of her brush with death would wear off completely and she'd be working herself into an early grave again. But he wasn't about to say so. Why burst her bubble?

"You're going to turn into a prune if you stay in there much longer," he finally said. "I'll leave so you can dry off."

He turned, but she stopped him, saying, "Jack, can I tell you one more thing before you go?"

He turned back, hoping whatever she had to say was brief and commonplace like, "Throw me that loofah sponge."

No such luck.

"Jack, I don't think I've ever really thanked you for last night, but I—"

"You thanked me," he said, cutting her off.

"No, not like you deserve to be thanked." She gave him a heartfelt smile over her bubbles. "You gave me another chance to live. And to show you how grateful I am—and I know this is going to sound as corny as Kansas—I'm going to live every day as if it were my last."

"Sounds exhausting," he muttered, one side of his mouth lifting in a reluctant grin.

"Just watch," she promised with a mischievous glint in her eyes. Then she puckered her lips and blew the bubbles in her cupped hands into the air, sending the sudsy foam flying in all directions. "Now get out, Stonewall," she said, laughing as he whisked some suds off his chin, "before I *really* embarrass you."

Jack turned and left, shutting the door behind him, then leaning against it with his eyes closed, trying to catch his breath.

"Excuse me, Jack."

Startled, and feeling as guilty as Sylvester caught with a mouthful of Tweety Pie, Jack opened his eyes to find Ginger peering at him through her magnifying bifocals. She had one arm curved around a makeup case, and the other arm was holding a comb, a brush and a giant can of hair spray against her chest. Obviously, she wanted to get by.

"Uh... hello, Ginger," he said, still propped against the door. He smiled nervously.

"Hello," she replied, returning his smile. She waited a minute as if expecting him to move. When he didn't, she said, "I just thought I'd spruce up a bit before dinner." She raised her thin, penciled brows.

"But you already look lovely," he said, trying to delay the inevitable.

Now Ginger's brows lowered as she studied him. "Jack, did you know you have bubbles in your hair?"

"I do?" He laughed, the sound as genuine as a plugged nickel. "I can't imagine how—"

"Wait a minute," Ginger said suddenly, cocking her head to the side. "I hear music. And I think I hear someone singing, too."

Of course she heard music and singing. So did Jack. Oblivious to the jostling going on just outside the bathroom door, Teri was singing along with the radio to the tune of "Wild Thing" by the Troggs, belting out the words with the gusto of a torch-song performer.

Now Ginger was giving him a whole different kind of look. Did sweet old ladies smirk? he wondered.

"It's all right, Jack," she said with a knowing chuckle. "When I saw you leaving the bathroom, I naturally assumed it was empty." She leaned forward and whispered, "Apparently I was mistaken. But it's no problem . . . no problem at all. I can certainly wait a few more minutes to fix my face and tease my hair."

"You don't understand, Ginger," Jack began, then gave a huff of exasperation when he realized he wasn't sure how to explain what had just happened between him and Teri and make it sound innocent. It *was* innocent, wasn't it?

"Oh, but I *do* understand," Ginger replied with a sly nod, scooting down the hall in her fuzzy, lop-eared bunny slippers and bulky pink chenille robe. "Don't worry about it, Jack. I have very modern views. See you at dinner!"

Jack felt like a lech who preyed on women in bathtubs for nefarious purposes. And if he had the *name,* he ought to be able to play the *game,* he thought peevishly. Only things weren't that simple. Rubbing the back of his neck, he walked down the hall, away from Teri and a tub full of temptation.

As TERI DESCENDED the stairs on the way to dinner, she slid her hand along the glossy oak rail, admiring its antique craftsmanship and beauty. Over the past month, she'd shown the house to dozens of clients and Realtors, pointing out the special amenities of the antebellum mansion, but never really appreciating them. Now the house seemed to her like a storeroom full of treasures and memories that had been passed down through generations of Tremains. But then, her newly heightened senses were making her see a lot of things—and people—with a higher regard.

At the bottom of the stairs, Teri found herself pausing, then instead of turning right toward the dining room, she turned left toward the library. She hadn't seen the portrait since her glimpse of it during a flash of lightning last night, just before she keeled over and quit living. The expressions on the painted faces of Stephen, Caroline and even little Samuel, had appeared disapproving and accusatory. Now she suspected that her own feelings of guilt had led her to imagine that the subjects in the portrait were actually watching her and passing judgment on her actions.

Now that she'd met them in person—or should she say in spirit?—she wondered how she'd feel coming face-to-face with the portrait again.

The door was open, the hurricane lamps were lit, and there was already a fire crackling cheerfully in the fireplace. Obviously, this was where Beau intended everyone to retire after dinner. Teri had never liked the room before, but today as she entered it, she was filled with a sense of peace.

Her first view of the portrait was from the side, so she had to walk to the center of the room and right up to the picture to actually be able to connect eye-to-eye with her new friends.

When she finally stood in front of the mantel, staring up at the faces in the portrait, she felt none of the creepiness she felt before. She saw what other people had always seen in the portrait and what *she* had always missed; she saw the love Stephen and Caroline and Samuel had for each other and for their home . . . so grand and lovely in the background. And she saw something else, too. She saw friendly recognition in their eyes as they looked back at her.

Wait a minute. . . . As they looked *back* at her?

*There I go again!* she chided herself. *Giving painted images human qualities and abilities. They aren't actually looking at me, for heaven's sake! It's just not possible!*

But the longer Teri looked, the less sure she became. There seemed to be something magical about the painting, something eerily beautiful and otherworldly. But none of that stuff scared her anymore. She knew now that she had nothing to be afraid of—not even death.

When Jack stepped inside the room, he stopped and waited for Teri to notice him. While he waited, he simply enjoyed the view.

She was wearing one of the sweaters she'd bought at J-Mart, a pale pink, cotton-knit turtleneck she'd tucked into a pair of snug-fitting jeans. Her hair was fluffy and shiny and curled in shaggy wisps at her nape.

She was standing with her hands clasped behind her, her shoulders back and her chin up. Her profile was quite alluring; a pert nose, pointed chin and small, firm breasts were outlined against a pale gold vintage-print wallpaper.

Her lips were curved in a faintly bemused smile as she stared at the portrait over the mantel, her absorption in the painting giving him an idea. But first he needed to catch her attention.

"Teri?" He stepped farther into the room. She still didn't move a muscle. *"Hellooo,"* he said, stretching out the word. "Earth to Teri? Earth to Teri?"

She turned, her eyes slightly dazed as if she'd just awakened from a pleasant dream. "Oh, hi, Jack. I didn't hear you come in."

"You didn't hear my squeaky loafers in the hall? Jeez, Teri, you had enough concentration going on in here to commune with the dead."

She smiled and said, "And why not? Most of them are probably very nice people."

"Well, since you probably met some while you were visiting the spirit world last night, you would know, I guess," he retorted with a wry lift of one brow.

"Your sarcasm doesn't faze me, Stonewall," she coolly informed him. "As a matter of fact, I did meet some dead people last night. *Nice* dead people."

He gave her a beleaguered look. "Let's not go there, Teri. We'll just argue." He had a different agenda in mind. He motioned toward the portrait. "Would you like to know a little bit about the people in the picture? They ought to fascinate you. They're dead, too."

Teri hesitated. She was probably debating whether to have the pleasure of arguing with him or getting along with him long enough to learn about his ancestors. "Yes, I would like to know about the people in the picture," she finally admitted in a tepid tone, but the eager light in her eyes indicated how curious she really was. Teri sat down on the sofa and patted the cushion next to hers. Now, suddenly, she was looking coy as hell. "Sit down and tell me everything you know," she said invitingly.

Jack was nervous about being so close to her, but he knew it might help his cause if he was friendly and cozy. He only hoped it wouldn't disturb his concentration. He took a chance and sat down. "Dad knows a lot more about them than I do," he began, "but he's finishing up dinner preparations. I suppose you know they're the Tremains that originally built Oak Meadows in 1855?"

"I heard your father telling clients that when I showed the house. Almost everyone paused to look at the portrait."

"Did he ever explain how they died?"

"If he did, I was either not in the room or I was on a call. Or I just wasn't listening."

Jack nodded, believing the latter to be the likeliest possibility. "Well, most people are surprised to learn that Stephen, Caroline and Samuel all died shortly after the portrait was finished."

Jack stretched his arm along the back of the sofa. Teri turned her head and her hair brushed his bare forearm. He wished he could run his fingers through those golden locks....

Teri's brows drew together. "Well, that would certainly explain why Samuel was still a child when I met him," she murmured.

Jack firmly corralled his wandering thoughts and said, "What did you say about Sam?"

Teri shrugged and looked away. "Nothing. I was just talking to myself. You were going to tell me how the Tremains died, Jack. Please go on."

"It's kind of a sad story. Are you up for it?"

"Sure," she said with another shrug, but Jack could tell she was really interested. This was a great opportunity for him to try to convey to Teri how important Oak Meadows had always been to the Tremains. And why it should stay in the family.

"As you can tell by Stephen's uniform, he was in the Confederate Army. It's simple for us now to see the importance of the abolition of slavery, but back then, things were much more complicated. Stephen believed in fighting for his home and his family, and that meant fighting against the Union."

"If you're afraid I'll be prejudiced against him for being a Confederate soldier, you're mistaken, Jack," Teri said. "I know he's a very nice man."

"You *know* he's a very nice man?" Jack repeated with a quizzical look. "You speak of him in the present tense, Teri, but he's been dead and buried for over a hundred years. You couldn't possibly *know* him. Or maybe he was one of the dead people you met during your NDE?''

Teri was trying hard not to get ticked off by Jack's continued sarcasm and patronizing attitude about her NDE. She wanted to tell him how narrow-minded she thought he was, but she wanted to hear Caroline and Stephen's story even more, so she held her irritation in check and said, ''Just get on with the story, Jack.''

''Well, it's pretty brief, actually. Stephen was killed early in the war in 1862 when Admiral Farragut forced open the mouth of the Mississippi and Federals took over New Orleans and Baton Rouge. Shortly after that, perhaps within a day or two, drunken Yankee soldiers paid an unauthorized visit to Oak Meadows on their way upriver, and Caroline and Samuel were fatally injured defending their home. They were all dead within a week.''

Teri nodded and stared up at the portrait, admiration and sympathy for the Tremains welling in her chest. ''Who inherited the estate after the war? Obviously, they couldn't be direct descendants of Stephen and Caroline.''

''Stephen's brother, Thomas, survived the war and was able to make Oak Meadows one of the few profitable farms in the area after slavery was abolished. But I suspect his motivation for working so hard to preserve the place had less to do with financial reasons—after all, he had other property and means of support—and more to do with honoring his brother's memory.''

''They must have been very close,'' Teri said softly. She wondered how it would feel to be part of a close-knit family.

Jack nodded. ''Thomas made this place his home, growing to love it as much as Stephen had. His children carried on the tradition, farming the vast fields belonging to Oak Meadows. As the years passed, however, and with the financial pressures of the Depression and the changing economy, chunks of the land were sold off as the need arose and the estate dwindled to its current ten acres. But you already know that part, don't you? As Dad's real-estate agent, you had to know how much land came with the house."

"I had what I thought were all the pertinent facts," she acknowledged. Then she sighed heavily and confessed, "But I never thought of Oak Meadows as a home. I only thought of it as prime property to be sold to the highest bidder."

Jack grabbed Teri's hand. "Am I getting through to you, Teri?" he implored. "Do you finally understand how my dad feels about this place?"

Teri looked down at their joined hands. She liked the feel of his long, strong fingers curved around hers. "I understand how *you* feel, Jack," she said at last, determined not to let her attraction to Jack sway her decision one way or the other. "After all, you're the one trying to convince me to encourage Schofield to back out of the deal. But *you* don't even live here."

"What do you mean I don't live here? I grew up here. Hell, it's my *home!*"

Teri looked up at him and shook her head. "But you don't *live* here. You live on the road."

He made an impatient sound with his tongue. "I won't *always* live on the road."

"Oh? And when will you start living at home?"

Jack hadn't expected this line of questioning. Hell, he didn't know when he'd get tired of living out of a suitcase. After Pamela died, work had been the addictive drug of choice, the anesthesia that numbed him so he could get through each day without sinking into despair.

And now, over a year later, he supposed he was still using his busy schedule as an excuse to keep from getting too involved in life.

When he was home for more than a week, he grew restless. He didn't like having so much time to think. And he wasn't used to sticking around and being a full-time dad. The truth was, the idea scared the hell out of him.

"That's not the point," Jack said at last, frustrated by the turn the conversation had taken.

"The point is that your dad's lonely, Jack. And so is Sam...who, by the way, deserves to have a father around at least half the time."

"Since when have you become a family relations shrink?" Jack asked caustically, withdrawing his hand from her warm clasp. "Is that what you did in Heaven last night, Teri? Sit in on some psychobabble workshops headed by Jung and Freud? Save it, please. And, if you don't mind...mind your own business."

"My business is selling houses," she coolly reminded him.

He stiffened. "Is that a warning?"

"It's just a reality check. I don't want to see the house sold and turned into a...a...commercial venture any more than you do, but—"

"So I have convinced you?" Jack brightened.

"You and, er, others have convinced me, but—"

"What others?"

Teri wanted Jack to believe she'd had an NDE. She wanted him to give her the credit she deserved for knowing the difference between a hallucination and a real encounter with the afterlife. But she wasn't ready to tell him that she'd actually visited briefly with his ancestors. So she sidestepped the question and continued her probing instead. "What are you going to do about your dad,

Jack? I won't be a party to something he doesn't completely approve of. And besides that, I really worry about his being lonely if he stays on at Oak Meadows."

Jack looked thoughtful. "I never considered this before, but judging by his influence on Ginger, I suppose my father might still have a certain appeal to women. If he hired a baby-sitter now and then, and took some nice woman to dinner, who knows what might happen?"

"Maybe he doesn't like leaving Sam with a sitter," Teri suggested.

"So, since I'm not here to properly take care of my son," Jack snarled, "you're saying that it's my fault my dad has a nonexistent social life?"

"You really have a guilt complex, Stonewall, or you wouldn't get so defensive every time I try to make a point," Teri replied evenly.

"I'm not being defensive," Jack objected. "And furthermore, I don't want to argue with you."

Exasperated, Teri exclaimed, "You were never shy about arguing with me in high school. Do you think you're doing me a favor now by backing away from a friendly little disagreement? I won't keel over and die, Jack. I promise you."

"I'm not so sure about that," he groused. "Besides, what happened to your good intentions? Your new lease on life? I thought you were going to live every day as if it were your last. Are you planning to argue right up to your last day on earth?"

Teri laughed. "If you're around, I probably will." Then she sobered. "I'm not trying to fight with you, but I do have some opinions about what's going on in this house. For example, why do you think your dad needs to go out somewhere to find a woman? What's wrong with Ginger? She's right here and she's crazy about him."

Jack frowned. "You think so, too?"

"It's as plain as the nose on my face."

Jack looked worried. "Do you really think Ginger is my dad's type?"

Teri grinned. "Believe me, there have been odder matches and stranger bedfellows. As long as two people love each other, a little diversity can lend a certain spark to a relationship."

As soon as the words left her mouth, Teri was concerned that Jack might think she was also referring to them and their always-ready-to-spar relationship. And by the troubled, intense look he was giving her, her concern was perfectly justified. Luckily, Jack's father chose that moment to make an entrance.

"Hey, you two!" Beauregard Tremain shouted cheerfully, striding into the room sporting a huge white apron emblazoned with a picture of Graceland. "Dinner's ready, and since I don't cook up such a wagonload of food every day, I expect you to come to the table with hearty appetites."

"You won't have to worry about me, Beau," Teri assured him, standing up. "I'm starving!"

Jack followed Teri and his dad out the door and down the hall toward the dining room. He was eager for dinner not so much because he was hungry, but because he was interested in observing his father's behavior in general, and around Ginger in particular. He had Teri on his side—which was bound to be a first, considering their combative history—but now he had to convince his dad to stay on and fight for Oak Meadows, too.

Jack realized that even if his father returned Ginger's romantic interest, he couldn't hope for a whirlwind romance and sudden wedding plans to change his father's perception of Oak Meadows as a lonely shell, as he'd so bleakly described the place. But a fun flirtation might remind his father that even though he'd lost a wife he'd loved dearly, there were still other wonderful women on the face of the earth.

Jack had to pause for a minute and consider why it had never occurred to *him* to apply the same logic to his own lonely life.

BEAU SAT AT THE HEAD of the long cherry table, with Ginger to his right and Viv to his left. Sam was seated between Ginger and Jack, and Teri was next to Viv. Beau had gone all out, setting the table with antique china and crystal and sterling silver, all shown off to elegant perfection by a white damask tablecloth and candlelight.

"You went to a lot of trouble, Beau," Teri said, smoothing her hand over the tablecloth with an appreciative smile. "Everything looks—and even feels—really beautiful."

"This lovely table reminds me of the elegant dinner scenes in *The Age of Innocence*," Ginger commented, beaming at Beau.

"But the atmosphere here is definitely less stodgy," Viv added.

Beau's face was flushed from a combination of bustling about and standing over a hot stove as well as plain and simple pride. "I don't have company very often," he said, "but when I do, I like to put on the dog, so to speak."

*Especially when there's a female you want to impress,* thought Teri, throwing Jack a significant look.

"We're not eating *dog,* are we, Gran'pa?" Sam asked with a horrified look.

Beau chuckled. "It's just an expression, Sam," he explained. "Putting on the dog means doing things fancy. Now before we get started—"

"Oh, I un'erstand!" Sam interrupted. "This really *is* fancy, Gran'pa." Pushing up on his elbows, he leaned as far across the table as he could and said to Teri, "Usually we eat in the ki'chen, and lots of times we have my fav'rite—macaroni and cheese. An' a vege'ble, of course. Gran'pa al'ays makes me eat vege'bles for dinner."

"I'm sure Teri's glad to hear that, Sam," Jack said, speaking close to Sam's ear, "but I think Grandpa wants to say something important before we start, so let's listen, okay? And please get your elbows off the table, son."

Sam obediently did as he was told and trained his big eyes on his grandfather.

Beau stood up and lifted his wineglass. "I'd like to make a toast or two tonight in honor of such a delightful gathering of guests. But I advise you to hold off tapping your glasses together and taking sips till the end...or else we'll all be too tipsy to eat."

Everyone chuckled, especially Ginger, who was dressed to kill in peach chiffon and couldn't take her adoring eyes off Beau. He'd left his apron in the kitchen and was spiffily dressed in a white, Western-cut jacket, with his usual string tie. He looked like a lean, mean, smooth-shaven Colonel Sanders.

"First to my son, Jack, who is back—thank God—safe and sound, in the good ol' U.S. of A. It's always a pleasure to have you home, son."

"Thanks, Dad," Jack said.

The two men smiled, the affection they felt evident in the softening of their eyes. Despite their disagreement over the sale of Oak Meadows, there was no denying that father and son cared deeply about each other.

And they were both very handsome men, Teri couldn't help but notice for the hundredth time that day. Jack looked especially attractive, and rather European, in his tan sport jacket with an off-white banded-collar shirt underneath. The candlelight picked out the russet highlights in his dark hair.

She supposed that when Jack was seventy, he'd have the same silver abundance of hair his father had. She just hoped he wouldn't wear it in an Elvis do, like Beau did. Remembering the print of Graceland on Beau's apron, Teri was beginning to see a trend. She wondered if he was a closet Elvis-the-Pelvis devotee. But when she considered how genteel and soft-spoken he was, Teri couldn't imagine his being crazy about the legendary rock-and-roll icon.

"My next toast is to Sam for keeping us all young," Beau continued.

"An' Bartholomew, too!" Sam chirped, lifting his ever-present buddy above his head so everyone could see.

"Bartholomew, too," Beau amended with a chuckle. "And to these two lovely ladies, Ginger and Vivien, who have brought liveliness and beauty back into my home."

The potato chip sisters blushed and pshawed and tittered.

"And last but not least, I want to make a toast to your health and future happiness, Teri." Beau's eyes rested on her warmly. "You scared us nearly to death last night, missy, and we're happy as crows in the corn that you gave old St. Peter a rain check. You just stick around with us mortals for a while and see what happens." He winked.

Teri smiled. "Thank you, Beau."

''To new beginnings,'' he finished, lifting his glass at last.

Everyone picked up their wineglasses—except for Sam, who performed his toast with a small tumbler of lemonade—and indicated their hearty approval of Beau's sentiments. But Teri could see a troubled look in Jack's eyes. Maybe he was wondering if Beau was still stubbornly determined to start his new beginning at some place other than his beloved Oak Meadows.

She sipped her wine, relishing the rich, fruity flavor, while making a firm resolution. Even if Beau was regretting his decision to sell Oak Meadows, Jack might not be able to convince his father to make the effort to get out of the deal. He was a stubborn man and a staunch believer in keeping his word no matter how devastating the results. But Teri had certain facts that might convince Beauregard Tremain that keeping his word to her was no longer an honorable obligation.

Teri marveled that, suddenly, it was just as important to her as it was to Jack to keep Oak Meadows in the family. He had convinced her that the Tremains belonged there. And somehow she knew Stephen and Caroline and Samuel would agree.

# Chapter Seven

Sam fell asleep ten minutes after they'd finished dinner and were settled in the library.

Ginger gazed fondly at the tender scene of Sam curled up in his grandfather's lap in the overstuffed chair by the fire. "He's very attached to you, Beau," she remarked.

"We've been constant companions the past couple of years," Beau replied, smoothing Sam's hair off his forehead. "And we've become the best of friends."

Teri saw a flash of pain pass over Jack's face. While Sam seemed to love his father, he was obviously closer and more comfortable with his grandfather. Just the sheer amount of time they'd spent together had to have forged a close and loving relationship. Maybe Jack was regretting all the time he'd missed with his son. *He should be,* Teri thought.

"I'll carry him upstairs," Jack said, rising from his favorite spot on the floor by the fire. He picked Sam up and cradled him against his chest, then stared quizzically down at Beau. "He's a lot heavier than the last time I was home," he remarked. "He must fall asleep down here all the time. How do you get him upstairs without straining your back, Dad?"

"Slowly, son," Beau admitted with a wink at Ginger, who was sitting next to Viv in their usual spot on the sofa. "I'm no young buck anymore, that's a fact. But I can still do everything I used to do...only slower."

Jack seemed embarrassed at the idea that his father was attempting a double entendre, and he quickly turned and left the room. Viv looked up from her knitting—she'd explained that she had several ski caps to knit for her grandchildren by Christmas—and telegraphed her amusement to Teri, who sat across from them in a wing chair. Ginger, who was apparently the only one who'd missed his meaning, simply continued to gaze adoringly at Beau.

"While I helped you set the table tonight, Beau," Ginger said, eagerly moving on to the next topic, "I noticed a print of Graceland on your apron. Are you an Elvis fan?"

"Yes, I am," Beau admitted with a shy grin. "Although I don't usually advertise the fact. Some folks'd think I'm foolish, I suppose, but—"

"He made a great contribution to rock-and-roll music," Viv stated matter-of-factly, busily clicking away with her knitting needles. "And some of his movies *were* rather entertaining. In my opinion, the only one that had any socially redeeming value, however, was *King Creole*. Circa 1958, I believe. Elvis showed some real acting talent in that one."

"Oh, I think he showed acting talent in *all* his movies," Ginger enthused.

Beau beamed with satisfaction. "Do you?"

"Well, of course," Ginger replied. "*G.I. Blues* was *my* favorite. He was so *smoooth* and dapper-looking in that uniform! Were you ever in the service, Beau?"

"Yes. I was in the air force during World War II. I was a tail gunner on a B-24 Liberator."

Ginger's eyes sparkled with admiration. "Elvis served his country, too. He went into the army. You know, there's a *lot* of similarities between you and Elvis...besides your good looks, of course."

"I thought you said Beau looked like Rory Calhoun?" Viv interjected.

"He does." Ginger cocked her head to the side, regarding her idol. "But I suspect Beau has a soulful personality, like Elvis."

"As long as he doesn't start indulging in fried peanut-butter-and-banana sandwiches," Viv murmured. "We don't want him losing his youthful figure and that Mel Gibson derriere."

Oblivious to her sister's humorous mutterings, Ginger finally gushed, "You could even say Oak Meadows is your Graceland, Beau!"

This impetuous comment caught them all off guard and resulted in an awkward pause in the conversation. Beau's smile slid off his face like hot syrup off a stack of pancakes.

Realizing her blunder, Ginger stuttered, "Oh, I...I shouldn't have said that. You...you told us you were selling Oak Meadows. It was very insensitive of me to make the comparison between Graceland and...and—"

"Nonsense, Ginger," Beau said gruffly, interrupting her flustered apology. He rose and went to stand beside her, then took her hand and patted it. Ginger turned pink with pleasure. "It's an apt comparison, m'dear. I'm sure I love Oak Meadows just as much as Elvis loved his Graceland. I must say, though, he'd probably rock and roll in his grave if he knew what a commercial sideshow they've turned it into, wouldn't he? But sometimes circumstances compel us to make decisions we don't especially like, but that are nevertheless quite necessary."

"Selling Oak Meadows isn't necessary," Teri stated flatly.

Since this was the first remark she'd made in ten minutes, and since the remark itself was rather remarkable, everyone turned and stared at Teri.

"What do you mean?" Beau asked her.

"Just what I said," she returned confidently. "It isn't necessary for you to sell Oak Meadows."

Beau shook his head and returned to his seat. "I don't like to contradict a lady, but that's just not true, Teri. I told you all my reasons for selling Oak Meadows."

"Yes, you did. And one of the major reasons you mentioned was loneliness. But living at Oak Meadows isn't the cause of your loneliness, Beau. You've been so wrapped up in raising Sam and taking the place of both his mom and dad, you've managed to isolate yourself."

"That happens to new mothers all the time," Viv observed. "In *Baby Boom* Diane Keaton bought that big old house in rural New England and moved there with that darling baby girl she inherited when a cousin died. She nearly went nuts! The next thing she knew, she was telling some veterinarian about her lack of a sex life, while a horse waited in the wings for the next empty examining room."

"Um...an interesting comparison," Teri murmured politely, then turned her attention back to Beau. "But you don't have to be lonely, Beau—"

"I should say not!" Ginger broke in, then blushed bright pink. "I mean, anyone would *love* to, er, keep company with *you*, Beau..." Her voice trailed off in confusion.

Beau threw Ginger a grateful—and affectionate?—look, then turned back to Teri. "I admit I've questioned my decision a hundred times since last night." He glanced over at Ginger and Viv. "I'd forgotten how much I love this place when it's filled with interesting people."

"And maybe your loneliness made you forget how much you love Oak Meadows even when it's empty," Teri suggested.

Beau nodded soberly and sighed. "You're a smart filly, Teri. And maybe you're right about all this, but there's one little problem."

"I know. You gave me your word."

"Exactly."

"But what if I've decided not to hold you to your word?"

"I might think you're still a bit woozy since that episode last night. I don't intend to take advantage of your vulnerability."

"I *have* changed my way of thinking about the sale of Oak Meadows just since last night, Beau. But the fact of the matter is, I've changed my way of thinking about a *lot* of things. But that doesn't mean—"

"You're confused, m'dear." Beau jutted his chin out and clamped his lips tightly together in that signature Tremain pose of stubbornness. "And besides that, I'm honor-bound to keep my word."

Teri took a deep breath. She could see she was going to have to bring out the big guns. "Are you honor-bound to keep your word to someone who hasn't been totally honest with you?"

Teri could feel everyone's eyes fixed on her. She was ashamed to disclose how low she'd sunk to clinch a real-estate deal, but she had no choice.

"What do you mean, Teri?" Beau finally prompted her.

She shifted uncomfortably in her chair. "Oh, technically I didn't do anything wrong or misrepresent the facts, but there were things I knew about the buyer—about Mr. Schofield's intentions—that I conveniently kept to myself. I was afraid they'd sour the deal, and the deal was the most important thing to me."

"What things?" Beau inquired gruffly.

"Things that might... No, things I'm *sure* would have made you change your mind about selling Oak Meadows... or at least change your mind about selling Oak Meadows to Schofield."

"But what are these *things?*" Viv demanded, sitting forward, her knitting needles forgotten and abandoned in her lap. Ginger just stared, her eyes bigger than ever behind her magnifying lenses.

"Schofield's broker, Ken Jacobs, led Beau to believe that his client planned to turn Oak Meadows into an upscale, elegant, very charming bed-and-breakfast establishment."

"He isn't?" Beau said, looking baffled and anxious.

"He isn't?" Jack repeated, pausing at the entryway.

"No, he isn't," Teri admitted, feeling more guilty than ever as Jack walked into the room.

But he'd hear the truth sooner or later, so it might as well be sooner. He stopped by the fireplace and leaned his shoulder against the mantel. He had taken off his jacket and rolled up his sleeves. He looked scrumptiously sexy... and more than a little suspicious.

"He does plan to renovate the upstairs and rent those rooms out, but the downstairs will be a bar, a restaurant and—" she sighed "—a casino."

"A casino?" Ginger repeated, dumbfounded. "These beautiful rooms turned into a...a...*casino?* With slot machines and roulette wheels and card tables?"

Teri could feel her cheeks burn with shame, but she had to tell them the rest. "And the grounds will be made into an amusement park—a theme park called the Yanks and the Rebels. They'll reenact battles between the Union and the Confederacy, giving it a...well...*lighthearted* twist."

"I've never heard anything so insulting in my life!" Viv exclaimed indignantly. "Lighthearted, indeed! There was nothing lighthearted about the Civil War. And they'll violate this lovely home, turning it into a parody of its former self. It's criminal, I tell you. *Criminal!*"

Viv and Ginger had left no doubt about what they thought of Schofield's plans for Oak Meadows. Teri had expected similar outbursts from Beau and Jack, but the men just stared at her, their expressions grim and disbelieving.

"Beau, I can't tell you how sorry I am," she told him, biting her lip nervously.

She decided not to brave another look at Jack for a while. One angry Tremain was disconcerting enough.

"I should have told you what Schofield planned to do with Oak Meadows, but I was afraid you'd nix the deal. And up till last night, that's all I cared about. I didn't care about you or your family or its history or *anything*. But things are different now. I want you to fight to keep Oak Meadows, and if your promise to me is the only thing holding you back, I've given you sufficient reason to take back your word. Tell me you'll fight, Beau! Don't make *me* the reason Oak Meadows was turned into the Yanks and the Rebels Amusement Park and Casino!"

Teri held her breath while Beau stared holes into the floor, the wall, the portrait above the fireplace, and then turned his sober gaze back to her. "I'll do whatever it takes to keep Oak Meadows out of Schofield's hands," he said. "Under one condition."

Teri swallowed hard. She wouldn't be surprised if Beau told her to remove herself and her J-Mart clothes from the premises pronto. He had every right to be angry with her, and she had no reason to hope he'd ever forgive her. He barely knew her, and most of what he knew about her was less than flattering.

"What's the condition, Mr. Tremain?" she asked him, automatically reverting to the more formal manner of address.

His face changed by slow increments from grim soberness to sweet tolerance. As he smiled, Teri's heart seemed to take flight. "I'll fight for Oak Meadows if you'll help me figure out how."

Teri smiled back, sure she didn't deserve a second chance but thrilled to get one anyway. "I'm honored to be included, Mr. Tremain."

He scowled again. "Hell's bells, girl, I told you to call me Beau."

She laughed, then darted a glance toward Jack. She was enormously relieved when she saw him shake his head at her, a half-reluctant smile tilting his lips as if to say, *I don't know why, but I forgive you, too.*

She smiled gratefully back, and for the first time since last night, her heart seemed to race out of control. But instead of feeling like fainting, she felt like tackling Jack Tremain and practicing a little mouth-to-mouth while she was conscious enough to enjoy it.

But Jack must have read her thoughts—perhaps he even shared them—because his smile faded away. She knew then that he was afraid to kiss her again, and for more reasons than the mere technicality that he'd kissed her once and she'd been stupid enough to dampen his ardor by dying in his arms.

THEY SPENT THE NEXT HOUR planning their strategy to discourage Schofield from buying Oak Meadows. Then Teri called Ken Jacobs—who was thrilled to finally have his many calls returned—and set up a meeting with Schofield at the house the following day at two o'clock in the afternoon. Schofield was flying in from his home in Las Vegas tomorrow and had specified that he wanted to walk through the house and over the grounds at least once before closing the deal.

Jacobs had assured Teri that there was no chance his client would back out. Supposedly, Schofield implicitly trusted Jacobs's endorsement of Oak Meadows for his proposed venture. He just wanted to see the place for himself and "feel the karma" before moving on to the planning phase of the theme park and casino. Apparently, Mr. Schofield was a very superstitious man.

"Everything's settled for tomorrow," Beau announced as he stood up and stretched his back. "And since we can't start preparations till morning, I propose we forget all about Schofield for the rest of the evening and enjoy ourselves."

"What shall we do, Beau?" Ginger asked eagerly.

"Do you like Elvis's music, m'dear?" Beau inquired.

"*Do* I? Was there ever a snappier tune than 'Jail House Rock'?"

"I like his mellower melodies." Viv gave her opinion from the sofa where she was still hard at work on a ski cap.

"I've got them all on disc, but they're stored in the parlor with the CD player. Would you ladies like to repair to the other room for a little impromptu sock hop?"

"I've been wanting to dance since I got up this morning," Teri admitted. "What are we waiting for?"

"I'll just watch from the sofa in the parlor," Viv said, gathering her yarn. "I've got five more caps to finish before Christmas."

As everyone headed for the door, Jack lagged behind. He wasn't as eager as everyone else was to cut a little rug to "Love Me Tender." He was bound to be partnered with Teri, and he wasn't sure he was up for any more torment that day. Hadn't he met his quota yet? Ever since the bubble-bath encounter, he'd been having these fantasies—

"Jack? You coming?"

Teri was standing in the doorway, her hands braced on her slim hips. The light from the hall haloed her shining cap of blond hair. Though she looked like an angel, Jack was of the opinion that she could more accurately be described as a heavenly temptress. There was a gleam of challenge in her eyes. Did she know what she did to him? Watching her from a safe distance while she enjoyed a hot dog at lunch or, as she'd described them at dinner, the "creamiest mashed potatoes in the world" was one thing, but holding her in his arms was something else entirely.

"I'm kind of tired," Jack said, sure his excuse sounded lame and unconvincing.

Teri's smile faltered and the challenge in her eyes faded. "You're still angry with me."

"Teri, I'm not—"

"I know it was wrong of me to keep that information from your father, and I have no excuses for my behavior. None at all. So if you—"

Jack crossed the room in three long strides and grabbed Teri's arms. "I'm not angry with you! You told the truth when it really mattered. You've convinced Dad to hold on to Oak Meadows. I'm not angry, you idiot, I'm damned grateful to you."

Teri stared at him, her mouth parted in surprise. Standing so close, smelling her lavender-scented skin and looking into her disbelieving blue eyes, Jack wanted to kiss her more than he'd ever wanted anything in his whole misbegotten life. But to give in to his urge would be foolish . . . and possibly dangerous.

*Dangerous for Teri or for you?* his heart taunted him. *Who are we really worried about here, Tremain?*

"If you're not angry with me, why don't you want to dance, Jack?" Teri finally asked, the gleam of challenge returning to her eyes full force.

Jack had no idea what to say. She'd asked a reasonable question, and no reasonable excuse sprang to his mind.

"I haven't danced since my P.E. class in the seventh grade," she continued with a coy smile, reaching up to playfully toy with the top button of his shirt. The pressure on his Adam's apple was strangely arousing. He swallowed hard. "Learning how to clog might have been good for me, aerobically speaking, but I'm sure slow dancing with you will be much more *fun*. You chastised me earlier for purposely missing out on the prom in high school, and now when I want to dance and there's a perfectly able-bodied male on the premises—" she flitted a hot glance over his chest and shoulders "—are you really going to deny me the pleasure of a few turns around the dance floor?"

Jack truly didn't want to deny Teri much of any-thing...least of all pleasure. But that was precisely the problem.

"Come on, Jack," she whispered in his ear. "I dare ya."

"One or two dances won't kill me, I guess," Jack groused wryly, unable to refuse a dare from his high school nemesis. "But I really am dead on my feet, you know."

"Your enthusiasm is overwhelming, Jack. And your morbid conversation thrills me to *death*," Teri quipped. "Just call me Morticia. Come on, Gomez. Show me what I missed at the prom. Is there a rose I can hold in my teeth?"

As the evening flew by and one or two dances turned into too many to count, Jack really began to feel like a high school kid again, raging hormones and all. The music was great, the slim girl in his arms was pretty in pink, and he was falling in love...or at least in lust. He'd prefer the latter. Lust was something that was easily cured. Love wasn't.

Starry-eyed, Jack was nearly oblivious to his father's and Ginger's presence in the room, despite the fact that the two of them were fox-trotting and jitterbugging themselves loopy. Viv had had the good sense to go to bed hours ago.

Every couple of songs, Jack took Teri's pulse. It was always fine, so he didn't even have the excuse of a slightly elevated heart rate to stop the fun.

Finally, sometime around midnight, Jack's father handed Teri and Jack a single large bowl of double fudge truffle pecan ice cream and two spoons, bade them good-night, then escorted an exhausted but giddily happy Ginger into the hall and up the stairs.

"It's kind of late for dessert, isn't it?" Jack said, staring uneasily at the mound of rich, gooey ice cream.

"Are you kidding?" Teri returned. "I've worked up an *enormous* appetite. Isn't this what the kids did after the prom—go to an ice-cream parlor and chow down?"

*No,* thought Jack. *Most of them made out in a parked car or on the couch at home.*

"Let's turn the lights out in here and go back to the library where it's cozier," Teri suggested, and Jack tamely followed like a man who knew his fate was sealed. Teri sat down on the sofa with one leg folded under her and the other leg swinging. She patted the cushion next to her. "Sit close so we can share."

Jack shook his head. "No, that's okay. I really don't want any."

Teri looked at him as if he was crazy. "Well, sit down anyway, in case you change your mind," she ordered.

Jack obeyed like a housebroken puppy and sat down. He knew he shouldn't, but he couldn't seem to help himself. He loved being near Teri, talking to her, absorbing her zest for life. Watching her eat . . . He was really beginning to fear he'd developed a weird fetish!

Teri scooped up a spoonful of ice cream and waved it in Jack's face. She smiled impishly. "Sure you don't want some?"

"No, you eat it," he urged, so she finally just shrugged, then popped the spoon into her mouth. The hoped-for reaction was immediate.

"Ummm, this is *heaven,*" she murmured. "This double fudge truffle is to *die* for!"

Jack licked his lips and Teri dipped her spoon back into the bowl.

"Oh, wow!" She rolled her eyes and smiled dreamily as she savored the second bite. "The pecans are *perfect.*

They're a nice crunchy surprise right in the middle of a creamy mouthful of fudge. Gives your teeth something to do." She snapped her small, perfect white teeth together to demonstrate.

Jack's pulse accelerated.

As Teri tasted her third spoonful, her eyes drifted shut with ecstasy. "I *love* this. I absolutely *love* this! My taste buds are exploding. Jack, you've got to try a bite."

Jack wanted to try a bite, all right. But not of ice cream.

She scooped some up, mounding it high on the spoon. "Open wide, Jack. The train's comin' to the tunnel," she ordered playfully.

Jack opened his mouth, but there was too much ice cream to clear the tunnel and a thick dollop of it dropped onto his chin. Laughing, Terry caught the falling ice cream with her finger, then stuck it into her mouth.

"Don't want to waste any of this good stuff," she explained, smiling sheepishly around her finger.

"Yeah, but that was rightfully mine," Jack asserted, keeping a deadpan expression. "You owe me another bite."

Teri smiled, dipping her spoon into the bowl again. "I knew I'd win you over. I told you it was good, didn't I?"

But when she offered him the spoonful of ice cream, he shook his head. "No. I don't want it on the spoon. I want it on your finger."

She paused, surprised at first. Then she laughed again, willingly dipped her finger in the bowl and offered it to Jack. He grabbed her wrist, took her finger in his mouth and slowly sucked off the ice cream.

When he didn't immediately release her finger, Teri's smile fell away. Jack watched as her blue eyes grew wide and her lips parted and her shoulders gave a delicate little shudder. He hoped her response was arousal. He knew *his* was. Every muscle in his body was tightening, every nerve was on fire, and every breath was quicker and more shallow than the last.

He released her finger but kept hold of her wrist, turning over her hand and pressing a kiss into her palm. She didn't move; she just watched as if she were mesmerized. Then he pushed up the sleeve of her sweater and trailed lingering kisses up her smooth, white arm to the tender, scented skin inside her elbow. He was following the same soft-as-silk path those lucky bubbles had made just hours before as he'd watched enviously from the sidelines.

Teri sat still as a statue. She was afraid that if she moved, Jack would stop. She didn't want him to stop. Wherever his warm lips touched her skin, it tingled with pleasure. It felt better than eating ice cream, better than anything she'd ever experienced.

He stopped kissing her just above the elbow when he couldn't push the sleeve up any farther. He lifted his head and gave her a searing look, then he took the ice-cream bowl out of her hand, set it on the coffee table, and gently took hold of her other hand, kissing the palm, then duplicating his actions by kissing his way up that arm, too.

Teri decided that she liked a thorough man. She closed her eyes and, with no effort at all, blocked out every sensation except for the light, titillating pressure of his kisses.

After he was through with her arm, Teri experienced a strange mixture of tension and relaxation . . . a sense of urgency and a soothing languor at the same time. She kept her eyes closed and let her head loll back against the sofa back. Then she felt Jack's hands on her shoulders and his lips were on her neck, kissing, nuzzling, nipping.

He moved closer. His chest made contact with hers, his shirt creating an erotic chafing sensation against her hardened nipples.

He worked his way up her neck, around to her ear and across the ridge of her cheekbones. By now, Teri's lips pulsed with need. She waited, her lips parted and expectant.

He kissed her chin.

He kissed her forehead.

He kissed her chin again. Damn, how much longer was he going to torment her before—

Teri heard a deep sigh as Jack pulled away. She opened her eyes. He had scooted clear to the opposite end of the sofa.

Blinking against the soft light of the single hurricane lamp, Teri tried to decipher Jack's expression and analyze his behavior.

"Jack?"

"Hmm?"

"Why did you stop? Couldn't you tell . . . I *liked* what you were doing."

He sighed again, wearily. "I liked it, too."

"Then why—"

"Because . . ."

"Because?"

"Because I think we're moving too fast, Teri." He sat up and propped his elbows on his thighs, dangling his clasped hands between his knees. His head hung down like a condemned prisoner's on execution day. "Hell, we shouldn't be getting involved at all."

Teri pulled both legs up and under her, sitting pretzel-style on the sofa. She wrapped her arms around her chest, feeling a sudden chill in the air now that Jack had physically and emotionally pulled away from her. "Why do you say that, Jack? Both of us are free of other commitments...aren't we?"

What had started as a statement had turned into a question. Jack *was* free, wasn't he? Or was there another woman? Suddenly, it was very important to Teri to know the answer to that question.

"I'm not presently seeing another woman, if that's what you're wondering," Jack answered in a grudging tone. "But that still doesn't make me free to...to...get involved with you, to care about you."

Up until two minutes ago, Teri hadn't known her own heart. Now, in an unexpected moment of self-revelation, she knew she cared more for Jackson Tremain than she'd ever thought possible in such a short time. Or maybe her feelings about Jack went clear back to high school when they'd fought and debated and competed. Maybe all along it had been a sort of prickly mating dance. And maybe she'd been crushed when he'd thrown himself at the dainty feet of a woman so diametrically opposite to her that it seemed like a personal affront, a figurative slap in the face.

But the bottom line was this: she did care about him and it would be a heck of a lot easier on her heart if he felt the same way about her. But he was saying he couldn't care about her and perhaps didn't want to get involved at all. Why?

But she thought she knew why.

"Jack, I'm not a porcelain doll," she said gently, reaching over and placing her hand on his shoulder. "I won't break if you hold me or if you...kiss me."

Jack turned his anguished face to her. "But you *did* break, Teri. You passed out. You quit breathing. Your heart went into fibrillation, for crying out loud! If I hadn't given you CPR, you'd be a goner. What if that happens again?''

Teri stared at him, shaken by the depth of his fear. ''It was a freak thing, Jack. The doctor said that if I look after myself, it won't happen again. And I *will* look after myself. I'm a new woman, Jack!''

''Yeah, but for how long?''

Teri sighed. ''Was the old me *that* bad?''

''No...at least not in high school. I liked the old you a lot. We argued, but it was fun...kind of like the way we argue now. But you turned out to be a little too ambitious, Teri. You tried to waylay my dad into a bad real-estate deal and nearly killed yourself to boot.

''And bits and pieces of that overambitious side of your personality are going to come back to haunt you more and more every day. So you're going to have to deal with it. You're going to have to incorporate your old need to *work* hard into your new need to *play* hard. 'Cause if you don't, you're going to—'' He cut himself off and stood up, moving to the fireplace to lean against the mantelshelf.

''I'm going to what? Die? Is that what you're afraid of? Jack, I'm *not* going to die. At least not any time soon. I promise!''

''No one can make that kind of promise, Teri,'' Jack told her, shaking his head miserably. ''Not you, not anyone.'' Then he turned and stalked out of the room without another word or even a backward glance.

Teri stared at the empty doorway for several minutes, as if Jack might miraculously come back. He didn't. So she turned and stared up at the portrait. She could feel the sympathy radiating from all three pairs of painted eyes.

"He's right, of course," she told them. "No one knows when they're going to buy the farm. I could die tomorrow. Or I could keel over when I'm ninety-five and playing shuffleboard on the *Love Boat*. But does that mean a person is supposed to go through life avoiding the possibility of caring about someone because he's afraid that someday she'll up and die on him?"

*Like Pam died on Jack?* A familiar voice drifted into Teri's subconscious . . . the sweet Southern drawl of Caroline Tremain.

And then Teri understood.

# Chapter Eight

"The repairs on the bridge were completed just this morning, Mr. Schofield," Teri said brightly. "So now the approach to Oak Meadows is as good as new. Isn't the view lovely from here?"

Mr. Schofield grunted. Grunting had so far been the extent of his comments during their trip from the airport.

As he'd stashed Schofield's luggage in the trunk, Ken Jacobs had told Teri in a harried whisper that his client was a little out of sorts because of a last-minute flight schedule change. Apparently, he'd ended up on a plane with a flight number that included the double use of a certain digit—to remain nameless, Ken added judiciously—which he considered very unlucky. It was just the sort of situation he always took great pains to avoid, but since he was eager to close the deal on Oak Meadows, Schofield braved getting on the plane and probably worried about crashing the whole time.

Although she felt rather guilty about rejoicing in another person's temporary misery, Teri couldn't have been happier. The edgier Schofield was, the better. Snatching a glance at his luggage ticket, she noted that he'd arrived on flight 1544, so that meant "four" was Mr. Schofield's unlucky number. She stored away that information to be used later.

On her way to the airport, Teri had stopped at her New Orleans apartment and changed into a gray tailored suit and black pumps. She would much rather be in her casual clothes, but she needed to look professional for the one day of her vacation she intended to work.

But it wasn't really work, Teri reasoned. Getting back in the real-estate saddle to keep a buyer from buying was definitely not what she routinely did for a living. If it were, she'd be broke.

Jack had only grudgingly approved of Teri's participation in "the plan." Last night, she'd slept in the room next to his, and although he'd been very standoffish, he'd taken her pulse before retiring. Then he'd taken it again three times that morning before allowing her to get in the car without him, and had made her promise to check in with him by cellular phone on a regular basis. Despite their almost-amorous encounter last night and the resulting awkwardness afterward, Jack had continued to fuss and watch over Teri as if she were a chick and he were the mother hen.

But Teri had never felt better. And now that she'd met Schofield in person, she was more firmly resolved than ever to make sure the sale of the Tremain estate did not go through. She realized that Schofield didn't appreciate Oak Meadows any more than he'd appreciate any other piece of profitable real estate. It was just a means to an end for him...just as it had been for Teri before she'd floated down a cool, dark tunnel toward the light.

But as much as she disliked Schofield, Teri was determined to play to perfection the part of an eager, obsequious salesperson. In order for things to work out the way Jack and Beau wanted them to, Schofield had to be

completely in the dark about Teri's collusion
Tremains to sabotage the deal. In fact, he had to th
they were *all* eager to say adieu to Oak Meadows.

Schofield—a portly man in an expensive but flamboy-
antly tailored blue pin-striped suit, with a loud tie and
shiny white loafers—was ensconced in the front seat of
Teri's luxurious Lincoln Continental, smoking a fat
Havana cigar he'd lit up without asking Teri if she
minded. She *did* mind, but since she was being obsequious, she refrained from asking him to toss the smelly
thing out the window.

Ken Jacobs, the broker—a thin, balding man with a
perpetual twitch in his right eye and a phony smile on his
lips, which Teri could swear had been attached to his face
by the miracle of plastic surgery—sat in the back, con-
tinually popping his head over the seat to engage Schofield's attention and putting in a good word for Oak
Meadows. His groveling made Teri determined never to
be so desperate to impress a client that she'd stoop to such
pathetic kowtowing.

As they pulled into the circular drive behind the Ford
Explorer, Teri was happy to see that Jack was back from
dropping Sam off at Mikey's house, his friend from their
old neighborhood. As Jack had mentioned earlier, the
boys still got together occasionally for a sleepover or a
marathon play day.

Jack and Beau had decided it would be best if Sam
wasn't around while the grown-ups participated in a little playacting. It was bound to be confusing for him. Besides, Mikey's mom was helping the boys put together
their costumes for Halloween trick-or-treating, an exciting event for Sam and Mikey that was little more than
twenty-four hours away.

The minute Teri killed the engine, Jacobs hopped out to open Schofield's door. Schofield clamped the cigar between his yellowed teeth and heaved himself out of the car, then stood and looked at the front facade of Oak Meadows through narrowed eyes.

"I told you you'd be impressed, Mr. Schofield," Jacobs remarked eagerly. "Isn't it a handsome building?"

"It'll do," Schofield growled, the very modest comment of approval only a slight improvement over the grunts. But Teri was under no illusion that Schofield didn't like what he saw. She suspected he was the type who projected a gruff, disapproving image just to intimidate people and to finagle better deals. He knew Oak Meadows was a prime find and a bargain or he wouldn't have hopped on a plane with an unlucky flight number and flown all the way from Las Vegas to give his final okay.

They walked slowly up to the porch as Schofield took in the impressive view of the verdant expanse of lawn. Realizing the place spoke for itself, Jacobs remained silent and smug. Obviously, he felt the deal was in the bag.

"Yoo-hoo! Miss Taylor! Over here!"

Teri's heart fluttered nervously. The play had begun. She just hoped she would remember all her lines or at least be able to improvise when necessary.

"Who's *that?*" Schofield gruffly inquired, staring at the unexpected sight of an elderly woman in striped coveralls and a large straw hat, who was approaching them dusted from top to toe in some of Louisiana's rich, dark soil and wielding a dangerous-looking garden tool.

Teri had been pretending to ignore Ginger, and now she pretended distress at being forced to acknowledge her at all.

"She's a boarder staying at Oak Meadows for a few days," Teri whispered out of the side of her mouth. "Don't pay any attention to her or to anything she says." She made a surreptitious gesture, twirling her finger in front of her ear to indicate that Ginger had a screw loose, then she headed for the door.

Just as Teri had hoped and expected, Schofield and Jacobs stared at Ginger with increased curiosity and suspicion as she continued in their direction.

"Miss Taylor! Miss Taylor! *Yoo-hoo!* Can't you hear me? It's Ginger!" By now, Ginger was standing on the porch directly behind them. There was no way she could be ignored.

Teri pressed the doorbell, gave Schofield and Jacobs an aggrieved look, then turned to face Ginger with a strained smile.

"Hello, Ginger. Puttering in the flower beds again, I see. I thought Mr. Tremain asked you not to—"

"I'm not upsetting any plants, Miss Taylor. Oh, *no*, I wouldn't dare harm Mr. Tremain's award-winning roses. Actually, I'm digging in a promising-looking spot near the bayou," Ginger babbled with a maniacal look in her magnified eyes. She wiped her sweaty face with a bandanna, smearing wet dirt across her cheek. "I know if I just keep looking, I'll find a bone or two. With so many Indians buried in one spot, there are bound to be *hundreds* of bones lying around just waiting to be unearthed!"

When Schofield and Jacobs turned to Teri with alarmed expressions on their faces, she chuckled nervously and jabbed the doorbell again.

"I'm glad to hear you're enjoying this sunny afternoon," Teri said, addressing Ginger in the slow, carefully articulated voice used by certain people when speaking to small children and dumb animals. "And I'd love to talk with you about your, er, treasure hunt, but some other time. I'm very busy with clients right now, Ginger." Teri indicated Schofield and Jacobs with a slight inclination of her head and raised brows.

Ginger seemed to notice Teri's companions for the first time. She blushed quite convincingly and pulled on a frizzy coil of permed hair sticking out from under her straw hat as if she were embarrassed. "Oh. Sorry, Miss Taylor. I just get *so* excited about what I'm doing, I forget where I am, whom I'm with, and what a *fright* I must look! Good afternoon, gentlemen," she said, vigorously nodding. "I won't disturb you again...unless I find a bone, of course! A nice fibula or tibia would be *excellent!*" Then she turned and left the porch, disappearing around the corner of the house.

Jacobs clamped a hand on the back of his neck to knead away the sudden tension that had knotted his muscles and said nothing. Any minute now, he'd be popping his ulcer medication, as Teri had known him to do on stressful occasions.

But Schofield had no reason to restrain himself and immediately asked, "What was that all about, Miss Taylor? That woman seems to be under the impression that Oak Meadows is built on Indian burial grounds. And, more to the point, *is* it?"

Teri gave the doorbell another couple of jabs. "Mr. Schofield, I had hoped that Ginger and her sister, Vivien, wouldn't be around when you came to see the place, but Mr. Tremain has such a soft heart, he can't bring himself to send them packing to the nearest motel, despite their strange idiosyncrasies."

"What are they doing here? They don't *live* here, do they?"

"No, of course not. They were stranded here by the storm the other night. You remember my mentioning the car stalled on the bridge, don't you? It was their car. Until its repaired, they're a fixture, I'm afraid." Teri paused, then added, "The mechanic said it would take *four* days."

By the way Schofield winced when she said "four," Teri was determined to say it as many times as possible that afternoon.

"But where did she get the idea that Oak Meadows was built on Indian burial grounds in the first place?" Schofield persisted. "Not that I'm superstitious, mind you, but—"

"Good grief," Teri interrupted, pressing the doorbell again. "Where *can* Mr. Tremain be, I wonder? I've rung the doorbell at least *four* times already!"

Schofield winced again. "The burial grounds, Miss Taylor?"

Teri faced Schofield and answered sincerely, "As far as I know, Mr. Schofield, Oak Meadows is *not* built on Indian burial grounds. Besides, if it were, surely bones or artifacts would have been discovered by now and the area descended on by archaeologists."

Teri had spoken truthfully, so naturally Schofield was dubious. He had to be aware of her reputation as a gung-ho Realtor, and Jacobs had probably told him that she'd kept his plans for a casino and amusement park a secret from Mr. Tremain as a precaution against jinxing the sale. Teri could see Schofield's mind clicking away. He was probably thinking that a devious little operator like herself would have no compunction about keeping things from *him*, too . . . especially if it meant making a big, fat sales commission.

He said nothing more, but he stubbed out his cigar on the porch and frowned. The seed of doubt had been planted.

Finally, Beau came to the door. "Sorry to keep you folks waiting," he said, out of breath or pretending to be. "I was upstairs taking care of some matters. But never mind that. Come in! Come in!"

Beau ushered everyone into the hall...right under a ladder that was placed directly in front of the door.

"What the—" Schofield blurted when he saw what he'd just done. "Why in heaven's name have you got a ladder in front of the door? Don't you know it's bad luck to walk under one of those things?"

Beau lifted his brows and shrugged. "I've heard something to that effect," he admitted. "But I don't pay much attention to that sort of hoo-haw. I was fixin' to change that light fixture above the door before you got here, but I was called away. The only way I can reach the blasted thing is with a ladder, so there you have it. Besides, I'm not a superstitious man, Mr. Schofield. Would you folks like some tea before we take a tour of the house?"

By now, Schofield was darting uneasy glances around the room, as if expecting bad luck to hit any second. He pulled a rabbit's foot from his jacket pocket and began to furtively stroke it.

"Isn't this a beautiful entryway, Mr. Schofield?" Jacobs weakly offered, a trickle of sweat wending its way down his temple. He dabbed a handkerchief to his brow.

"Yes, yes, it'll do," Schofield replied, obviously distracted by other thoughts. "I'd like that tea, Tremain. Or preferably something stronger."

"Certainly, Mr. Schofield," Beau replied cordially. "Come in and make yourself at home. It'll be yours soon enough, won't it?"

Schofield did not reply.

Beau guided them into the parlor where he'd placed a tray of tea and assorted goodies on a round table in front of the antique sofa and chairs. Schofield sat down, and after two jiggers of Southern whiskey and three cookies, he seemed to be feeling much better.

As he'd been reviving himself with food and drink, his gaze had wandered around the large, beautiful parlor. He couldn't be immune to the charm of the house and its potential as a unique tourist trap in the form of a nostalgic-style casino. Teri was sure he was trying to rationalize away his uneasiness over the mention of Indian burial grounds and the several unlucky incidents that had already occurred that day.

Teri and Beau exchanged conspiratorial glances. They were simply lulling Schofield into a false sense of security.

Teri picked up the plate of cookies. "Another one, Mr. Schofield?" she inquired sweetly.

He patted his paunch. "Better not. I've already had three."

"I believe you've had *four*. But who's counting?"

Schofield's frown returned and he waved away the plate. "No, thank you," he said firmly, then turned to Beau. "I'm ready for that tour now."

Beau stood up with every appearance of eagerness and they headed for the hall again, with Jacobs enthusiastically pointing out the gilded cornices on the ceiling and the graceful, arched entryways at both ends of the parlor. Apparently, he was no longer confident that he could rely on the house to speak for itself.

They were about to ascend the stairs, which were, as Teri remarked with the ardency required of her role as obsequious Realtor, "made from the finest oak in the country and in mint condition," when they were stopped in their tracks by the appearance of a strange vision on the landing.

There was nothing ethereal about this apparition. It wasn't a ghost, although it did appear to be something from a long-ago era...or perhaps Walter Cronkite in period drag. But Teri knew it was only Vivien posing as a fair facsimile of Norma Desmond, the legendary but faded silent-film star in the movie *Sunset Boulevard*.

Viv was admittedly a bit plumper than Gloria Swanson, who had originated the role, but there was no mistaking the turban, the drapey dress, the heavily lined and shadowed eyes, the dark red lipstick and the stiletto-style cigarette holder. And there was no mistaking the slow, vampish slink down the stairs as she grasped the rail with one hand and held her cigarette at a dramatic angle with the other.

"What the hell is going on here?" Schofield muttered.

"That's what I'd like to know," Jacobs added with a troubled look in Teri's direction.

"I warned you about Vivien," Teri whispered into Jacobs's ear. "Just tell Schofield to ignore whatever she says. She's a little eccentric...just like her sister."

"A *little?*" Jacobs repeated doubtfully.

"Beauregard!" Viv belted out in a throaty voice as she reached the last few stairs. She threw the group before her a haughty, disparaging glance. "Who *are* these people?"

"This is Mr. Schofield, Vivien," Beau began. "He's—"

Vivien waved her cigarette. "Oh, never mind! The question was rhetorical. I don't really *care* who they are. But I suppose they're the reason you didn't return to my room and attend to that little matter we discussed."

Vivien widened her eyes, flared her nostrils and clenched her teeth in the classic Norma Desmond pose. Teri wanted to laugh out loud, but she somehow kept a straight face.

Beau leaned close to Vivien and whispered loudly, "There's nothing I can do, Vivien. I searched your room and there's no one in there besides that blasted cat of yours."

As if on cue, a black cat darted down the stairs, right past Schofield's feet. Teri heard Schofield suck in his breath and saw him openly squeeze his rabbit's foot in full view of the others. This lack of self-consciousness smacked of desperation.

"At least the cat *was* in there the last time I looked," Beau amended. "But unless there's something about your cat I don't know, no man or animal has been moving your things, Vivien."

"Are you saying that my things—my toiletries and makeup in particular—are moving around the room of their own accord?" Vivien inquired with a disdainful toss of her head and a drag on her cigarette. "Not likely," she puffed out in a cloud of smoke. "I can *never* find them where I left them. And since I *never* leave my door unlocked, I can only assume it's those naughty poltergeists playing tricks. It's bad enough seeing their dreary faces in the mirror when one is least expecting it, and having one's bathwater turned off and on at their whim, but I really *detest* the little ghouls playing hide-and-seek with my Polident!"

"What's going on here, Teri?" Jacobs demanded in a strangled voice. "Is this some kind of a joke? 'Cause if it is, I'm not laughing!"

Teri grabbed Jacobs by the arm and pulled him out of earshot of the others. "You're right, Ken. It must be some kind of sick joke!" she whispered vehemently. "If I were you, I wouldn't believe a word Vivien says. She's obviously putting on a show. No one in their right mind could honestly believe there are *poltergeists* in the house!" She glanced nervously over Jacobs's shoulder and saw Schofield eyeing them with a suspicious and troubled air.

"I've always considered myself in my right mind," Jacobs replied fretfully. "But I don't know whether I believe in ghosts or not. I've been in the real-estate business long enough and in so many houses, old and new, I have to admit that sometimes things go on that can only be explained in a supernatural context."

Teri raised her brows. "So you think Oak Meadows really is *haunted?*"

"I don't know and I don't care! What matters is what Schofield thinks. You know how superstitious he is, Teri. And, by the way, you keep repeating his unlucky number!"

Teri blinked innocently. "I do?"

"Yes. It's four. So cut it out, will you? It's making him crazy!"

"Certainly, Ken. But what are we going to do about Vivien?"

"Get Tremain to take her away, then you and I will finish showing Schofield the house. After he gets an eyeful of the place, I'm sure he'll make the effort to forget all this supernatural stuff."

"Jacobs!" Schofield bellowed, startling both Teri and Jacobs. "What the hell are you two in a huddle over? I demand to be included in every discussion!"

Jacobs and Teri scrambled over to Schofield.

"You're right, Mr. Schofield," Jacobs apologized meekly. "We were just discussing the very best...the most comfortable and convenient way to show you the house." He turned to give Teri a significant look. "Miss Taylor is going to speak briefly to Mr. Tremain, then we'll begin the tour."

While Vivien struck an imperious pose, impatiently tapping her foot on the carpet and looking like miffed royalty, Teri dutifully pulled Beau to the side. "He thinks I'm begging you to get Vivien out of sight," she whispered. "I think our plan is working, but it can't hurt if you insert the number four into the conversation as frequently as possible."

Beau nodded, then looked past Teri's shoulder to the top of the stairs. "I will if I get the chance, but Jack's center stage now and Ginger's in the wings, so I may not need to."

Teri turned and followed Beau's gaze up the stairs. Jack was standing there, sopping wet, with a large white towel wrapped around his waist and a puddle of water forming around his bare feet. His arms were crossed over his broad chest, his wet hair was slicked back from his forehead, and he was scowling like a peeved potentate.

Teri's heart skipped a beat, then started again with a hard thump she felt clear to her toes. She had been expecting Jack to show up in a towel; it was part of the plan. But she'd apparently underestimated her reaction to the sight of his bare chest and long, sexy legs. The man was gorgeous. He was lean and tan and had just the right amount of sleek muscle to make him look movie-star macho.

"Now what?" Jacobs muttered.

"Gentlemen," Beau said, "this is my son, Jack. He's just returned home from assignment in Eastern Europe. He was gone *four* months."

Jacobs groaned and Schofield clasped the rabbit's foot to his chest and looked faint.

"Nix the introductions, Dad," Jack called down in a beleaguered voice. "I'm not exactly dressed for company."

"What's the trouble, son?" Beau returned. "I thought you were taking a shower."

"I was. But someone is either playing a practical joke, or the water pipes in this old joint are finally shot. The water keeps going off and on, off and on." He heaved a long-suffering sigh. "Or maybe it's the poltergeists."

"Well, of course it's the poltergeists, you idiot," Vivien interjected with a superior sniff. "*I* knew it all along."

Beau wrung his hands and looked anxious. "Jack, this is Mr. Schofield. Remember I told you we had a buyer for the house? *This* is *him!*"

Jack's eyebrows shot up in surprise. He uncrossed his arms and looked uncomfortably aware of having blundered. "Oh! Well...!" He forced a nervous smile. "You're getting a heck of a house, Mr. Schofield. You're going to *love* it here!"

Schofield did not look convinced. In fact, he reminded Teri of a groom at a shotgun wedding...desperate to be anywhere other than opposite the bride. He cleared his throat and made a stab at looking calm, collected and in control. "I might or I might not love it here," he gruffly asserted. "But that depends on whether or not I'm satisfied with your explanations."

"What explanations?" Beau inquired innocently.

"To begin with, I want to know why everyone keeps talking about Indian burial grounds and poltergeists! Is this house built on a burial ground or not? *Is* this house haunted?"

"I assure you, Mr. Schofield," Beau began in a placating tone, "there's certainly no proof to be found in official documents concerning Indian burial grounds on the Oak Meadows estate. And as for poltergeists—"

"No proof in official documents, you say?" Schofield snapped. "But what about word of mouth, Tremain? Have you known all along that Oak Meadows was a playground for prankster poltergeists? Tell me the truth!"

Beau raised his hands in a helpless gesture and looked sheepish. "Mr. Schofield, I *am* telling the truth. I don't know what else to say that would ease your—"

Suddenly, the front door burst open and Ginger stumbled into the room. With a look of elation on her grimy face, she held up two bones, one in each hand, and exclaimed, "I did it! I found some bones!" She waved one at them and announced, "This is a femur!" She waved the other and added with pride, "And *this* is a rib!"

"That's it, Jacobs," Schofield said grimly as he strode toward the door. "I'm outta here!"

"But Mr. Schofield," Teri exclaimed, following the two men as they made their exit, "what about your contract?"

"To hell with my contract," he bellowed back. "You can keep the earnest money. It's probably jinxed anyway. Now, if you don't mind, I'd like a ride to the airport."

Teri didn't mind. No, she didn't mind one little bit.
"Be right there, Mr. Schofield," she called, then she
turned and gave her favorite collection of grinning luna-
tics a triumphant wink before heading out to the car.

## Chapter Nine

Jack had been waiting impatiently for Teri to return from the airport when he finally saw her tank of a car crossing the bridge and heading for the drive. He breathed a sigh of relief. Although she'd called as soon as she'd dropped Schofield and Jacobs off at the terminal, then called again just fifteen minutes ago, he'd still been worried about her.

Jack felt he'd been derelict in his duty by allowing her to drive such a distance without him along to assist her if she happened to have another arrhythmia attack. But she'd been doing so incredibly well since the incident, most people would have had a hard time believing it ever happened in the first place. Even his dad and the potato chip sisters seemed to have forgotten that Teri had keeled over and quit living less than forty-eight hours ago.

But Jack would never forget. He'd always remember how helpless he'd felt while trying desperately to revive her. And now, if something similar happened, it would be even harder for him to handle . . . because he had feelings for her. Or maybe he'd had feelings for her all along, ever since high school, and it took his nearly losing her to bring them to the surface.

It was a hell of a way to realize you were falling in love with someone, he thought wryly as he stood at the parlor window and watched Teri get out of the car and walk briskly up the porch steps. Her stride was so springy, she practically bounced. She was smiling a secretive, self-satisfied smile, as if pleased with herself and with life in general. She radiated an aura of health and contentment.

Jack sighed. Maybe *he,* too, needed to have an NDE and get a new lease on life. Obviously, he didn't have the confidence Teri had about facing whatever came his way. He still felt compelled to shield himself from the kind of hurt he'd suffered when Pamela died . . . the kind of hurt he could be setting himself up for again with Teri. With her Type A personality just barely kept in check by her recent brush with death, he knew it was only a matter of time before she was working herself to death again. Yes, a relationship with Teri would definitely be high risk.

He walked into the hall to meet her. She had set her briefcase on the hall table and was fluffing her bangs in the mirror above it when she saw his reflection behind her. Her smile widened and her eyes lit up like stars. He felt a painful twist of joy and longing.

"Jack!" She turned around and extended her arms. "Hey, give me a hug, will ya? I think I deserve a little pat on the back. And so do you. You were great! All of you were great!"

Unable to resist an armful of sunshine, Jack walked helplessly toward Teri. She grabbed him around the chest and pressed her cheek against his shirt. His arms automatically wrapped themselves around her slender shoulders and he rested his chin on the top of her head. He closed his eyes and breathed in the floral scent of her shampoo and enjoyed the feel of her soft curves against him.

She was so vibrant and alive. But life was so fragile . . . and could be so fleeting. Pam's death had taught him that.

She pulled away just far enough to gaze up at him. Her face was so aglow it hurt his eyes—and his heart—just to look at her.

"Why the gloomy face, Stonewall?" she inquired with an arched brow. "You should be happy."

He finally allowed himself to smile. He pushed aside his worries and decided to let Teri's happiness and love of life flow over him like a warm tidal wave. All anyone ever had was the moment, and Jack decided to enjoy this one . . . no matter how fleeting it was.

"I *am* happy," he assured her, still holding tight. "And I owe it all to you."

She gave him a teasing smile. "You sure do, Stonewall. I played the avaricious real-estate agent to the hilt, didn't I?"

"It wasn't much of a stretch," Jack couldn't resist retorting with a grin.

Teri shrugged, still smiling but suddenly looking a little uneasy. "I'm not like that anymore, Jack." Then she pulled away and turned to fiddle aimlessly with the latch on her briefcase.

Jack put his hands on his hips and stared at her slender back. "Yeah, you've changed, Teri, or you wouldn't have helped us save Oak Meadows from the grip of a greedy entrepreneur. But you haven't changed *that* much. You enjoyed the thrill of duping Schofield, didn't you? It must have been similar to the feeling you get when you make a big sale. Admit it, Teri."

Teri turned to face Jack. "Sure, I enjoyed it," she said, a little defensively. "But that doesn't mean I'm suddenly going to revert to my old ways. I believe in balance now, Jack—a balance between my career and my personal life. Can you say the same thing?"

Since Jack planned to call his agent that very afternoon to arrange for another assignment—less than a week after he'd completed his last assignment—he couldn't really defend himself with much surety.

They stood for a long moment, not speaking, their gazes locked in a sort of battle. She was challenging him, as she always did, and he was putting up a "stone wall."

Finally, she sighed and smiled wistfully, as if realizing that it was time to ease off... at least for now. "I'm glad that Schofield backed out of the deal. Thank goodness things went just the way we planned," she said.

"Yeah," Jack agreed, then added pointedly, "In life, things seldom do." Jack wasn't trying to be profound, and he hated clichés. But there was a wealth of meaning in his words and a wealth of feeling in his heart. And by her suddenly pensive look, he guessed Teri was experiencing the same sad-yet-happy war of emotions that he was. She must understand, then, that even though they were obviously drawn to each other, it wasn't a good idea for them to get involved. At least, it wasn't a good idea for *him*.

Abruptly, the expression in Teri's eyes turned from pensive to provocative. She smiled mischievously. "You know what I can't wait to do right now?"

"What?" he inquired, bemused by her sudden change in mood and enchanted by the way she was never more than a smile away from playfulness.

She leaned forward and whispered, "I can't wait to get out of these clothes."

Jack swallowed hard. "Here? *Now?*"

Teri chuckled throatily. "No, Jack. In my room...you know, the one next to yours?"

Of course Jack knew. He'd been up checking on her half a dozen or more times during the night, and she'd always been peacefully sleeping. He'd been tempted to lie down beside her just as he'd done the previous night, but that would just be asking for trouble.

"I want to change into something more casual," Teri continued, facing the mirror again and scrutinizing her reflection with a tiny, critical frown between her brows. She shrugged and squirmed inside the padded shoulders of her tailored gray suit. "This thing feels like a strait-jacket. Would you believe I've practically lived in getups like this since I graduated from college? The only really fun clothes I own are the ones I bought yesterday."

Jack lifted his brows and crossed his arms. "So what are you going to wear when you go back to work next week? Cutoffs and a midriff top like Cousin Daisy wore on 'The Dukes of Hazzard'?"

"Funny, Stonewall," she retorted dryly.

He grinned and shrugged. "Hey, you'd be comfortable. And I'm sure you'd sell even more houses than you already do."

"Oh, you think so, do you?" Teri said with a quirked brow. "Maybe I don't care about selling houses anymore. Maybe I'm ready to change professions completely."

Jack stared. "You're kidding, aren't you?"

Teri looked just as surprised as he did. "Well, I was at first. But come to think of it, there are a lot of other things I'm interested in. Selling real estate has been lucrative and challenging, but it's not terribly...well... creative."

Jack was about to pursue this intriguing turn of conversation, when Viv and Ginger and his dad danced into the hall from the kitchen in conga-line formation, all decked out in party hats and blowing on whistles and horns. Ginger was still wearing her striped coveralls and Viv was still dressed like Norma Desmond.

"What's all this?" Teri cried, delighted.

"It's a celebration," Beau informed her with a huge smile as he danced to a halt in front of her. The potato chip sisters broke formation, giggled and tried to catch their breaths. "We nearly lost Oak Meadows, and now that it's in my family again for keeps, I feel like a man with a new lease on life."

"The other night at dinner when you toasted new beginnings, you were probably thinking about moving away and starting fresh somewhere else," Teri said, returning Beau's smile. "But I suppose you realize now that you can stay at Oak Meadows and still make a fresh start, have a new beginning."

Beau slid a fond glance toward Ginger's flushed, happy face, then turned back to Teri, grinning more broadly than ever. "You can bet your sweet life on that one, m'dear."

"Let's not bet Teri's life on anything," Jack objected.

Beau clapped Jack on the shoulder. "Don't tell me you've become superstitious, too, son?" He gave a bark of laughter. "Did you see the way Schofield kept pawin' that rabbit's foot? What kind of goldarned silliness was that?"

What followed was a boisterous fifteen-minute play-by-play recap of Schofield's fateful visit. Beau laughed a lot, the sisters giggled, Teri smiled, and Jack kept his arms crossed and looked cranky.

"You were a wonderful Norma Desmond, Viv," Teri said.

"Thank you, *dahling*," Viv drawled, her words dripping with melodrama as she easily slipped back into her faded-film-star persona.

"I thought I was a pretty decent amateur archaeologist, too," Ginger piped up, looking expectantly at Teri for approval.

"You certainly were," Teri agreed. "I thought you all did wonderfully well at your various roles."

Viv turned her keen gaze in Jack's direction. "Looks like Jack's still in character," she observed. "Standing at the top of the stairs in that towel, with his arms crossed like they are now, his hair slicked back and a royal sneer on his face, like now, he reminded me and Ginger of Yul Brynner in *The King And I*."

Jack unfolded his arms and shifted uncomfortably.

"The sexiest bald man in the movies," Ginger added, oblivious to Jack's embarrassment. "Not even Captain Picard in 'Star Trek: The Next Generation' can hold a candle to Yul Brynner. Did you see him in *The Magnificent Seven?* What a presence!"

"I'm sure he had presence in all his movies," Beau said, patting Ginger fondly on the arm. "And speaking of movies," he continued, smoothly taking control of the runaway conversation, "I think Teri deserves a night on the town for all her trouble. Don't you, Jack?"

Jack flicked a nervous glance at Teri, then cautiously replied to his dad's question. "Well, I don't know. What kind of a night on the town are you talking about?"

"That's up to you and Teri to decide," Beau returned nonchalantly. "You're the one who's supposed to keep tabs on her, so it stands to reason that you'd be the one to take her out on the town."

Teri could swear Jack was panic-stricken. She wasn't sure whether she should be flattered by his fear of going out with her, or insulted. She'd find the whole thing rather amusing... if her heart weren't beating so hard at the thought of actually going on a bona fide date with Jack.

"I have to pick Sam up from Mikey's house," Jack finally said, hedging.

"No, you don't," Beau said decisively. "Mikey's mom called a while ago and asked if Sam could spend the night. He and Mikey are still working on their Halloween costumes and they're having so much fun that Pat didn't want to break things up. She suggested that Sam stay till tomorrow night so the boys could go trick-or-treating together in your old neighborhood. Since it'd take a week of going house to house out here to fill up Sam's candy sack, I agreed."

"*You* agreed?" Jack repeated.

Beau seemed to immediately understand Jack's implication, but he didn't back down. "Hell's bells, son, I'm used to making decisions about Sam when you're gone—and that's ninety percent of the time—so what makes you think I can just up and quit the minute you show your face on the premises? Besides, we all know you'll be gone again soon enough. No point confusin' the boy about who's got the last word around here."

"Did it ever occur to you that I might want to take Sam trick-or-treating?" Jack inquired icily.

"No, son, it didn't," Beau admitted with painful honesty. "But it did to Pat. When she heard you were back in town for a spell, she suggested that you come over to the house about seven tomorrow night and go along with Mikey's dad... what's his name?"

"Rick," Jack supplied, still stone-faced.

"Yeah, that's right. She thought you might want to go along with Rick when he walks the boys from house to house." He paused and eyed his son keenly. "So, are you going to do it?"

"Of course I am," Jack said curtly. "Dad, you ought to know by now that I want to spend as much time with Sam as I can when I'm home. Try to remember that when you're making plans for my son, okay?"

Beau nodded perfunctorily, but he said nothing more. The question about how long Jack intended to stick around before he accepted another assignment hung in the air, but neither man broached the explosive subject.

The atmosphere had gone from festive to grim. Even the potato chip sisters were minus their usual ear-to-ear smiles. It was obvious that Jack and his father had unresolved issues between them that circumstances would force to the surface. But even when a conflict arose, Jack and Beau didn't really face the issues. Father and son just circled each other like a couple of sparring partners, jabbing and feinting, then backing off. Someday they were going to have to quit circling and start talking.

Teri suspected that the biggest point of contention they'd have to resolve was Jack's avoidance of full-time parenting, which she was sure was a major part of the reason he accepted all those long-term assignments. And now she had a feeling he was running away from something else, too. Her, perhaps?

"So, when can you be ready to go?" Jack suddenly asked, turning to Teri with a stern look.

Teri made an effort to lighten the mood. "Are you asking me out, Jackson Tremain?" she inquired in an exaggerated soft Southern drawl and with a coy smile.

His lips twitched, but he maintained his severe demeanor. "Yes, I'm asking you out," he practically snapped.

Teri clasped her hands together and cocked her head to the side, giving him a shy-Di look and batting her lashes. "Well, I never could resist a sweet-talkin' man," she cooed. "Is seven o'clock okay?"

Jack's mouth tilted in a reluctant grin, breaking the tension. Beau guffawed and the potato chip sisters tittered appreciatively.

"Then seven it is, Miss Taylor," Jack said, bowing from the waist. "Shall we go formal or casual?"

"Since all I have in the house is this suit or my new play clothes, we'd better go casual," she replied. "Unless you want to leave at five and take me shopping first?" Teri threw Jack the most imploring look she could muster.

Jack could feel himself relenting. Even though he knew he was in for a torturous hour or two if he took Teri shopping again, he couldn't resist the challenge in her eyes, so cleverly conveyed behind a facade of playful coyness.

He sighed the sigh of a man resigned to his fate. "Meet you in the hall at five," he said grumpily. Then he turned and left before Teri had the chance to thank him by throwing her arms around his neck and pressing that sweet, soft body of hers against his.

BY FIVE O'CLOCK, Jack was dressed in a charcoal gray, light wool jacket over a white open-collared shirt and black slacks, and waiting in the hall. His palms were clammy and his heart was doing a cha-cha worthy of a ballroom dance competition. He was excited. He was scared. And he was determined to maintain control of the situation no matter what.

He hated being a grump. He wanted to relax and have fun on this so-called date with Teri, but that would be too risky. He'd always have to be on his guard, constantly struggling to temper his reaction to Teri, to downplay the thrill he felt whenever he touched her. But it would be damned hard and he groused to himself for the umpteenth time that it was extremely frustrating to be attracted to a woman who was a walking powder keg just waiting to go off.

He definitely didn't want to fall in love with her, even though he suspected he was already halfway there. But even if he did allow himself to care about her and to let that caring grow into something stronger, it wouldn't make him change his mind about not getting involved with her. A romantic involvement with Teri would just make it harder to leave when he accepted his next assignment. And that would be soon... very soon.

He'd talked to Iris, his agent, that afternoon, and a major magazine wanted him for another assignment in Eastern Europe. They wanted him to leave the day after tomorrow. Held back by a surge of longing to spend more time with his son, Jack hadn't given his answer yet, but he was sure he'd end up accepting. He always did, didn't he? But he'd try to make the next couple of days special for Sam.

As for Teri... Before leaving the States, Jack wished he could just kiss her again. Once, just once. But he didn't dare touch his lips to hers, much less make love to her...which is where kissing might ultimately lead them. And here he was, destined to spend an entire evening with her, starting at five o'clock and ending who knew when.

This was definitely a dilemma. How the hell was he going to keep his hands off the most beautiful, radiant woman in the world? Maybe if he took her to a very public, noisy restaurant in the French Quarter, then walked her up and down Bourbon Street till all hours, dropping into lounges to dance and listen to music, he'd wear her out and she'd go to sleep on the way home. If she was asleep, surely then he'd be safe from the temptation of kissing her.

He discarded that plan immediately, however, when he considered the possibility that he might tire her out too much and bring on some sort of arrhythmia attack. The doctor had assured him that Teri wasn't that fragile, but Jack still worried. He hated worrying. He just didn't want to care that much about someone. It was too damned painful.

As he paced the parquet floor, he kept glancing up the stairs. Finally, Teri appeared at the top in jeans and a clingy white sweater that was cropped at the waist. She looked sweet sixteen again. But she was a woman—a consenting adult—and way too sexy for words.

"You look great, Jack," she said, sliding her purse strap over her shoulder. "I'll have to find something black or red so we'll complement each other."

Jack did not reply. He just watched as she skipped blithely down the stairs. She stopped a foot away and frowned up at him.

"You're not going to be a grump tonight, are you?"

In that moment, Jack impetuously decided that, no, he was not going to be a grump. Since he apparently couldn't turn off his feelings for Teri by pretending indifference and nurturing irritation, he might as well enjoy the short time they'd spend together. Since he'd be gone soon, he reasoned fatalistically, what would be the harm in letting himself enjoy being in love for just one night?

Jack recognized the gaping holes in his logic, but he ignored them and smiled brightly at his high school nemesis, the self-proclaimed NDE survivor and girl with the glow. "I'm not going to be a grump," he promised her. "I'm going to have as much fun as you are, Teri."

Teri's face lit up. "That's pretty tall talk, Stonewall. I hope you've got the energy."

"What? Are you kidding?" he called, following her outside to the Ford Explorer.

By six o'clock, Jack was marveling at Teri's stamina and wondering about his own. They'd been to three department stores, and Teri had tried on every slinky dress east of the Mississippi. And she'd looked drop-dead gorgeous in every one of them.

He finally realized why he felt as if he'd been running a marathon. Watching Teri having a ball as she tried on red silk, gold lamé, black leather and white chiffon kept his heart going ninety miles an hour. Or, as Captain Picard would say, going warp speed. No wonder he felt weak in the knees.

When Teri finally settled on something, he decided she'd chosen well. It was a mere slip of a red dress, sleeveless and short. The salesperson helping Teri had found some nude hosiery and red suede T-strap heels to finish the outfit. She was already wearing small diamond studs in her ears, which added just the right amount of jewelry for understated elegance.

The bright, pure color and the simplicity of the ensemble brought out the classic beauty of Teri's blond hair, pale, flawless complexion, clear blue eyes, long neck and slender arms. She was model thin—a little too thin in Jack's opinion—and she looked as if she'd just stepped off the runway at a Paris fashion show.

"Do you like it?" she asked, smiling demurely but still managing to do a pretty snazzy turn to show off the flared skirt.

"Do chickens have lips?" he returned.

"No, Jack, chickens *don't* have lips!" Teri chided with a laugh.

"Bad example," Jack admitted. He grinned. "How's this? Does Sam like Bartholomew?"

Teri's eyes twinkled. "He *loves* Bartholomew."

"And I love that dress. It makes you look…" *Elegant. Sophisticated. Young. Carefree. Scrumptious. Sexy.* "Hell, Teri, let's just say it's perfect for you. Or, better said, you're perfect for *it*."

Teri smiled. "You sure know how to turn a girl's head, Stonewall. Are you ready to go to dinner?"

"Not until you buy a wrap or a coat or something to keep you warm. There's not much to that dress…not that I'm complaining."

"I have just the thing," the hovering salesperson offered, then she rushed off and returned in minutes with a short, swingy, black velvet coat that topped the outfit perfectly, and a small velvet clutch for Teri's essentials.

"Now all you need is that black cat we borrowed from the farm next door to drape over your arm," Jack suggested. "You could walk down Bourbon Street with your cute little nose in the air and everyone would think you were vacationing royalty."

"So that's where you got the cat that put Schofield in a dither," Teri observed, unfazed by his flattering reference to royalty. "I knew I hadn't seen it at Oak Meadows before." As they left the department store arm in arm, Teri leaned close to Jack's ear and whispered, "You know, I've never worn anything this daring before. I've always been tailored and practical and businesslike. But I think I *like* being daring.''

Jack couldn't help but think Teri's comment did not bode well for a problem-free evening. And the biggest problem would be resisting taking her in his arms at the first dark alley as they strolled the streets of the romantic French Quarter. But that's where they'd find the best restaurants in town, and Jack wanted Teri's newfound love of eating to be justly rewarded with some excellent gourmet food.

They stashed Teri's jeans, sweater and casual purse in the car, then headed for Mr. B's Bistro, Jack's favorite New Orleans restaurant, which was just a few blocks away.

It was a pleasant walk. Dusk had come and gone moments before and the night air was brisk and refreshing. The crowds on Bourbon Street were thin compared to the usual influx of visitors at other times of the year. Jazz and Cajun music drifted from bars, restaurants and intimate nightclubs. The spicy smells of shrimp Creole, gumbo and black beans and rice wafted on the breeze that rolled in from the river.

Jack was reminded again of how much he loved his home state, and New Orleans in particular. And he wondered again why he kept running away from it to the most distant corners of the earth. Sure, he loved and was committed to his work as a photojournalist. But he knew there were just as many news and human interest stories to be covered in the United States as there were in Europe, Africa and Asia.

Jack didn't make a habit of analyzing his behavior, and now was not the time to start. He was with a beautiful woman and he was about to share some fabulous food with her. Trouble was, once they got to Mr. B's, they were told that without reservations they'd have to wait an hour or more for a table.

"Sorry about this," Jack said. "I guess I'm not the only one who likes this restaurant."

"It's no big deal," Teri assured him. "Just give them your name and we'll come back in an hour."

"What are we going to do in the meantime?" Jack asked her after he'd left his name with the maître d'.

"My condo is only five minutes away by car. Would you mind if we went by there so I could pick up my mail? I was in such a hurry earlier today that I didn't check my mailbox or my phone messages."

Jack gave her a searching look.

"No, I'm not anxious about missing calls from clients, Jack," she informed him with a wry smile. "My boss is taking care of that. I'm just worried my mom might call and get irritated if I don't call her back. Or some bill will get ignored too long and I'll have collectors breathing down my neck. I promise it will only take a few minutes. Okay?"

Jack agreed although he had grave misgivings. The idea of being alone with Teri in her condo, with very little chance of interruption, seemed risky. He really didn't know exactly how Teri felt about him, but he was crazy about her. He wanted to touch her, kiss her. Hell, he wanted to make love to her till the cows came home.

They drove to her condo in silence. Teri seemed content to gaze at the play of moonbeams on the river, humming some whimsical little tune under her breath. On the other hand, Jack was gripping the steering wheel, feeling as tense as a mattress spring.

He was nuts, he told himself. He was stark raving mad to be going to Teri's condominium.

Too late. They were there, and headed toward a ground-level, Spanish-style unit with a thick wooden door. With the money she made and her knowledge of real estate, Jack was frankly surprised that Teri didn't own something fancier. She could easily afford a house on a golf course somewhere, but she chose to live in a nice, but basically unremarkable, condominium complex. Her modest choice was hard to understand.

When Teri unlocked the door and Jack followed her inside, he understood. Teri's place wasn't a home; it was merely a pit stop alongside the fast lane.

Teri flicked on the light, but instead of heading for the answering machine to check messages or stooping to collect the mail strewn on the floor through the mail slot, she just stood in one spot and stared. She seemed as struck by the barrenness of her so-called home as Jack was.

"My God, Jack," she whispered. "Have I been *living* here?"

Jack looked around at the meager furnishings, the bare walls devoid of paintings and the cold fireplace without any family photos to clutter the mantel. He noted the absence of green plants and throw pillows and dog-eared, well-loved books randomly scattered. It looked like a motel room, only not quite as cheerful.

"That's the point, Teri," Jack began, trying to reassure her. "You weren't really *living* here. My bet is you came home only to sleep and change your clothes, not stopping to look at anything...like this afternoon. You've probably never entertained or even fixed yourself a meal here. Am I right?"

Teri nodded mutely. Jack peered at her face and he didn't like its pale look. Where was the radiance she'd carried with her like an inner light for the past two days?

He took her hand; it was cold as ice. "Come and sit down on the sofa, Teri," he urged. Zombielike, she followed, her eyes full of pain.

As soon as she sat down, he took her pulse. He was relieved to find her heart beating at a normal rate...perhaps even a little slower than normal. Everything about her seemed suddenly dull and listless. Lifeless.

"What's the matter, Teri?" he whispered, forcing her to look at him by gently cupping and turning her chin.

"It's this place, Jack," she whispered brokenly. "It scares me."

"Why?" he asked her.

"It's so cold and lonely here. And it reminds me too much of what I was like before...before..."

"Before your bout with a problem heart?"

"Yes. And I'm afraid I'll—"

"Change back?" Jack finished for her.

Her gaze darted around the sterile room, then locked with his. The expression in her eyes was heartbreaking. So sure of herself before, she was suddenly filled with doubt. She was reaching out to him for comfort. He couldn't resist. He took her into his arms and held her close.

"No, Teri," he murmured soothingly into her ear. "No, sweetheart, you won't change back."

But he knew he was probably lying.

She pulled back and searched his face, seeming to seek reassurance. Jack didn't know how sincere he looked, but he knew the love he felt for her must be written all over his face. And whether or not she was responding to that love, he didn't know and didn't care. All that mattered was the glow that suffused her skin with life and color again, the returning sparkle in her eyes and the sweet upward tilt of her lips.

"Jack," she whispered, "I'm going to close my eyes and pretend that I'm back at Oak Meadows." Her thick, tawny lashes fluttered down. "And to help me remember how good I've felt there for the past two days...I want you to kiss me. Please, Jack. Kiss me *now*."

# Chapter Ten

Jack was as human as the next guy. He couldn't resist such a sweet plea. Besides, he'd been wanting to kiss her for eons, but he'd been held back by fear. Whether he was afraid she'd die in his arms again or whether he was afraid for other, more selfish reasons, he wasn't sure anymore. All he knew was that there was no longer a choice. Kissing Teri the Terror was apparently his immediate destiny.

He leaned forward, closed his eyes and tentatively pressed his lips against hers. The resulting jolt of pleasure that coursed through him had enough electricity in it to stop the heart of a two-ton bull. He pulled quickly back. "Are you all right?" he asked her, anxiously searching her face.

Teri slowly opened her eyes. Her expression was dreamy, but with a touch of amused impatience. "I'm all right, but I could be a lot better. That kiss was *way* too short, Stonewall. Give it another try, will ya?"

She looked fine—more than fine—but Jack couldn't resist taking her pulse. He pressed his middle fingers against the carotid artery in her neck. His brow furrowed. "Your heartbeat is strong, but it's a little fast," he said.

"Of course it's fast," Teri said dryly. "I'm turned on, Stonewall, turned on by a guy who only wants to take my pulse. Could we get on with things...please? I promise you, I'm not going to croak in your arms. On the other hand, if you don't kiss me again, right this minute, I just might die waiting."

Jack hesitated for only a second. He wanted to kiss Teri more than he wanted his next breath. And according to the doctors they'd consulted, the chances of her repeating that dramatic death scene from the other night was next to nil. Maybe it was worth the chance....

Jack pulled Teri close and kissed her. When that jolt of electricity hit him again, he felt an accompanying surge of anxiety and had flashbacks of doing CPR over her inert body. But when he stiffened and would have pulled away again, Teri held on tighter. Then she parted her lips and invited him to kiss her more deeply.

Jack accepted the invitation, then lost himself in a flood of emotional and physical sensations. Her mouth opened willingly and he probed the sweet, sensuous lining of her lips. She tasted so good....

She pressed herself against him eagerly and he could feel her small breasts, the nipples hard and erect, through the thin material of his shirt. The longing that had been a steady flame over the past few days burst quickly and suddenly into a blaze of desire. His hunger for her was more than an ache; it was a sharp pain that twisted in his gut and demanded to be satisfied.

Such a fierce and desperate need for a woman scared the hell out of him, especially since that woman was temporarily not herself. The time would surely come when she'd feel at home again in this mausoleum of a condo, with a cellular phone perpetually glued to her ear, her delectable little body hidden inside a tailored suit with the appeal of a prison uniform.

She'd be trapped again by her ambition and on the road to ruin. He didn't want to see that happen, so he resolved then and there to call his agent in the morning and accept the new assignment, even though he hadn't spent as much time with Sam as he'd wanted to. But he'd make it up to his son by moving heaven and earth to be home for the holidays.

Jack pulled back. His breath was labored. His heart was hammering against his ribs. "This is crazy," he rasped. "This is wrong. Nothing can come of this, Teri. I'll be leaving soon."

Teri's face was radiant. Her lips were rosy from their ardent kisses. She smiled . . . and Jack nearly melted.

"This may be crazy, Jack, but it's not wrong," she whispered, luxuriously trailing her fingers through his hair and down his neck, then resting her palms flat against his chest. "Sometimes a little craziness is exactly what the doctor ordered. And judging by the way your heart's beating, you want me as much as I want you."

"How fast is *your* heart beating, Teri?" he asked, hoping to curtail her passion by alluding to her medical condition.

She took his hand and pressed his palm against her chest. She arched a coy brow. "How does it feel, Jack?"

"Your heartbeat?" he asked, gulping down a lump of nervousness like a teenager.

"Of course," she answered with a chuckle.

Her heartbeat felt strong and healthy. The rhythm was faster than normal . . . but what was normal when you were in the throes of passion? Wouldn't it be *ab*normal to have a slow heartbeat under these circumstances?

*Thud, thud, thud.* The beat vibrated against his palm, loud and clear and bursting with life. It felt good. And her firm, small breasts, rising and falling with her rapid breathing, felt pretty damned good, too.

"Don't worry, you won't hurt me, Jack," she whispered, lifting his hand to her lips and kissing his knuckles. "In fact, by making love to me, you may be the best over-the-counter preventive medicine around."

Jack swallowed hard. "How do you figure?"

"I asked Dr. Benson if sex was beneficial, and—"

Jack choked out a laugh. "You *what?*"

"Don't laugh," she said, grinning. "I asked him if sex was a good form of relaxation or if it was taboo, and he—"

"Told you it was a great idea," Jack finished dryly. "And I'm sure Dr. Benson had no ulterior motives whatsoever. The guy has the hots for you."

Teri smiled demurely and shrugged, her slender shoulder rolling seductively. Jack wanted to slip his finger under her shoulder strap and pull it down, then bend to kiss the pale, silky skin he'd exposed.

Teri must have somehow read his thoughts, or followed his hungry gaze and figured out what he wanted, because she slipped her own finger under that tantalizing strap and pulled it down herself.

Jack stared at her bared shoulder, then gazed, speechless, into Teri's eyes. Then, in a move that was somehow both bold and shy, Teri slipped her hands inside Jack's jacket and slowly pushed it off his shoulders. "I don't know how Dr. Benson felt about me, Jack, but there was no attraction on my side. The only man I really care about is you."

Jack felt a thrill shoot through him at her words, a sensation that seemed dangerously like joy. He hadn't felt joy in years . . . not since before Pamela died.

Teri eased the sleeves of his jacket down his arms, and he automatically straightened his elbows and slipped free. Then she tossed it on a nearby chair. "You saved my life, Jackson Tremain." Her smile was shy, but still lethally seductive. "Now make it worth living," she challenged.

In that moment, Jack lost the war. But, oh, what a sweet surrender.

He picked her up and carried her through the open door of her bedroom. En route, Teri kicked off her shoes.

Like the rest of the place, the bedroom was furnished sparsely and the walls were bare. The color scheme was muted, consisting of a mix of beige and ivory and pale gold.

Just enough light streamed in from the living room, so Jack didn't bother to flick the switch before he laid Teri down in the middle of the bed. He was about to join her there when she said, "Turn on the lights, Jack. I want to see you."

Having detected a disarming shyness beneath her eager passion, Jack was a little surprised by this request. But considering her fascination with everything since her alleged NDE the other night, it stood to reason that she'd want to get all her senses involved in something as pleasure filled as lovemaking. And he wasn't about to argue the point.

Jack did as she asked and large, ugly clay lamps on either side of the bed lit the room to a moderate brightness.

He started for the bed, then he stopped, fascinated by the scene before him. Looking at Teri on the bed was like looking at a picture painted by an avant-garde pop artist. The background was brushed in broad strokes with washed-out colors of beige and white. Then, as the focal point of the picture, just off center, was a vibrant splash of red . . . Teri's dress.

And inside that dress was the embodiment of life. Thrumming, vital, sparkling life. Teri was a masterpiece.

He went to her. He toed off his shoes, then lay down beside her. He took her in his arms and she lifted her face to his. They kissed.

Teri decided that you didn't have to die to go to heaven. She was there.

Jack covered her face, her neck and her shoulders with kisses, then returned to hungrily capture her mouth again and again. Teri pressed close as the ache of desire mounted higher and higher. She explored his body, reveling in the tight muscles in his arms, his back, his buttocks. She pulled out his shirttail and slipped her hands underneath, tangling her fingers in the silky mat of hair on his chest.

Jack gasped with pleasure and Teri's heart tripped into a faster rhythm. She wanted to touch him everywhere, to kiss him from top to toe.

Jack caressed her back in sensuous circles, then slid his hands up her ribs and over her breasts. He ran the pad of his thumb over her hardened nipples and she arched against his palms, moaning. He responded by cupping her hips and pulling her against the evidence of his arousal. Teri was awash in pleasure.

Then he was unzipping her dress. In no time at all, he slipped it over her head and tossed it unceremoniously to the floor.

"So much for my designer duds," she whispered teasingly.

"And so much for these scraps of lace called lingerie," he said, undoing her bra, then dexterously removing her panties and hose.

Lying naked beneath him, a willing slave to his skillful hands and lips, Teri had never felt so free or so alive. If life was like a necklace with moments strung together like pearls, she thought, this moment had to be one of the finest. A perfect pearl.

And it got better.

Jack pushed himself to a sitting position and sat back on his heels. She looked up at him, at his tousled hair, his chiseled features, and at the almost fierce gleam of desire in his eyes, and she knew she was completely and forever in love. Ever since that stormy night at Oak Meadows, her life had been a whirlwind. But she wasn't going to fight it. Finally, she was really living.

When he started unbuttoning his shirt, she caught his hands and said, "No. Please let me do it, Jack."

Jack smiled ruefully. "Okay, but hurry, will ya?"

Teri sat up and rested on her heels, facing Jack. He didn't touch her, but there was a tingling trail of awareness on her skin wherever his gaze wandered. She was just as eager as he was to consummate their lovemaking, but she purposely took her sweet time undoing his shirt. After releasing each button, she bent forward and kissed his bare chest on each newly exposed area.

"You're trying to drive me crazy, aren't you, Teri?" he murmured roughly.

"Is it working?" she whispered as she nuzzled his chest and laved a taut, wine-colored nipple with her tongue.

"I'll return the favor," he warned her, gasping as she opened his shirt completely, curled her hands around his waist, then bent and lingeringly kissed each of his ribs.

"Promises, promises," she crooned.

"Okay, sweetheart," he finally said, taking her by the shoulders. "Now it's my turn."

"I'm not worried, Stonewall," she said, lying back on the pillows and taunting him with a come-hither smile. "I can take whatever you dish out."

Jack undid his trousers and slipped quickly out of them. Dressed only in his briefs, he returned her smile with one equally playful and sexy. "Still egging me on to do my best with those challenges you throw at me, eh, Teri the Terror? No problem. I always rise to the occasion."

"That's what I'm counting on," she returned, grinning. Then he took off his briefs and Teri no longer felt like indulging in teasing repartee. She was awed by the beauty of the man, and all she felt like doing—possibly for the rest of her life—was making love.

She opened her arms and he came to her, now fully aroused. As their lips met again, passion overwhelmed them. Teri couldn't wait any longer, and neither could Jack. He entered her with one long, deep thrust and Teri bit her lip to keep from crying out.

Bracing himself on his elbows, Jack looked searchingly into her face. "Don't tell me you're... Teri, are you a *virgin?*"

"Not anymore," she joked weakly.

"If you'd only said something, I'd have been gentler," he explained, distressed.

"What? And advertise the fact that I was a twenty-eight-year-old virgin? If the tabloids got word, my face would have been plastered all over their cheap sheets."

Jack shook his head and smoothed her hair away from her damp forehead. He looked tenderly into her eyes. "Joke all you want, Teri, if it makes you feel better. But are you okay?"

She ran her hands up and down his smooth, muscled back and smiled. "In every way, Jack. But the fun's just begun, hasn't it?"

He smiled back. "Oh, yeah."

And like his dad, Jack was a man of his word. Only what happened between them was so much more than just fun. As Jack moved inside her, Teri's body responded with a building pleasure that became mindless and all-consuming. But her heart responded, too, nearly bursting with joy as she clutched Jack to her and felt for the first time that she wasn't alone in the world. That she wasn't competing for love or attention or praise. That she didn't have to prove herself. She was just *being* herself... and loving a man to distraction in the process.

Teri's release came first and it rocked her with the awesome force of a mini-earthquake or a small typhoon. It was a new experience and Teri immediately ranked it even higher than eating double fudge truffle pecan ice cream... and that was saying something.

Then she watched Jack as he found his release, his face arrestingly beautiful as pleasure and satisfaction played over his features.

Afterward, curled up together on the bed, the lights switched off and the room awash in soft moonlight, Teri had never felt so connected to someone, so peaceful, so happy. And she was no longer frightened that she might return to her old workaholic ways. She'd found out how wonderful life could be when you took the time to enjoy it, to discover new things and to risk involvement with the people around you. She could never turn back into the person she was before.

Jack insisted on taking her pulse, and finding it perfectly acceptable—given the circumstances—he sighed deeply and pulled her more fully into his arms. By his deep breathing, Teri could tell he'd dozed off. It felt so intimate, so cozy, so right to be sharing a bed with Jack, whether they were making love or sleeping.

Since her NDE, Teri had found out what it was like to fall deeply in love. Trouble was, there was a distinct possibility that she might also find out how it felt to have a broken heart.

Teri was pretty sure she had Jack all figured out. Just like her, he'd been running away from life ever since Pamela died. While she had been afraid to take the plunge to begin with, Jack had risked loving someone too much when he married Pam, then he was devastated when he lost her.

Now he was afraid to love again, and he was even skittish about getting close to his own son. While he might be escaping some of the worry and heartache of raising a child, Jack was also missing out on all the joy.

*Joy.* Wasn't that what everyone wanted? Teri thought, growing drowsy herself.

*And wouldn't it make a great name for a little girl?*

Snuggling against Jack's chest, her eyelids drooping sleepily, Teri mentally cautioned herself not to get carried away. Before she could ever hope to convince Jack that he wanted desperately to marry her and bring more children into the world, he had to quit running away from the family he already had.

But a girl could dream, couldn't she?

JACK WOKE UP, blinked against the bright morning sunshine peeking around the bedroom drapes, pushed himself up on his elbows, then looked down at Teri. She was lying on her side, facing him, her legs slightly drawn up and her hands tucked against her chest. Her skin was radiant with color, and he could swear she was smiling in her sleep.

As he'd admitted to himself last night when he'd first kissed Teri, he was, after all, only human. So he supposed it wasn't surprising that he felt somewhat responsible for Teri's present state of well-being. Apparently, their lovemaking had agreed with her, or she probably wouldn't be having dreams that made her smile. Was it egotistical of him to feel a little . . . pride?

And he'd been her first. That part was humbling. He couldn't believe such a beautiful woman had managed to stay out of the sack for so long. But then, she'd been more than a little busy being top Realtor of the year . . . year after year after year.

Jack eased down in the bed, turned on his side toward Teri and propped his head on his hand. Then he just looked at her.

The covers were tucked under her arms, just barely covering her breasts. Her white shoulders and the curves of her slim waist and hip under the pale bedding just begged to be touched, traced, tantalized. It would wake her up, then they could make love again.

Jack frowned, nixing that idea fast. Sleeping with Teri last night was bad enough. Making love with her again this morning would only make things worse. Considering the fact that he'd be leaving Louisiana quite soon, and for who knew how long, he already felt like a first-class cad. Teri might think there was something more to their relationship than Jack was willing and able to give. Even though he cared for her, he wasn't ready to start wearing his heart on his sleeve again.

Besides, Teri was a definite risk. As soon as she got back into the swing of buying and selling at Sugarbaker Realtors, she'd more than likely fall into her familiar rut.

It was a shame, too. A damned shame. And he didn't want to stick around to see it happen.

Teri shifted and moaned, rolling on her back and exposing one small, creamy breast. Jack felt himself tightening with arousal, and he knew he'd better get up and into the shower right away before his resistance was completely demolished.

Jack slipped out of bed and into the bathroom. He found clean towels in the cupboard, then turned the shower on full blast. By the time he got inside the stall, the glass was opaque with steam. He stood under the stream of water and drenched his hair and face, then soaped up all over.

Suddenly, he felt a slight draft of cold air, then two slim white arms snaked around his chest. He could feel Teri's naked body pressing against his as she kissed his back.

"Good morning, Jack," she murmured against his skin. "Do you mind if I join you? I've never showered with another person in my whole life." He could feel her lips curve in a smile. "It would be another new experience to add to my list."

Instantly, uncontrollably aroused, Jack turned in the shower and pulled Teri into his arms. He'd give her one more new experience to add to her list, all right... or maybe two.

LATER, DRESSED IN the same black slacks and white shirt as the night before, Jack stood in the kitchen and drank a cup of instant coffee. Teri walked in wearing the jeans and cropped sweater she'd had on before they'd bought that little red number that had ended up so quickly on the bedroom floor. Her hair was still a little damp and she was smiling radiantly.

"Good morning...again," she said with a provocative lift of one brow.

"Good morning," Jack replied, feeling awkward. His first instinct was to take her into his arms and give her a big kiss, but he'd gone that route already and his control had proved to be less than adequate. "Hungry?"

"Very," Teri answered promptly. "We missed dinner last night."

"I know. Sorry about that," Jack said sheepishly.

"I'm not," Teri said, grinning.

"Neither am I," Jack had to admit, returning her grin. They stood there and smiled at each other way too long for Jack's comfort, then he motioned toward his cup of java and said, "I hope you don't mind if I helped myself. Does it bother you if I drink coffee in front of you?"

"Not a bit," Teri assured him. "I suppose it was the only thing resembling food on the premises?"

"Your cupboards are bare, Mother Hubbard," Jack agreed.

"After breakfast, let's go shopping again," Teri suggested eagerly.

Jack frowned. "Not for clothes, I hope."

"No, not for clothes."

"For food? But I thought you were going to stay at Oak Meadows till the end of the week?"

"I am. But when I come back here for keeps, I don't want it to be such a shock when I walk in the door. I won't buy groceries till I officially move back in, but I want to buy some things for the condo to brighten it up a bit, make it look more homey. Don't you think that's a good idea, Jack?"

Jack nodded thoughtfully. "I think it's a great idea." Maybe by making the place more inviting, Teri would be a little more tempted to spend time at home relaxing instead of out on the real-estate trail roping clients.

"So you don't mind if we stay in the city for the day instead of driving back to Oak Meadows before you go trick-or-treating with Sam?"

Jack shook his head. "I don't mind. I'll call Dad and let him know what's going on. He worries about you, too, you know. I'm glad I remembered to call him last night, er, in between things."

Teri blushed like a new bride.

*Bad simile,* Jack thought with an inward grimace. Then he forced himself to continue the conversation as though he hadn't been tempted to grab her and make her blush even more.

"You realize I won't be through with Sam till about nine?"

"That's fine," Teri said. "I can wait here at the condo till you get back, or..." She smiled and suggested brightly, "I could go with you when you take Sam trick-or-treating."

Jack's immediate reaction was to happily agree to the plan. Sam liked Teri a lot, and having her along could only make things more fun for both Sam *and* himself. But it would be a kind of "family" activity, creating speculation on the part of Mikey's parents, Pat and Rick, both of whom had known Pamela. But worse than creating speculation among his friends, he could be raising Teri's hopes that their relationship was going somewhere. Somewhere serious.

"If you have to take so long to consider the suggestion, you must not like it and are trying to think of a tactful way to turn me down," Teri joked, but he could detect a suggestion of hurt in her eyes.

He hated to hurt her even slightly, so he quickly said, "I was just wondering if you'd ever gone trick-or-treating before, or if it was another new experience I could introduce you to."

His heart did a grateful little tap dance when the hurt disappeared from her eyes. "I wasn't a total washout as a kid. I went trick-or-treating for a few years, then I stopped when I was eight."

Jack's face showed his surprise. "That's awfully young, Teri! Why?"

She shrugged. "I was too busy. I quit going out the year I won first prize at the science fair. I made this spectacular volcano out of putty, but it took every minute of my spare time. Then, after that, it seemed silly to dress up and troll for candy when I could be using my time more productively."

Jack raised a brow. "I gather you don't feel that way anymore?"

"No, I don't. Frankly, I can't think of anything I'd rather do tonight than troll for candy." Teri moved close to Jack and wrapped her arms loosely around his waist. "Can you?"

Jack could think of *one* other thing he'd rather do, but he was determined not to make love to Teri again before he left on his next assignment. It just wouldn't be fair. But she was making honorable abstinence a very difficult objective.

"We'd better get going if we want to have breakfast and refurbish your entire house by seven o'clock," Jack reminded her, summoning up all his self-control to pull out of the embrace.

Teri looked a little puzzled by his reluctance to cuddle, but she quickly became enthusiastic about their shopping spree. As they locked up the condo and headed for the car, she chattered away about all her ideas for sprucing up the "morgue," as she facetiously referred to her living quarters.

It was another beautiful fall day. They had beignets at an outside table at the Café du Monde, then hit the department stores and garden shops. Teri couldn't buy enough plants.

"My houseplants have been like my relationships with men," Teri said with self-derisive humor as they inspected a flourishing ivy. "They all dried up from neglect. After a while, I just gave up on them."

"Men or plants?" Jack inquired.

"Both."

"Well, I don't think you'll have that kind of trouble anymore," Jack suggested.

Teri turned to him and gave him a puzzled smile. "With men or plants?"

"Both," he answered.

She didn't reply, but turned back to the ivy plant, gently touching the supple leaves and testing the dark, moist soil with her finger. But Jack could tell she was mulling over his words, as if he'd implied—which he had—that she was free to pursue other relationships. And he could tell she wasn't sure how to react.

Jack gritted his teeth. He wanted to take her in his arms and tell her not to give another man a single thought for the rest of her life. But he didn't. He couldn't. He refused to commit himself, only to wish he hadn't. Even though it was damned lonely, remaining emotionally unfettered was the best choice.

After lunch at Mr. B's Bistro, Jack and Teri drove back to her condo and unloaded all the shopping bags. Then Teri bustled about, calling out cheerful orders until they'd given the place a whole new look.

Coral and turquoise throw pillows livened up the living-room couch. Fresh, colorful seashore prints graced the walls. Plants were scattered all over the place, and several hardback books recommended by the clerk at the bookstore were lined up on the mantel. Two of them were romances that Teri vowed she couldn't wait to get to.

In the kitchen, she'd adopted a sunflower motif. The throw rugs had sunflowers on them, as well as the dish towels and dishcloths. Bright yellow mugs hung from a mug tree, and several different kinds of magnets that had struck Teri's fancy adorned the refrigerator.

For the bedroom, Teri had chosen a floral bedspread in cornflower blue. She'd replaced the big, ungainly-looking lamps on the nightstands with delicately worked Victorian lamps with frosted globes. At the foot of the bed she'd placed a handmade quilt and a hope chest. On the walls she'd hung reproduction Victorian prints that evoked a distinctly nostalgic charm.

"Oak Meadows got to you, didn't it?" Jack marveled, looking around the room as he stood at the end of the bed.

"In more ways than one," Teri admitted, giving him a soft look Jack would be a jackass to misinterpret. Which meant they'd better be getting out of the bedroom pronto or he'd lose control again.

"It's five-thirty, Teri," he said, peering pointedly at his watch. "If we want to catch a bite before we meet Sam at Mikey's, we'd better get going." Then he hurried out of the bedroom like a man with a rabid dog nipping at his heels.

Teri sighed. She'd be crazy not to recognize the fact that Jack didn't want to get intimate with her again. For all she knew, he'd already called his agent and lined up another overseas assignment. He was definitely running scared.

She moved to the mirror and briskly ran a comb through her hair and put on a dab of lipstick. She recognized the stubborn set of her jaw. This wasn't the first time she'd butted heads with Stonewall Jackson Tremain, and she wasn't about to back down any time soon...no matter how much it hurt. Jack might not know it, but Teri had a distinct premonition that they were destined to be butting heads together for the rest of their lives.

# Chapter Eleven

"Daddy, how d'ya like my costume?" shouted a green-and-purple miniature dinosaur running down the sidewalk toward Jack.

For the first time in hours, Teri watched Jack drop his cautious, controlled facade and show some honest emotions. His face lit up with pride and love as he bent and balanced on the balls of his feet, holding his arms out to Sam.

"Hey, son, you look great!" Jack enthused, squeezing Sam's shoulders and peering behind him at the long dinosaur tail. "You're a Brontosaurus, right?"

Sam nodded vigorously. "Right! I eat vege'bles."

"And I'm a meat-eater!" crowed Mikey, who had followed Sam outside. *"Groowwll!"*

"T-rex, I presume?" Jack said, tousling Mikey's carrot red hair.

From the open front door, the hall light streamed out into the gathering dusk and the smell of apple cider wafted on the air. Childish cutout Halloween decorations festooned the door and windows of the traditional-style, two-story house where Mikey lived, and a garishly carved jack-o'-lantern, with a candle where its brains used to be, grinned at them from a bay window.

Appearing at the door was a dark-haired, attractive woman in her late twenties or early thirties. "Hi, Jack," she called cheerfully, then she smiled pointedly at Teri as Jack took Sam's hand and the three of them walked up the pavement to the door with Mikey tagging along behind.

"Hi, Pat," Jack said. "It's good to see you again." He touched Teri on the arm. "This is a friend of mine, Teri Taylor. Teri, Pat Johnson."

"She's a friend of mine, too," Sam added. "Are you gonna go tricker-treatin' with us, Teri?"

Teri laughed and said to Pat, "Pleased to meet you." Then she looked down at Sam and said, "If it's okay, I'd really like to go with you...unless this outing is strictly for the guys. You know, just you and Mikey and your dads?" Suddenly, Teri was wondering if maybe she'd be horning in on a father-son thing. She definitely didn't want to be in the way of a bonding experience.

"My daddy can't come," Mikey announced in a petulant tone. "He has to work at the dumb ol' police station."

Pat placed her hand gently on Mikey's head. "Mikey, I explained why your dad had to work tonight." Mikey just crossed his arms and stuck out his bottom lip. Pat looked at Teri and Jack and shook her head. "There's a flu epidemic going on down at the station. Rick requested this night off months ago, but he, along with a lot of other off-duty policemen, had to go in to help cover for everyone that called in sick. And as I'm sure you understand, no one wants New Orleans to be understaffed with police on Halloween."

"We understand, of course, but I guess it's harder to understand stuff like that when you're only four years old," Teri said quietly.

Pat nodded, then invited them in, shooing the boys ahead of her. "Why don't you two go and get Sam's backpack so his dad can put it in the car before you go treat-or-treating?" she suggested, obviously trying to get rid of them so the adults could talk freely.

The boys quickly disappeared down the hall, their tails flipping back and forth.

"You did a fantastic job on those costumes," Teri said as they walked into an inviting living room.

"Thanks," Pat said. "But I had lots of help." She shook her head again. "I took pictures so Rick could see how cute and excited the boys looked. He's really taking it hard that he can't be with Mikey tonight. And Mikey hasn't made it any easier for him. He's so used to his dad being there for him all the time—at his T-ball games and preschool functions—he's really disappointed when Rick just can't make it. He's a little spoiled."

Teri could sense how uncomfortable Jack was feeling. He was probably thinking about how he was hardly ever there for Sam.

Pat seemed to suddenly realize that she might be treading on sensitive territory and she quickly changed the subject. She asked Jack about his work and got some polite, but very brief answers in reply. Then she asked Teri some getting-acquainted questions, and they chit-chatted until the boys barreled into the room again, their crayon-decorated candy sacks clutched in their hot little fists.

After some last-minute admonitions to Mikey to always stay within sight of Jack and Teri, not to open and eat anything till he got home and not to cross the street without supervision, Pat waved goodbye from the door as they headed down the walk.

"All that stuff Mrs. Johnson said to Mikey," Jack said, briefly pulling his mite-size dinosaur to the side, "goes for you, too, Sam." Sam nodded agreeably and they were off.

Mikey may have been disappointed not to have his father along, but he was obviously having a great time anyway. The weather was perfect with clear skies and just a nip of autumn in the air. Scores of trick-or-treaters were racing up and down the streets of the family neighborhood, with moms and dads trailing along behind the smaller ones. Doorbells rang and children's voices chorused, "Trick or treat, smell my feet, give me somethin' good to eat!"

Teri would have been having a great time if she weren't so attuned to Jack's sober mood. To try to cheer him up, she commented on all the funny costumes, the antics of the kids as they collected their treats, and Sam's near delirious enjoyment of the evening. He came up to Jack every three or four houses and, with wide-eyed wonder, showed his father how full his sack was.

"He's having a wonderful time, Jack. And he loves being with you," Teri said.

Jack smiled grimly. "But he's definitely not spoiled like Mikey, is he? He knows better than to expect *me* to be around all the time."

"You could change that, Jack," Teri flatly suggested.

Jack shook his head and gave her a very direct and challenging look. "No, I can't, Teri." And Teri knew that he meant that message for her, too.

*Get it through your head, Teri. He's not going to change his life to include you and Sam.* But Teri wouldn't accept that.

After a while, Teri's continued good humor and Sam's excitement seemed to work their magic on Jack. He got in the spirit of things, loosened up and had a good time.

By eight-thirty, the boys had enough candy to sink a ship and they were definitely dragging, so Jack and Teri headed them back in the direction of Mikey's house.

By the time the boys got out of their costumes and had a few of their treats, neither of them was able to keep his eyes open. While Jack carried Mikey upstairs and put him in his bed, Sam crawled into Teri's lap and fell fast asleep.

When Pat came back downstairs with Jack, she was carrying a baby.

"Oh, I didn't know you had another child," Teri said, keeping her voice low so she wouldn't disturb Sam. The baby was dressed in pink, so Teri supposed it was a girl. But since Teri was an only child and had no experience with children, she couldn't estimate how old the child was. All she knew for sure was that Pat was carrying the cutest baby she'd ever seen and she was itching to hold her.

Pat walked over to Teri's chair. "This is Caitlin," she said, smiling into the baby's rosy face. Caitlin still looked half-asleep. She leaned against her mother's chest and stared at Teri with a sort of dazed expression in her china blue eyes. She had curly red hair just like her brother.

"She's beautiful," Teri whispered in an almost reverent tone, then added teasingly, "I gather your husband has red hair."

Pat laughed. "How'd you guess?"

Teri smiled. "How old is she?"

"Seven months old next Tuesday," Pat answered proudly.

Jack watched this exchange with a lump in his throat. Apparently, Teri not only liked dolls, she liked the real thing, too. And judging by the way Sam had instantly taken to her, she'd probably make a wonderful mother. But Jack still wasn't sure the Teri he had been enjoying for the past few days was the "real" Teri. She'd certainly shown no indication that she was changing back to her old self, but there was always that chance. He was willing to take chances in his professional life, but his personal life was different.

And there was the fact that he'd liked and been attracted to Teri even before her supposed NDE. So he was afraid he'd still love her no matter how ambitious, success-oriented and work-driven she became again. Returning to her former life-style would be like committing slow suicide. He couldn't bear to stand helplessly by and watch another woman he loved die.

Jack shook free of his morbid thoughts. He wanted to enjoy what time he had left with Teri and leave her with pleasant memories of their days together.

"I'll take Sam," he said, moving forward with a smile. "I need to put him in his car seat anyway. Then you can hold Caitlin for a few minutes before we leave."

"Oh, that would be great," Teri said, her face lighting up at the prospect. But then she turned to Pat. "Would that be okay? Do you think she'll come to me?"

"She won't go to everyone," Pat admitted. "But we can give it a try."

Teri nodded enthusiastically, but she still gave Sam a loving look as Jack took him out of her arms. "He looks like an angel when he's sleeping," she said.

"They all do," Pat said dryly. "I think it's God's way of helping us to forgive them for shattering our nerves while they're awake."

Teri stood up and Pat handed Caitlin over to her. The baby went to Teri willingly enough, but she gave her mother a doubtful look. Then, as Jack stood and watched with Sam asleep in his arms, Teri's charm took over and she won Caitlin's heart in a matter of minutes.

Teri's face was full of animation as she talked to the baby, walking her around the room and pointing out the Halloween decorations and talking in a sweet, cheerful tone. Teri was obviously a natural because, by her own admission, she'd had no opportunity or desire in the past to learn how to woo a baby.

When Teri finally, reluctantly, handed Caitlin over to Pat, the baby seemed disappointed that the fun had ended.

"Bye, sweetheart," Teri crooned and waved as they left moments later and Caitlin gave her a big smile.

Behind Teri's back, Pat caught Jack's eye and mouthed the words, *I like her.*

Jack wasn't surprised by the endorsement, but he wasn't pleased by it, either. Like all his well-meaning friends and relatives, Pat obviously thought he should get married again. He acknowledged her approval with a nod and a smile, then took Teri firmly by the elbow and guided her out the door.

With Sam buckled securely and comfortably in his car seat, Jack and Teri headed for home.

*Home.* Yes, that's what Oak Meadows was, all right. And it seemed especially appropriate that he was headed for that particular destination with Teri beside him. It was a good feeling...and a scary one. He'd be glad when he was back on the road again, where home was a distant, idealized vision that drifted through his dreams at night, instead of a real place with real people in it who had real needs, made real demands and presented real risks. Because dealing with all that would take *real* commitment.

On the other hand, real people were nice to be with most of the time. He treasured every moment he'd spent with Sam and his dad on this trip home, and especially with Teri. With her newfound love of life, she'd brightened up his world and made him feel like a whole person again. But all good things must come to an end...right?

Jack kept his responses to Teri's attempts at conversation brief and unencouraging. Teri caught on that he didn't want to talk and finally she just sat back and stared out the window. He wondered what she was thinking, but at the same time he was glad he didn't know.

As they pulled off the highway and crossed the bridge, Teri spoke her first words since leaving New Orleans. "What's going on at Oak Meadows?"

Jack was wondering the same thing. It was nearing ten o'clock, but light streamed out of the parlor and dining-room windows and several cars were parked in front of the house. It looked suspiciously like his father was throwing—

"A party!" Teri exclaimed. "Your dad's throwing a *party!*"

"You make it sound like good news," Jack groused.

As they neared the house, the inside of Jack's car brightened and he could see Teri's face. She was beaming. "It *is* good news, Jack. Your father is doing what he should have done all along. He's socializing. If this keeps up, you certainly won't have to worry about his being lonely."

She had a point.

"I'm going to take Sam in the back way, through the kitchen," he told her. "Hopefully, it will be quieter in there than in the main rooms. I don't want him to wake up."

"I'll go with you, but then we can come back down to the party, can't we?" Teri implored, looking at him expectantly.

"What makes you think we're invited?" he asked with a wry grin.

"Don't be silly, Jack," Teri admonished. She looked wistfully toward the house. By now, faces were peering out at them from the parlor windows. "I've never been to a Halloween party before."

That settled it for Jack. He couldn't resist sharing first experiences with Teri. Besides, from what he could remember, his dad threw great parties.

Teri followed Jack as he carried Sam up the back stairs to his room. The little guy didn't stir at all as his father settled him in bed. Then Jack and Teri went to their separate rooms to freshen up before going down to the party. Teri changed her clothes, putting on an oversize burnt-orange sweater and black leggings. If everyone was in costume, she could at least feel she had on appropriate Halloween colors.

When Jack knocked on her bedroom door, Teri opened it excitedly. She took one look at Jack and had to force herself not to throw her arms around his neck and give him a big kiss. It wasn't just that he looked wonderful in the brightly patterned ski sweater he'd put on; he always looked wonderful. But just in the fifteen minutes they'd been apart, she'd missed him.

They'd made love last night—and this morning in the shower, too—but Teri had felt awkward with Jack ever since breakfast. She realized that he was pulling back, but she also recognized that he had mixed feelings. She could tell by looking in his eyes right now that he wanted to kiss her as much as she wanted to kiss him.

With a groan that signified surrender, Jack reached for Teri and drew her into his arms. They kissed eagerly and thoroughly, like lovers who had just been reunited after months apart.

"Why do you fight it, Jack?" Teri whispered breathlessly against his cheek.

"Because I don't want to hurt you," he answered gruffly.

"But you won't." She chuckled. "You should know by now that my heart's not going to stop just because you kiss me, or. . . or even if we—"

Jack caught her by the shoulders and held her at arm's length. "You'll be happy to know I'm not that worried about your heart anymore. At least not in the way you're suggesting. As long as you take care of yourself, I'm sure you'll be around a long time, no matter how many men kiss you."

Teri frowned. "I don't want to be kissed by half the world's population, Jackson Tremain. The fact that I was a virgin when you made love to me ought to prove that I'm pretty picky about whom I kiss."

He sighed and smiled at her affectionately. "Here we go again... arguing. Just like in high school. And all I wanted to do when I knocked on your door just now was to give you—" he reached down and picked up a glossy shopping bag with a department-store logo on the front "—this," he finished.

"What is it?" Teri asked, taking the bag and peering inside.

Jack grinned and shrugged. "It's a gift."

Teri's lips formed a delighted smile. "For me?"

"Of course for you. You were so eager that I buy Sam whatever he wanted the other day in the toy department at J-Mart, but for some reason you wouldn't buy yourself the thing you wanted most. Today, while you were engrossed in picking out kitchen curtains with that salesperson, I paid a visit to the toy department and bought you what you wouldn't buy for yourself."

Jack had been waiting for this moment all day... and he wasn't disappointed. Teri's face lit up with excitement and curiosity. She set the bag on the bed, reached inside, parted the tissue paper, then pulled out a newborn baby doll in a long, frilly white christening gown.

The look on Teri's face would be a memory Jack would treasure forever. It was like a child's face on Christmas morning, full of wonder and awe and heartfelt delight.

"Oh, Jack, it's beautiful!" Her gaze darted from the doll, to Jack, then back to the doll, as if she couldn't decide which of them fascinated her the most. "I felt kind of foolish, you know, when I was so smitten by the dolls the other day. After all, I *am* a grown woman." She cradled the doll against her chest, looking sheepish.

"Lots of women have doll collections," Jack countered gruffly. "It's normal for women to like—" he gestured ineffectually "—those kinds of things."

"I didn't like them before my NDE," Teri confessed, gazing into the doll's lifelike porcelain face with a tenderness that wrung Jack's heart. "I can't imagine why I've become so sappy." She traced her finger along the doll's rounded cheek and puckered mouth. "Maybe it's just my maternal instinct kicking in."

Jack had instincts, too. And right now he had the strongest urge to gently remove the doll from Teri's arms, then carry her to the bed and make passionate love to her, giving her a real baby to hold and gaze at lovingly. *His* baby.

But as luck would have it, he was saved from such an unwise and impetuous act by...Elvis.

"Say, are you two comin' to my party or not?" his dad said in a reasonably good imitation of the King of Rock and Roll.

Teri couldn't believe her eyes. Beauregard Tremain, genteel landowner and Southern gentleman, was decked out in a white satin pantsuit covered with sequins. The outfit also boasted flaring bell-bottoms, a huge rhinestone belt buckle and a stand-up collar. He was wearing sunglasses and a sneer, and he had his pompadour moussed up to an incredible height.

"Beau, you look fabulous!" Teri exclaimed.

"Thank ya, baby," he drawled, Elvis-style. "Thank ya vera much."

"Dad, where'd you find that getup?" Jack inquired, laughing.

"I've had it for years," Beau admitted. "I bought it through a costume company catalogue."

"Why haven't I seen it before?"

Beau drew off his sunglasses and raised a brow. "It's not exactly something I could wear to the grocery store, Jack. You haven't seen it before because I haven't had occasion to wear it before." He grinned sheepishly. "Well, except for the odd night or two when Sam was in bed and I put some of the King's songs on the CD player and practiced my routine."

"What routine?" Jack asked suspiciously.

"The show's about to start. Why don't you two quit playin' house up here and come down for a spell?"

Teri blushed and put her doll down on the bed, self-consciously making sure it was propped on a pillow and had its christening gown arranged attractively across the bedspread. Beau watched with an interested expression, but he didn't say anything, displaying a restraint for which Teri was very grateful.

She and Jack followed Beau down the stairs to the hall, where a mostly geriatric crowd milled about, spilling over into the parlor and dining room. Some of the guests were in costume and some weren't, but most of them recognized and called greetings to Jack.

Jack shook hands and introduced Teri around to various historical and theatrical luminaries, like an aging Madonna wearing a cone-shaped bra over her otherwise very respectable and modest outfit; a well-padded Henry VIII; a comical Pee-wee Herman; and the requisite Cleopatra.

In reality, Madonna was the leader of the church choir, King Henry was a bank president, Pee-wee sang bass in a barbershop quartet and Cleopatra ran a hair salon.

As Teri began to wonder where Viv and Ginger were, they suddenly appeared, arm in arm, threading their way slowly through the crowd. They had taken on the personas of the movie goddesses they were named for.

Ginger was wearing a blond wig styled à la Ginger Rogers, and was dressed in a flowing forties-style evening gown with padded shoulders. A gardenia corsage was pinned to her chest. Vivien was dressed like Scarlett O'Hara, the role Vivien Leigh was best known for. She wore a copper-colored wig of ringlets, a saucy hat with a long feather in it and a green velvet, corseted gown, circa the 1860s.

When the potato chip sisters caught sight of Jack and Teri, they hurried over and expressed their delight in seeing them again. "Did you have a good time in New Orleans?" Viv inquired with a wink.

"Well, we—" Jack began.

"You couldn't have had nearly as good a time as we've had at Oak Meadows!" Ginger gushed, unaware she was interrupting. "We've been so busy arranging the party and finding things to make up our costumes. You should see all the great stuff Beau's got in the attic!"

"I'd love to some time if—" Teri started to say.

"And now that all the guests are here," Ginger went on in a fever of excitement, "Beau's going to do a little routine, then Viv and I are going to show everyone our potato chip collection!"

Teri smiled. "Well, that sounds really—"

"Excuse me, folks. Excuse me!"

Beau was standing halfway up the stairs and calling for attention. The room quieted and everyone turned in his direction.

"As you all know, we've got a little show prepared for your entertainment."

There was a smattering of applause and cheers.

"Thank ya. Thank ya vera much," Beau said, aping Elvis again and making everyone laugh. "But after I do my routine and my special guests, Vivien Myers and Ginger Williams, display their unique collection of potato chips shaped like movie stars, the rest of you are invited to share your talents with us. And don't tell me you aren't prepared, 'cause I told you all about the show when I called you and invited you to this little shindig. Now let's get started!"

"He missed his calling in life," Jack whispered into Teri's ear, making a thrill go down her spine at his closeness. "He should have been a circus barker or had his own 'Gong Show.'"

Teri laughed and Jack took her by the hand, guiding her to a spot just opposite the area where performances were to take place. Then he leaned against the wall and pulled Teri back against his chest, nestled his chin in her hair and wrapped his arms around her waist. Teri found this position quite cozy and perfect for watching the show. In fact, she couldn't think of any other place she'd rather be.

Beau started the show by lip-synching Elvis's early hit, "You Ain't Nothin' but a Hound Dog." He put his whole heart into the performance, gyrating his hips, pivoting his knees, shimmying his shoulders and whipping his hair around in such a grand manner, the King himself would have been proud.

Glancing at Ginger, who was in charge of the CD player, Teri was afraid the smitten old lady would faint from the excitement. She was acting like a groupie, swaying and squealing. And she wasn't the only female in the room who was star-struck by Beau's performance.

Several white-haired women were squirming in their chairs and clapping their hands excitedly. . . much to the chagrin of their husbands and partners.

Even Teri had to admit that if she were quite a bit older, she, too, would be infatuated with Beau. For a man seventy years old, he could really move. But she was lucky enough to be keeping company with the younger Tremain stud muffin.

"He's going to feel like hell in the morning," Jack whispered in her ear.

"I think he'll consider the attack of arthritis worth it, don't you?"

"Yeah." Jack paused and watched with a grin on his face, then said, "But I wonder what made him come out of the closet with his Elvis obsession?"

"Ginger did it," Teri answered decisively.

Teri could feel Jack stiffen a little, then he asked, "I know she's crazy about him, but do you think the feeling is mutual? Has my dad fallen in love in just three days?"

"I can't speak for your dad, Jack. But, speaking for myself, falling in love in just three days is certainly possible."

Jack did not reply, but his arms tightened around her and Teri allowed herself to hope.

Beau's performance was followed by tumultuous applause and whistles. Then Viv and Ginger were on. Teri knew Jack had been dreading having to sit through a display of the potato chip collection ever since the sisters had arrived at Oak Meadows, but it was really quite interesting. Many of the chips actually did resemble movie stars.

"And I don't have to tell you who this is, do I?" Viv was saying, carefully holding up a large, misshapen potato chip with one especially protruding bump. Everyone leaned forward and strained to see.

"We'd pass it around, but sometimes people forget themselves and actually *eat* our movie stars," Ginger explained tactfully. "Or one of the fragile ears or noses breaks off. I'm sure you understand."

"Here are his large ears," Viv said, pointing with a pencil like a schoolmarm. "Here's his rather bulbous nose, and here's his trademark hat. Can't you just hear him saying, 'My little chickadee'? It's W. C. Fields!"

The potato chip collection was a hit, then several others took their turns performing. One man played the spoons, another played "Moon River" on the saxophone, and Madonna warbled "Flow Gently Sweet Afton" in a quivery soprano, accompanying herself with a twangy ukulele. She looked very incongruous singing the melodious, old-fashioned ballad in her cone-shaped brassiere.

After the entertainment, other more traditional Halloween games were played. Teri couldn't remember having so much fun. She bobbed for apples, threaded a spoon on a string through her clothes in a relay race and did a cakewalk. And Jack participated, too, leaving them both convulsed in laughter several times.

Food was served and Jack and Teri opted for sharing a caramel-candied apple, frequently taking the opportunity to kiss each other's sweet, sticky lips.

When the last guest finally headed for the door, Teri felt that the barriers Jack had built up between them since breakfast had received some direct hits. She was hoping he was feeling relaxed enough to stay a few days longer in New Orleans. And she was hoping that tonight Jack would sneak into her room and—

"Oh, dear! Something's wrong with Ginger!" Viv's strident voice rang out from the parlor. "Come quick, everybody!"

## Chapter Twelve

Beau had just waved farewell to his last guest when Viv's urgent call reached his ears. Jack didn't miss the look of sick anxiety on his father's face as they rushed into the parlor to check on Ginger. He couldn't believe they were having another emergency! He hoped Ginger had just gotten a little dizzy or something and wasn't having a heart attack.

"Get ready to call 9-1-1, if necessary," Jack said to Teri, grabbing her arm and pulling her close to relay the message as he hurried into the parlor. White-faced, Teri nodded and hovered near the phone in the hall.

Ginger was sprawled on the floor, her head in Viv's lap. Her complexion was pink—which was a good sign—but her eyes were closed and her mouth was slack.

"She just collapsed!" Viv exclaimed, not her usual calm self.

"Is she breathing?" Jack asked, checking her pulse.

Viv bent her ear near Ginger's mouth. "Yes. But it's fast and shallow."

"Her pulse is fast, too," Jack acknowledged. "I think she just passed out."

"Why would she pass out? It's still not a good sign, Jack," Beau fretted, kneeling beside Ginger and holding on to one of her hands. He was so agitated, he was shaking.

"No, but it's not as serious as what happened to Teri the other night, so don't get yourself in a stew, okay, Dad?" Jack entreated, glancing nervously at his father. "Trust me. She's going to be all right."

"Shouldn't we call 9-1-1?" Beau asked.

"Let's see what we can do to revive her first. Does she take medication, Viv?"

"No. She doesn't take a thing. She's as healthy as a horse, and she's never fainted before in her life . . . as far as I know."

"Teri, bring a cold, wet cloth," Jack called. "And a glass of water." He heard Teri rush into the kitchen to do what he asked. "She feels really warm," Jack commented, testing her cheek with the back of his hand. "Maybe she just got overheated, overexcited. . . ." His eyes roved over her prostrate body. Then Jack figured it out. He darted a glance at Viv. "Viv, did you ladies happen to find corsets in the attic?"

Viv's brow furrowed. "Well, yes, but—"

"You'll have to excuse me for being so nosy, but did you wear them tonight to, er, help squeeze into the dresses you're wearing?"

Viv shrugged. "All females wore corsets in the old days to nip in their waists."

"But if you're not used to wearing them, those things can make it pretty hard to breathe."

Teri came in just then and hovered nearby with the glass of water and a cold cloth.

"If Ginger's wearing a corset, my dad and I will be happy to turn our backs while you and Teri loosen it for her and take it off. I think that's what made her faint."

Viv nodded, suddenly brisk and businesslike. "Then let's get the darn thing off her!"

The men turned their backs and Teri and Viv went to work. A few seconds later, Jack heard a whoosh of air and then a grateful sigh. Ginger mumbled, "What happened? What am I doing on the floor?"

They soon had Ginger sitting on the couch, bundled in an afghan, sipping water and having her brow sponged with a cool, wet cloth. Beau was sitting next to her with a look of profound relief on his face, stroking one of her plump hands between his two.

"You gave me, er, *us* quite a scare, m'dear," Beau informed her. "You won't be wearin' that corset again, will you? Your figure is fine just the way it is. No cinchin' is necessary, do you hear?"

Ginger went rosy with pleasure. "Whatever you say, Beau."

"I'm glad you're feeling better, Ginger," Teri said, leaning over the back of the sofa.

"You're such a dear to fuss over me," Ginger said. She smiled around at everyone. "Thank you all." Then her smile fell away. "Although I must confess that while I was unconscious, I don't remember seeing or doing *anything*. I didn't float above the scene, or go down a tunnel toward a light, or meet any *dead* people like Teri did. It was quite disappointing."

"That's foolish talk," Viv reprimanded her sternly. "You have to be headed for the hereafter to see dead people, Ginger. You don't want to die, do you?"

"No, but Teri's near-death experience sounded so *fascinating!*"

"Don't you dare even think about dying, Ginger," Beau said gruffly. "And that's an order from your husband-to-be!"

A collective gasp sounded through the room as everyone's mouth fell open. And no one was more shocked and alarmed than Jack.

"Dad! What are you saying?" he choked out.

"I'm proposing, that's what!" he bellowed, throwing Jack a warning glance. "I hadn't intended to do it with an audience, and I definitely hadn't planned to ask for this sweet lady's hand in marriage while I was decked out in silver sequins and bell-bottoms. But, hell, life's short and I'm not wastin' another minute worryin' about conventions and traditions... except maybe this one."

Beau got down on his knees in front of Ginger, still clasping her hand. Her other hand was pressed against her ample bosom in a gesture of disbelief. Her mouth hung open and her eyes were wide with amazement.

"I love you, Ginger Williams. I'm an old coot, I know, but will you marry me anyway?"

Ginger's lashes started fluttering and she swayed a little.

"Good grief, she's going to faint again," Jack groaned.

But Ginger didn't faint. After an apparent moment of dizziness, she rallied her senses, focused and smiled. She reached down and laid her hand against Beau's cheek. "Beauregard Tremain, I've waited my whole life for a man like you. You've got the looks of Rory Calhoun, the soulful style of Elvis and the heart of an angel. I'd be crazy not to marry you."

"Is that a yes, Ginger?" he demanded tenderly.

"Yes, Beau. Yes, I'll marry you," Ginger said with feeling, her eyes welling up with tears.

When they fell into each other's arms, Viv bustled to her feet, blinked away her own tears and said briskly, "I think we should leave the happy couple alone, don't you? Come along now, Jack. Come along."

Jack, in a state of shock, allowed himself to be ushered out of the room and into the hall by Viv. He noticed that Teri had already left.

Viv closed the double doors to the parlor, then turned and sniffled into a tissue she'd pulled from the sleeve of her elegant dress. Having more or less gotten command of her emotions, Viv lifted her chin and announced, "I'm going upstairs to get out of this corset. One fainting female is enough. Don't disturb them, Jack, you hear?"

Jack nodded mutely, still feeling numb. Viv had climbed the stairs and was long gone before Jack was able to gather his wits and get his rear in gear. Then he decided to look for Teri. On a hunch, instead of going upstairs to check her room, he headed for the library.

BY THE LIGHT of a single lamp, Teri stood in front of the family portrait of the Tremains and stared up at it. The room was chilly and she had her arms wrapped around her shoulders to stave off goose bumps.

"Hi, folks," she said, smiling wistfully. "I missed you while I was in New Orleans. My condo seemed so sterile. It needed pictures on the walls, but none of the prints I bought could ever give it the family feeling you give Oak Meadows."

The painted eyes stared back and Teri felt a warm glow.

She looked directly at Stephen. "I hope you and Samuel don't mind, Stephen, but tonight I really need to talk to Caroline alone."

She waited until she felt comfortable doing it, then she looked into Caroline's eyes and spoke as if the pretty blond-haired woman was actually in the room with her. But then, maybe she was....

Teri sighed. "I left the parlor right after Beau proposed to Ginger. I knew she'd say yes, so I went away to let them have their privacy." She paused. "And the truth is, it was kind of painful being in there."

Caroline's eyes seemed to soften as if to say, *Go on.*

"First of all, I think I was a little jealous. Don't get me wrong. I'm absolutely thrilled for Ginger. She's waited so long to find the man of her dreams. I just hope *I* don't have to wait as long."

If paintings could come to life, Caroline might have nodded understandingly at this point. Teri could almost imagine she did.

"It was also painful because I could tell Jack wasn't happy about his dad's proposal to Ginger. Oh, I think he will be in time...but *he'd* never be that spontaneous. Jack would never take a risk and follow his heart. He's too afraid of getting hurt again. I just don't understand how a man can be so brave in his work and so skittish when it comes to love."

*Jack is a man of strong emotions. He loves deeply and he feels loss very deeply, too.*

Whether the thought was her own or whether it had somehow come from Caroline, Teri didn't know. But she knew it was true.

"Jack just doesn't get it," Teri went on, her voice tinged with frustration. "But Beau does. He understands that you have to live every day to the full-est . . . and now I understand that, too. You have to grab happiness when it passes close by or it just keeps on going. Why doesn't Jack understand? He should have learned that simple truth from Pam's death.''

*Accepting the reality of death liberates some people and frightens others.*

''But how do I help set Jack free from his fears?'' Teri wanted to know. ''Tell me, Caroline. I really don't know what to do.''

Teri searched Caroline's eyes and waited, but no profound answer came galloping, or even strolling, into her consciousness.

''Maybe I *can't* help Jack get over his fears,'' she finally mumbled to herself. ''Maybe he has to do it himself and my job is to simply love him and be patient.''

''Who are you talking to, Teri?''

Teri whirled around and discovered Jack standing just inside the library door. ''How long have you been there?'' she asked him, afraid he'd heard her conversing with the painting. He might decide that his suspicions about her being slightly crazy since her NDE had been confirmed.

He cocked his head to the side and peered at her questioningly. ''I just got here. I heard you mumbling something, but I didn't hear your exact words.''

Teri forced a laugh. ''Well, it wasn't worth hearing anyway. I was just thinking out loud.''

With his hands stuffed in his pants pockets, Jack sauntered into the room, frowning thoughtfully. ''You must have been thinking about my dad's proposal to Ginger. Can you believe he did that? He's only known the woman three days. Three days! I just hope she isn't after his money."

Teri was shocked and disappointed by Jack's distrustful attitude. "How can you be so cynical, Jack? They obviously love each other. Besides, I thought your dad didn't have any money to speak of. Wasn't part of the reason he wanted to sell Oak Meadows because he didn't have the money to do repairs and restoration?"

"Well, yes. But maybe she's thinking of what Oak Meadows is worth."

"She was delighted when the sale of Oak Meadows didn't go through. In fact, in case you've forgotten, she and Viv were instrumental in helping sabotage the deal with Schofield. We might not have been able to pull it off without their help. How can you suspect her of being mercenary? Jack, you're just looking for reasons to disapprove of the match. Don't you want your dad to be happy?"

Jack slumped into the overstuffed chair by the fireplace and rested his chin on his fist. "Of course I want him to be happy. But I thought he *was* happy living here with Sam. Now he's just got one more person—possibly two, if Viv moves in—to worry about. Ginger's no spring chicken. Dad could just get used to her being around, then..." He didn't finish. He didn't have to. "I saw the way he panicked when she fainted. Why would he want to set himself up for more heartache?"

Teri looked at Caroline and rolled her eyes as if to say, *Now you can see what I'm up against.* To Jack, she said, "There are two ways to look at things, Jack, and you persist in taking the negative view. Why can't you think about all the happiness your father will have with Ginger instead of imagining heartache?"

"There's always heartache."

"You're right, Jack. There's always a few bumps in the road. But if you twist and turn down life's highway, trying to avoid all the bumps, you'll never get anywhere."

"What self-help book chock-full of analogies have you been reading, Teri?" he asked sarcastically. "Save the pep talks for your next staff meeting at Sugarbaker Realtors. I don't need them."

Teri propped her fists on her hips. "Right again, Jack. You don't need a pep talk. You need a good swift kick in the rear! I thought I knew you, but apparently I was wrong. I always thought you were one of the bravest people I knew." Teri felt a lump of disappointment and defeat rise in her throat. "But now I realize you're nothing but a coward."

The look of hurt and shock on Jack's face was painful to see, but Teri couldn't tiptoe around the hard facts any longer. Despite her near-death experience, patience was clearly a virtue she still lacked. Besides, Jack had to realize what he'd become. He had to face the truth and change, or he was doomed to loneliness for the rest of his life.

"I'm sorry, Jack, but someone had to tell you," Teri said quietly, then she turned and left the room.

After Teri left, Jack just sat there. He felt betrayed. He'd sought her out to talk over his legitimate concerns about his father's whirlwind romance and precipitate marriage proposal, and she'd turned the conversation into a personal attack on *him*. How could she call him a coward? If she only knew the perils he faced every day while on assignment...

But he knew she wasn't accusing him of being afraid of physical danger. He knew she was talking about the

C-word—commitment. She was saying that he was afraid of relationships. But Jack thought another C-word could best describe his approach to emotional entanglements. The word was *cautious*. And was there something inherently wrong with being cautious?

While Jack sulkily defended himself to himself, he got the most uncanny feeling he was being watched. He looked toward the library door to see if Teri had come back or if his dad had finally managed to drag himself away from his ladylove, but there was no one there. He was the only one in the room. So who was watching?

Then his gaze was drawn to the portrait. Although he was sitting to the side of the fireplace and wasn't standing directly in front of the painting, it still appeared that its three subjects were looking straight at him. He'd heard of portraits where the eyes followed you no matter where you were in the room, but he'd never noticed that sort of optical illusion in connection with this one. It must be his imagination.

He looked away, then looked back. They were still watching. And he got the creepiest feeling they disapproved of him.

*Your logic is self-indulgent.*

*You're fooling yourself.*

*You really are an emotional coward.*

Were those his thoughts . . . or someone else's?

Jack rubbed his eyes, convinced that his mind was playing tricks on him because he was overly tired. He rose to his feet and headed for the door without a backward glance at the painting, flicking off the light switch on the wall. He didn't get very far down the hall, however, before he ran into his dad and Ginger.

"Jack!" Beau exclaimed with a big smile. "We were just looking for you."

Jack forced a smile. "I'm off to bed, Dad. Dead tired."

"Not too tired to give your old dad five minutes of your time, are you, Jack?"

Jack couldn't say no. And he couldn't deny that his dad and Ginger both glowed with happiness.

"All right, Dad, let's talk. But not in the library, okay? It's cold in there."

Boy, was it ever.

They returned to the parlor. Beau and Ginger sat on the sofa and Jack sat across from them in a wing chair.

"You were present during the proposal, so I don't suppose we need to announce our engagement to you, eh, Jack?"

Jack smiled wanly. "No. Congratulations, Dad, Ginger. I hope you'll be very happy."

Jack tried to sound sincere, but he recognized a certain flatness in his tone. Thankfully, Beau and Ginger were too happy and absorbed in each other to notice Jack's lack of enthusiasm. They thanked him, then grinned at each other for so long Jack was beginning to think he could slip away and they wouldn't even notice.

Then, suddenly, Beau turned back to Jack. "I have a favor to ask you—"

Ginger squeezed Beau's arm and looked at him adoringly. "But first, dearest, don't you think I ought to make my confession?"

Jack sat up straighter in his chair. A confession?

Beau kissed her lightly on the forehead. "If it will make you feel better, darling."

Make her feel better? Uh-oh. Maybe he was right all along to suspect Ginger of ulterior motives in falling in love so hard and fast with his father.

"What could a nice lady like you have to confess, Ginger?" Jack said, smiling amiably but feeling tense.

Ginger's brow furrowed. "Well, it's like this, Jack. My sister and I haven't been completely truthful with all of you. It's about our finances...."

*I told you so, Teri!* Jack said to himself, although not feeling any particular satisfaction in being right. It was a damned shame when cold cynicism was supported by colder facts.

When Ginger seemed embarrassed and hesitant to continue, Jack prompted her, saying, "Does this have anything to do with your job at the potato chip factory?"

"Partially..."

"You lost it?"

Ginger chuckled self-consciously. "Well, no. Actually, I never had a job there in the first place."

Here it comes, thought Jack. Now she's going to tell me she's flat broke and in debt up to her eyeballs.

Ginger took a deep breath and said, "I never worked a day at the potato chip factory in Boise. Viv and I *own* the blasted thing...lock, stock and fryer."

Jack blinked. "You *own* the factory?"

Ginger nodded miserably. "Yes. And there's more."

Jack blinked again. "More?"

"We own three other factories, one in Idaho Falls, another in Pocatello and a third just outside the resort town of McCall."

"In other words, you're—"

"Yes, we're rich. Filthy rich. But Viv and I didn't tell you because we never tell anyone. We hate it when people treat us differently just because we're plump in the purse." She sighed heavily. "You never know whether they like you for you or for your money. After all, Viv and I are just ordinary people. We want to be treated like ordinary people. You understand why we kept our wealth a secret, don't you? I don't want to start off my marriage with you thinking badly of me, Jack."

Jack felt like the biggest heel in the world. Thank goodness Ginger would never know what terrible things he'd been eager to suspect her of. That she was rich and didn't flaunt the fact just proved there was even more to admire about her.

"Do you forgive me for my little white lie, Jack?" she asked him, her big blue eyes looking imploringly at him through those funny glasses of hers.

"Believe me, Ginger, there's nothing to forgive," Jack assured her, smiling with genuine warmth this time. "Just be happy, you two."

"That brings me to that little favor I was about to ask," Beau spoke up. "Will you be my best man at the wedding, Jack?"

Jack was about to answer with an unqualified yes, assuming that the wedding would be a few weeks or even months away, and that he'd be able to work his schedule around it. But his father nipped that idea in the bud.

"We're getting married at Thanksgiving. We thought that would be a perfect time for Ginger's relatives to fly in for a long weekend." He smiled at his bride-to-be. "She has a whole slew of grandnieces and -nephews, you know. Sam'll love having 'em swarmin' all over the house."

"That's just three weeks away, Dad," Jack said. "I'm considering taking an assignment right away, and I'd be smack in the middle of things just about then."

"Take a few weeks off, Jack," his dad suggested. "You don't have to go back to work so soon, do you? You haven't taken a vacation in years, son. And I need you to be my best man."

Jack was between a rock and hard place. How could he turn down his father's request to be his best man? But how could he possibly stay in New Orleans for another month? He had to get away from here soon or he'd be tempted to stay forever.

Hell's bells, Jack thought, borrowing his father's favorite epithet. Is Teri right? *Am* I a coward? "Tell you what, Dad," Jack said, rising to his feet. "If I can manage it, I'll take a leave of absence from the assignment to attend the wedding, then go back and pick up where I left off. How does that sound for a plan?"

Jack could tell his father thought his plan stank. He could also tell by the way the sparkle in his eyes dimmed and his smile sort of slid off his handsome, Rory Calhoun face that his father was hurt, confused and disappointed. Jack couldn't deal with all that at the moment, so he hurriedly told his dad they'd talk more in the morning, bade him and Ginger good-night, then left the room.

Upstairs, Jack went to Sam's room first and tucked the blanket around his son's shoulders. As usual, Sam was holding tight to Bartholomew. Jack kissed him on the forehead and simply gazed at him for a while, as overwhelmed as ever by his love for Sam and as troubled as ever by the aching feeling he always got in his chest whenever he knew he was leaving again for an extended period.

Jack hesitated as he passed Teri's room on the way to his. He wanted nothing more than to knock on the door, have Teri open it dressed in a sexy negligee—or even a tattered T-shirt—and invite him in. It had been difficult restraining himself all day and all night when the only thing he wanted to do was make love to her. But since he'd never thought of himself as a love-'em-and-leave-'em kind of guy, the better part of valor would be to avoid further intimacies.

After all, he was calling Iris in the morning to tell her the assignment was a go. By tomorrow night, he'd be headed for the airport.

## Chapter Thirteen

Every morning since her NDE, Teri had awakened with a sense of happy expectation. After all, with each new day there were new experiences to look forward to. But this morning, Teri's happiness was tempered by the realization that it might be the last day she'd have with Jack before he left for a new assignment.

The signs that he was about to jump ship were all there. Last night when Beau had proposed to Ginger, Jack had been stunned and disapproving. He'd blamed his reaction on the whirlwind nature of their three-day courtship, but Teri thought it had more to do with his general negative attitude toward relationships and commitment.

And last night, he hadn't even stopped by her room to check her pulse before retiring. Although she'd made a lot of headway toward convincing Jack that she wasn't about to keel over and die any second, Teri knew he still worried about her. So it must have been a struggle for him to pass by her door without stopping for a look-see. That he willingly subjected himself to such a struggle meant he was determined to avoid intimacies with her again. Apparently, he'd felt as close to her as she had to him while making love. That's what scared him.

Teri stretched one more time in the large, antique iron bed, then whisked off the covers and walked to the window that overlooked the beautiful grounds sloping down to the bayou. In a few short days, she would return to her condo in the city, but she was determined to enjoy her time at Oak Meadows, despite her unhappiness over Jack's departure.

She was going to miss this house and everyone in it. But she hoped she'd be invited back for frequent visits, even though Jack would probably never be one of the party. He'd always be off on another assignment, risking his neck for a prizewinning photo, but unwilling to risk his heart for a prizewinning family.

Teri sighed and was about to turn away from the breathtaking view and head for the shower, when something caught her eye. Jack and Sam were walking slowly together toward the bridge. Their heads were down as if the conversation was very serious and absorbing. Sam was clutching Bartholomew tightly to his chest and Teri knew then with a surety that Jack was going away. He was probably telling Sam right now.

Instead of depressing her and slowing her down, this confirmation of her suspicions made Teri move faster than ever. Her philosophy was simple; she might not have Jack forever, but she was going to spend every minute she could with him until he left, and she was going to make sure they both thoroughly enjoyed themselves. And Sam, too. The kid deserved to have fun with his dad during the rare times Jack was around.

Teri quickly showered and dressed in jeans and a cerulean blue sweater that matched the color of her eyes. She hurried downstairs and headed for the kitchen.

She found Viv and Ginger seated at the big oak table by the window, eagerly discussing wedding plans while Beau presided over the stove, dressed in his Graceland apron. She could smell bacon frying and cinnamon-spiced muffins baking in the oven. She slid up next to Beau and slipped her arm in his, saying, "Ginger's one lucky lady, Beau. Not only are you movie-star handsome, you're a wonderful cook, too."

"Why, thank you, missy," Beau said, beaming. "But I think I'm the lucky one."

"Oh, Beau!" Ginger exclaimed, waving a disclaiming hand in their direction. "If we have to decide which of us is luckier, we'll end up having our first argument."

"That would never do," Teri said, opening a cupboard and reaching for a stack of dishes. "So let's just say you're both lucky." She carried the dishes to the table. "By the way," she added, smiling at Ginger as she set the table. "Did I congratulate you two?"

"Thank you, Teri," Ginger said, her eyes sparkling with happiness.

"Come here, sweetcakes," Beau called. "Will you hold this platter for me while I spoon up the eggs?"

Ginger was so eager to respond to Beau's request for help, she practically sprang to her feet.

After setting the table with silverware and glasses, Teri sat down beside Viv. Together they watched the two lovebirds dish up breakfast.

"They seem perfect together," Teri commented. "I'm so happy for them both."

Viv nodded and continued to gaze at the couple with satisfaction. "So am I," she said, but then she added, "I just hope they don't argue about the money."

Teri blinked. She wasn't aware that either of them had money to argue about. "What money?"

Viv looked at Teri and said ruefully, "That's right. You don't know yet. The fact is, Ginger and I are both quite wealthy."

Teri raised a brow. "I didn't realize that working at a potato chip factory was so lucrative."

Viv laughed. "We don't work at the potato chip factory in Boise," she admitted. "We actually own the place, as well as three other factories in Idaho."

Now Teri raised both brows. "I see. I, er, had no idea."

Viv nodded. "We don't tell people right away. We want people to like us for *us.*"

Teri grinned. "That's easy enough."

Viv smiled back. "Now Beau's joking that people will say he married Ginger for her money. I think he'd rather she were poor."

"If that's the case, why would they argue about money?"

"Ginger will want to help Beau with repairs and such around here, and I'm afraid he'll be too proud to accept her assistance. In case you hadn't noticed, underneath that gentle Southern facade, Beauregard Tremain is a stubborn man."

"It runs in the family," Teri said dryly. "But I don't think you need to worry about Beau and Ginger. They'll deal with the money issue because they know how lucky they are to have found each other. They've figured out what's important in life."

Viv cocked her head to the side and studied Teri with a smile. "So have you."

Teri shrugged. "I just wish..." She was going to say she just wished a certain other person would get a clue, but she didn't want to sound whiny or as if she were criticizing Jack. But Viv caught her drift anyway.

"I hear Jack's leaving tonight for another assignment," Viv said with a look of sympathetic understanding in her wise eyes.

"I hadn't actually heard, but I suspected as much," Teri admitted. "He must have called his agent late last night or this morning. When I saw him out on the lawn with Sam, I figured Jack was breaking the bad news. I feel sorry for the kid."

"I feel sorrier for Jack," Viv said. "Kids are resilient. Sam's secure and happy with Beau, and now he'll have a grandma, too. He'll miss Jack for a while, but he's grown used to his dad's being gone most of the time. Unless Jack curtails his traveling, the day will come when Jack will want to be close, but Sam will have different ideas."

Just then, Jack and Sam could be heard coming in the back door through the laundry room. "Wash your hands, Sam," Jack called and Sam streaked by to the bathroom. Judging by Sam's happy smile as he passed them like a comet, it seemed as though he was already bouncing back from the news of his dad's imminent departure.

When Jack walked in, his gaze immediately locked with Teri's. Apologies flowed unspoken between them. She was sorry for her hurtful words of the night before; he was sorry he couldn't stay and take the risk she wanted him to take.

"Hi," he said.

"Hi," she answered, smiling tentatively. "You didn't roll down the hill without me, did you?"

He smiled back and Teri's heart did a somersault. "Not on your life. How about we try that after breakfast?"

"Deal," she agreed.

She probably could have sat there for another hour just staring into Jack's eyes, but Sam got everyone's attention when he came back into the kitchen and tugged on Beau's apron, saying, "Gran'pa? Daddy says you're gettin' married."

Holding a platter of eggs and bacon, Beau smiled down at his grandson. "I sure am, buster. Isn't that great news?"

"Does that mean she's my gran'ma?" he asked, pointing shyly at Ginger, who was holding a basket of piping hot muffins.

"She sure will be, in about three weeks," Beau assured him. "And she'll be good at it, Sam. You can count on that."

Sam nodded thoughtfully, then turned and pointed a finger at Viv. "Will she be my gran'ma, too?"

Everyone chuckled. "No, Sam. I'll be your great-aunty," Viv told him.

Then Sam's gaze rested on Teri. "Who will you be?" he asked. "Will you be my mommy?"

This time no one chuckled. There was a poignant, awkward pause, then Teri said, "Come here, Sam." The little boy skipped over and Teri pulled him onto her lap. She bent her head and looked into his expectant face. "I won't be your mommy, Sam," she explained cheerfully, "but I'll still be your friend. I'll always be your friend. That's something else you can count on."

Sam nodded, still working out all this new stuff in his head. "But if you were my mommy, you could live here all the time. That's better than a friend."

Teri couldn't dispute that, so she changed the subject. "How's Bartholomew today?" she asked, poking the stuffed bear's stomach. "Is he hungry for eggs and bacon and muffins, too? Or does he just eat berries in the woods?"

While Sam was successfully diverted from the awkward line of questioning, Beau and Ginger covered the table with fragrant dishes of food.

Teri lightly spread some butter on a muffin, then sank her teeth into it, closing her eyes and savoring the delicate cinnamon seasoning, the cakelike texture and the light, creamy taste of real butter. When she opened her eyes, Jack was staring at her. There was no mistaking the hungry look in his eyes . . . and it wasn't for food.

Teri swallowed hard, and for the first time since her NDE, she wasn't tempted by the array of delicious food in front of her. All she could think of was how she and Jack probably wouldn't get a chance to make love again before he left. And even if they had the opportunity, he probably wouldn't take advantage of it. It was that Tremain honor thing. He'd decided that he couldn't promise her anything permanent, therefore, he wouldn't encourage her, or undermine his own determination, by making love with her.

Having completely lost her appetite, Teri pushed the food around on her plate to make it look as if she'd eaten something. But Jack wasn't fooled. He frowned at her plate, then at her, so she forced herself to eat a few more bites.

Sitting at a table and eating with a lot of people, no matter how much she liked them, wasn't what Teri wanted to do. Time was precious and it was ticking away. She wanted to be with Jack. She wanted to hold him, kiss him, make love with him. She wanted something more to remember him by during the lonely nights ahead.

He didn't seem to be eating much, either, Teri noted. Their eyes kept meeting across the table and it was obvious that they both just wanted to be alone together. The air was so charged with sexual tension, Teri was surprised the others weren't aware of it. But they were deeply engrossed in discussions about the wedding. Teri found herself imagining Jack as a groom, all decked out in a black tux with a rose boutonniere pinned to his lapel. Then her mind wandered ahead to the honeymoon....

"What's your favorite, Teri?"

Teri was prodded from her distraction by Ginger's question, but she had no idea what the woman was talking about. "Er, my favorite?" She looked to Jack for help, but since he'd been just as distracted, he didn't know what Ginger was talking about, either.

"My favorite wedding movie is *Father of the Bride*," Viv announced. "The old one, not the new one. Although Steve Martin did look pretty funny trying on that tuxedo he'd grown out of."

Teri should have known. Movies.

"I never thought about gettin' a tuxedo," Beau mused aloud, puffing out his chest as he contemplated the idea. "Might be fun to wear some fancy duds."

"In *Four Weddings and a Funeral*, my favorite dress was the one Heni wore," Ginger said. "You remember, she was the last bride...the one that socked Hugh Grant in the eye."

"You're not thinking of wearing white, are you, Ginger?" Vivien asked, her brows lowering disapprovingly.

Ginger looked offended, stuck her nose in the air and said, "Why shouldn't I? I've earned the right."

"Luis and Maria got married on 'Sesame Street,'" Sam mumbled around a mouthful of eggs. "Then she got a baby in her stomach. Are you goin' to get a baby in your stomach, Ginger?"

"You're too old, Ginger," Viv said.

Ginger turned pink. "Well, I should hope so! I know they're doing all kinds of in vitro experiments with gals my age, but I'm not a fool. I know I'm much too old to have a baby."

Viv clicked her tongue. "That's not what I'm talking about. You're too old to wear white!"

"Then I must be, too," Beau said, looking disappointed. "I had my heart set on a white tuxedo."

"Is Teri too old to have a baby?" Sam asked.

At this point, Teri burst out laughing, and so did Jack. Everyone looked at them as if they'd lost their minds.

"I wish I'd taped this conversation," Jack said. "You're all talking at cross-purposes. But go on, go on! It's very entertaining."

They did go on, and Teri gave Jack a look that said, *Aren't you going to miss this?* With a wistful smile, he acknowledged that he would, then they both pushed their food around on their plates some more.

After breakfast, Jack and Sam and Teri headed outside for the promised roll down the hill. Jack brought along a blanket to sit on in between the horseplay.

The day was just right for sweaters and they were each wearing one. They appeared very patriotic; Sam wore red, Teri wore blue and Jack wore white. There was a nice breeze, and colorful leaves swooped past them and tumbled at their feet.

Teri rolled down the hill not once, but four times, and it was just as exhilarating as she'd imagined. Then she and Jack and Sam played tag, hide-and-seek, Mother may I and leapfrog until they were all three exhausted. Sam had been up since six o'clock, so he was ready for a nap, or at least some downtime. Jack was about to settle him on the blanket for a snooze, when Viv showed up and announced that she was taking Sam inside for some quiet reading time.

"Come in the house with your Great-Aunty Viv," she said cajolingly. "I read out loud to a lot of grandkids, Sam, and I even know how to do the voices of the Power Rangers and all those creepy villains. You have a picture book about those guys, don't you?"

Sam's interest was piqued, just as Viv knew it would be. He happily accompanied her into the house, leaving Teri and Jack alone.

Jack was stretched out on his side and Teri was standing. She smiled ruefully. "We should have told Viv it wouldn't be necessary to lure Sam away. She doesn't know you don't want to be alone with me."

Jack shook his head. "You're wrong, Teri. I want to be alone with you more than anything."

Teri tried to ignore the thrill that shimmied up her spine and said, "That's not true, or you wouldn't be going away." She paused, then asked, "Why didn't you tell me?"

"I didn't get a chance. When I came in the house with Sam this morning, I figured someone had already told you."

Teri had been trying to keep things light, but she couldn't resist saying, "I don't buy that, Jack. You knew you were leaving before this morning."

"So did you," he challenged.

"What do you mean?"

"You've known all along that I'd be leaving again. It's the nature of my job."

"You mean it's your M.O.," she countered.

He shrugged.

"Let's be honest with each other, Jack."

"Fire away," he returned, his jaw setting in that stubborn way of his.

Teri lifted her chin and looked him straight in the eye. "I'm in love with you."

Jack's gaze didn't waver. "I'm in love with you, too, Teri. But that doesn't change anything."

"Why not?" she asked, the joy she felt at his words mixed with angry frustration. "Why are you afraid to have a family again?"

"I have a family. I've got Dad and Sam."

"And what about Sam?"

"He's fine. He's got my dad to rely on a hundred percent of the time, and now he'll have two grandmothers watching over him . . . one permanently settled at Oak Meadows, and one that visits frequently from Boise."

"But he misses you. Don't you miss Sam when you're away?"

He sighed heavily. "Yes, I miss him. And now I'll be missing you, too," he added miserably.

"It doesn't have to be that way." Teri eased herself down on the blanket and sat by Jack, close but not touching. "Jack, I don't really believe what I said last night. You're not a coward. But something's holding you back. Are you just against marriage in general, or does your reluctance have something to do with me specifically?''

Teri was just throwing out questions, but by the look that flickered over Jack's face after her last suggestion, she knew she'd finally hit the nail on the head.

She was incredulous. "It *is* me, isn't it? You're afraid of getting involved with me. Specifically with *me!* Why, Jack? I admit you had me pegged that first night. I had become totally self-serving and overly ambitious. But I've changed since my NDE. And I'm not going to go back to my old ways. You said so yourself—''

Teri stopped abruptly. Suddenly, she understood.

"But you didn't mean it, did you?'' she said quietly. "You don't believe I've changed for good. You were only agreeing with me, lying to me to make me feel better. You think I'll become that workaholic robot again.''

Jack sat up and grabbed her by the shoulders. "I don't want to believe it, Teri, but I'm no fool,'' he said. "You feel very strongly about this now but, remember, it's only been three days since your heart fibrillated and you passed out.''

"I died, Jack. How many times do I have to tell you . . . I *died.*''

Jack gave Teri a beleaguered look and his hands fell to his side. "If that's true, then it's some kind of miracle that you're alive and walking around now, isn't it, Teri?''

"Yes. I totally agree. It *is* a miracle.''

"I don't believe in miracles. I prayed for one once and it never happened.''

"With Pam?''

"Yes, with Pam.''

"But that doesn't mean—''

"I don't want to hear any more clichés about faith and hope and how 'bad things sometimes happen to good people.' None of those hackneyed sayings ever helped me get through a hard day. I've learned to rely on myself for that. I don't need anybody, and I don't want anybody to need me."

"Too late, Jack," Teri said. "Sam and I both need you."

"You'll meet someone else . . . and Sam has his grandfather when he doesn't have me."

Jack was staring out across the lawn, and Teri was saddened by the hardness of his profile. She was beginning to think it was hopeless, that she'd never get through Jack's protective armor, that it would indeed take a miracle to open up his heart again. Then it occurred to her that maybe she should tell him everything that happened during her near-death experience. She'd been hesitant about telling him before, worried that he'd think she was crazy. But maybe it would make a difference. . . .

"Jack, can I tell you exactly what happened to me when I was in cardiac arrest the other night?"

Jack didn't look excited about the prospect, but he smiled wanly and said, "If you want to. But, you know, Teri, I don't believe what you experienced was real. I think you were—"

"Dreaming? Hallucinating?"

"Yes."

"Well, I'm sure I wasn't. And I have proof."

While Jack patiently listened, Teri told him everything that had happened from the moment her spirit left her body. She told him what Beau and the potato chip sisters said and did as they witnessed Jack's resuscitation attempt. She told him about her pleasant journey down a dark tunnel toward a bright light. Then she told him about meeting Stephen, Caroline and Samuel Tremain.

"Hold on," Jack interrupted, shaking his head in patent disbelief. "Teri, how can you expect me to believe you had a conversation with my ancestors? You were just influenced by the painting, that's all."

"It's true that I've always had a fascination with that painting, but Samuel said something to me while I was...well, wherever I was...and what he said convinced me that I wasn't dreaming up the whole experience."

"What did he say?" Jack asked with a weary sigh.

"He told me to say hello to Bartholomew."

"Sam's bear?"

"Yes, Sam's bear. But it was Samuel's first. However, I didn't know what Samuel was talking about at the time. I'd never met a Bartholomew in my life."

Jack's eyes narrowed. "You never saw Sam carrying the bear around the house, or heard the story from Dad about how he got the bear?"

Teri laughed. "Jack, you've got to be kidding. Before my NDE, I was hardly aware that Sam was even alive. I didn't notice the child, much less the bear, and I definitely didn't know the bear's name."

Jack pondered this for a few minutes, then said, "All of this can be explained. Viv and Ginger must have told you what they said and did while you were unconscious, and since your memory is bound to be fuzzy after such a traumatic event, you just don't remember the conversation. The same could be true about Bartholomew. Somewhere in your subconscious you'd stored away the information, not realizing it."

"So just like that—" Teri snapped her fingers "—you explain away and discredit my story! According to you, it was just a bunch of disjointed dreams and buried memories doctored up by stress hormones released during my cardiac arrest. Thanks for believing in me, Jack," she finished bitterly. "Thanks for nothing."

On the brink of angry tears, Teri started to get up, but Jack caught her hand and pulled her down again. She turned her face away, but he forced her to look at him by firmly cupping her jaw.

"Teri, I believe in *you,*" he whispered fiercely. "I just don't believe in miracles."

"Jack, don't you understand?" Teri whispered back, placing her hands on each side of his head, a single tear brimming over her lashes and running unchecked down her cheek. "*I* am a miracle. And so are you and Sam and Beau. *Life* is a miracle."

Jack didn't agree, but he didn't argue the point, either. He simply kissed her.

At first, the kiss was tender and bittersweet. Then it seemed to catch fire, sending ripples of heat through Teri's bloodstream. She wrapped her arms around Jack's back and pressed closer as the kiss deepened and lengthened. It felt so good, so right to be in his arms again. But then, suddenly, Jack pulled back.

"I'm sorry, Teri," he said, his eyes filled with anguish. "But for both our sakes, this is not a good idea." Then he stood and walked away, headed in the opposite direction from the house.

# Chapter Fourteen

"Well, Caroline, I did the best I could," Teri said, staring up at the painting in the library. "I told him how I felt and I tried to convince him to stay, but it didn't work. He's upstairs right now, packing. He took Sam to his room an hour ago, read him a book and tucked him into bed, and now all he's got left to do is say his goodbyes to the rest of us."

Teri thought Caroline's face reflected sympathy.

"He doesn't believe me, you know. He doesn't believe that I met you and Stephen and Samuel. I even told him about Samuel asking me to say hello to Bartholomew, but he explained it all away with that darned logic of his. He's so implacable, Caroline . . . but I love him *so* much! Underneath all that stubborn cynicism, I think he really wants to believe in miracles."

Teri studied Caroline's eyes a little while longer, but no profound advice popped into her consciousness and no easy answers came to mind.

"Oh, well," Teri said, rubbing her arms distractedly, feeling a chill despite the fire Beau had built in the grate. "At least it helps to talk to you. I get things off my chest this way, and then what I need to do is usually a lot clearer to me." She smiled ruefully. "I know you can't fix things for me, Caroline. I know my life is my responsibility, but if you've got a spare miracle lying around that you're not using at the moment...just a small one, mind you...Jack and I could sure use one."

Teri stood in front of the portrait a minute longer, then she moved to the window, pushed the drapes back and looked outside. A storm was brewing. The wind had picked up since dinner. The limbs of the large oak trees that dotted the lawn were bending and swaying, and clouds scudded across a nearly full moon. The air seemed charged with expectancy, and Teri felt goose bumps erupt on her arms.

Beau and the potato chip sisters were in the kitchen, playing cards. Teri was all by herself in the library...but for some reason she didn't feel alone. And suddenly, as she watched an eddy of fallen leaves swirl past the window, a peaceful feeling crept over her. At least she'd be able to say goodbye to Jack calmly, she thought. Maybe that was the miracle she'd asked for....

JACK HAD FINISHED PACKING and was headed for Sam's room for one last look and kiss. Teri might think differently, but it tore him up to leave Sam time after time like this. But Jack didn't think he'd be a good full-time father anyway, so he reasoned that his frequent long absences weren't really harmful to the boy.

The door was open a crack so the hall light could shine in, which comforted Sam on stormy nights like this one. Jack crept quietly to the side of the twin bed with the Power Ranger blanket spread over it. Just enough light filtered into the room for Jack to see, and he gazed down at his sleeping son.

Just as Teri had pointed out last night, Sam looked like an angel. His face was all innocence, with his thick lashes feathered against his sleep-flushed cheeks and his hair a dark tumble against the pillow.

As usual, he was holding tight to Bartholomew. Seeing the stuffed bear brought to Jack's mind Teri's preposterous story about conversing with its original owner, little Samuel Tremain. He wondered how she could believe that any of what she'd described as happening during her NDE could possibly be true. She wasn't dealing with reality, and when she inevitably came to realize that, she might end up as cynical as he was. He wouldn't wish that on anybody.

Jack stooped and gave Sam one last kiss on the forehead and brushed his silky hair off his brow. Then he turned and left the room without looking back.

"I'll be back for the wedding, Dad," Jack said. "Somehow I'll schedule around it. I wouldn't miss being your best man for anything."

"That's good to hear, son," Beau answered, but Teri could tell by the sad look in his eyes that Beau wished Jack would skip this assignment and take the next month off. It was the only way to be certain he'd be there for the wedding.

"You take care of the old coot," Jack said to Ginger, bending forward to kiss her on the cheek.

"You don't have to worry about that, Jack," Ginger replied, looking lovingly at Beau. "I'm going to spend the rest of my life taking care of this old coot."

"I'll see you at the wedding, Jack," Viv said, stepping toward Jack to surprise him with a quick hug. "Now you be careful," she finished bracingly. "I'm going inside to get out of this cold wind!'' Then she did exactly that, pulling Ginger along with her.

Since there was nothing left to say, Beau and Jack embraced and mumbled their farewells, then Beau abruptly turned and went inside, too, leaving Teri and Jack alone together on the porch.

Terry had wrapped her arms around herself, shivering from the cold and the shock of actually having to say goodbye to the only man she'd ever loved. ''You made us all come out here to say goodbye so it wouldn't drag on too long, didn't you?''

''You'd better get inside, too, Teri,'' Jack murmured.

''Not till I get my kiss,'' she said playfully, though tears were stinging her eyelids.

Jack hesitated for only a second, then he pulled her into his arms and kissed her. He may have meant the kiss to be short and sweet, only a gesture, promising nothing. But Teri's eagerness and desire made that kind of moderation impossible. She wrapped her arms around his neck and pressed her body against his until he couldn't help but feel every curve.

He responded to her ardency with a kiss as thorough, as luxurious, as thrilling, as full of longing as Teri could ever hope for. But then it ended and he pulled away.

''How's your heart, Teri?'' he asked her.

''It hurts,'' she answered. When she could see her own pain reflected in his eyes, she added, ''If you mean how's my pulse . . . it's fine.''

He nodded. ''That's good. Promise me you'll take care of yourself, okay?''

''I promise. Believe me, Jack, I learned my lesson.''

He nodded again, seemingly satisfied.

"But who's going to take my pulse, Jack?" she teased. "I don't want just anybody doing it, you know."

Jack smiled wanly. "You'll find a good man with a watch," he said in a bleak, flat tone. "Goodbye, Teri." Then he grabbed his suitcases and hastened down the steps, loaded up his Ford Explorer and drove away.

Teri stood on the porch watching the taillights disappear around the curve of the drive, then she slowly turned and went inside.

JACK WAS RELIEVED when he finally parked the car at the airport. Now all he had to do was return the keys to the car-rental agency, check his luggage and find his boarding gate. He planned to read up on the political situation he was covering while he was in the air over the Atlantic, and hopefully, he'd be able to block out the feelings of loss that were eating at him like a cancer.

The drive in from Oak Meadows had been hell. His logical, practical side told him that leaving was the best thing he could have done for everyone concerned, including himself. His heart told him to go back....

During this past visit, Oak Meadows had never seemed more like home. Sam was a delight to be with, so full of energy and laughter...and questions! No longer a toddler, he'd turned out to be a bright, inquisitive child. Jack was going to miss him more than ever during this trip.

His dad was going to be okay because he had Ginger, but it sobered Jack to think about how lonely his father had been before the arrival of the potato chip sisters and how oblivious Jack had been to the problem.

Then there was Teri.... There were no words to describe how he felt about her. He loved her. If anyone could make him throw caution to the wind and take a stab at a commitment again, it was Teri…at least the Teri he knew since her supposed NDE. If he could believe— even just a little bit—in miracles, if he could dare to hang his happiness on the hope that Teri wouldn't return to her old ways and risk making herself sick, he'd marry her in a minute. But he didn't believe in miracles.

Jack wearily stepped out of the car and went to unload his bags from the back seat. He opened the door and reached inside… then his hand froze. There on the seat, next to the luggage, was Sam's bear, Bartholomew!

"How the hell did you get here?" he mumbled out loud, picking up the bear and staring at it incredulously. "When I left Sam's room, he had you in a headlock."

Jack stood up, held the bear in both hands and gazed at it in a state of shock for several minutes, his mind racing to make sense of things. Finally, a man passing by looked at him strangely and Jack decided to do his thinking inside the car.

Back in the driver's seat, Jack held on to the bear and puzzled over how it had gotten in his car. He didn't remember seeing it there when he loaded the luggage, but he'd been pretty upset after having just said goodbye to Teri, so maybe he just hadn't noticed it. But how could he *not* have noticed it?

And who would have put it in there? Sam was sound asleep just shortly before Jack left the house, so it couldn't have been him. And Sam certainly had no motivation to send his bear to Europe with his dad. On the contrary, it was the last thing he'd do with his most precious possession and best friend.

Jack couldn't believe Teri or his dad, or even the eccentric potato chip sisters, would stoop to a trick that might end up hurting a child. So that ruled out their placing the bear in his car in the hopes that he'd turn around and come back. Besides, all they'd have accomplished would be to make him miss his flight and delay his trip by a few hours. Not one of them was that calculating, that naive, or that cruel.

So, how the hell . . . ?

Jack glared at the bear as if willing it to fess up and reveal its secret for getting around on its own. But the button eyes only stared back, revealing nothing. It smelled as strongly as ever of mothballs and cedar, making Jack wonder how he'd overlooked the odor entirely during that long drive to the airport.

The whole thing was a mystery. Or was it a miracle?

*Careful, Jack. Don't get carried away,* he cautioned himself. *There has got to be a logical explanation!* But try as he might, Jack couldn't come up with one. And sitting in the airport all night wasn't going to help, he finally realized. Besides, Sam could wake up any minute and have a fit when he discovered Bartholomew was missing. It was storming in earnest now; Jack could see the sheets of rain falling just outside the covered parking lot. There was plenty of thunder and lightning, too. It was just the sort of night a four-year-old boy would want his best friend around for company.

Jack started the engine. He'd made a decision, and it wasn't nearly as hard as he thought it would be. It was simple, really. His family was more important than his work.

As he pulled back out of the parking spot and headed for the exit, Jack felt a surge of freedom. He felt energized, reborn! Suddenly, everything fell into place. He was going home and the very idea filled him with joy.

By the time Jack hit the freeway, he was having a very difficult time keeping the gas pedal off the floor. Speeding was tempting but stupid, so he tried very hard to control his eagerness to hot-rod it back to Oak Meadows. Besides, the hour's drive was a good opportunity for him to think through what was happening to him.

What *was* happening to him? Jack wondered. A stuffed bear mysteriously shows up in his car and suddenly he's thinking that all things are possible.

Being a full-time dad was possible.

Being a husband again was possible.

Taking the risk of loving someone, even if they might change—or worse, die—was possible.

But what risk was he taking that everyone else wasn't taking day after day? Life was a gamble. Everyone was living on the edge, but only a few people really knew that and lived their lives accordingly... as if each day could be their last. It might be exhausting living that way, but it would definitely be exhilarating. Hadn't the past few days been exhilarating? And that's how he wanted to live the rest of his life.

Jack smiled as he drove the rural highway, each mile bringing him closer and closer to everything and everyone he loved. He felt like laughing. He felt a little bit crazy. And he was as happy as a clam.

All this because of a stuffed bear.

It *was* a miracle.


TERI WAS HUDDLED on the overstuffed chair in the library under an afghan. She was trying to read a book she'd randomly picked from the shelf, the classic Thomas Hardy novel, *Tess of the D'Urbervilles*. Viv was knitting and Ginger and Beau were talking quietly together as they cuddled on the sofa. Outside, the storm raged on.

"That's not a very cheerful novel," Viv commented as Teri turned another page and glanced restlessly toward the window.

"It isn't?" Teri said disinterestedly. "I read it once, years ago. But I don't remember it."

"Did you see the movie version? It was called, simply, *Tess*. It was beautifully done, but so sad. She was, er, hanged at the end. Wouldn't you rather read something uplifting, dear?" Viv suggested tactfully.

"Have you got something in mind?" Teri asked, willing to do anything to divert her mind from the fact that the house seemed empty without Jack.

Viv set down her knitting and moved to the bookshelf. "Well, what about—" she began, but was interrupted by the library door slowly creaking open and Sam standing there in his "feety" pajamas looking half-asleep and lost.

"Gran'pa?" he called, rubbing his eyes.

"What is it, Sam?" Beau asked, rising to his feet.

"Bartholomew's gone!" he exclaimed. "The thunder woke me up, and when I looked for Bartholomew, I couldn't see 'im anywhere! I looked under the bed and ever'thin', but someone musta stole him, 'cause I can't find 'im!"

"It's okay, Sam," Beau said reassuringly. "I'm sure he's in your room somewhere. We'll go up and look together."

"I can go, too," Teri volunteered, smiling at Sam. "With three of us looking, Bartholomew's bound to show up. He's probably just hiding somewhere to tease you, Sam."

Sam managed a weak smile and Teri swooped him up and carried him into the hall with Beau right behind. They were at the bottom of the stairs about to head up, when they heard a pounding on the front door.

"Hell's bells," Beau muttered, surprised by the sudden noise. "Who could that be?"

Still holding Sam, Teri turned and watched and waited. Her heart was doing a funny little flip-flop, as if it already knew who was standing just outside. She held her breath, hoping against hope that her heart was right.

The door opened and a tall, dark man in a trench coat stumbled into the room, dripping water all over the place. It was Jack. And the scene was uncannily like the stormy night four days ago when he first showed up at Oak Meadows after his trip. Only this time, Teri wasn't going to repeat her journey toward the light.

"Jack!" Beau exclaimed. "Son, what are you doing here? Are the roads washed out?"

Teri was too stunned and happy to say anything. She was content just to feast her eyes on a beloved face she'd been sure she wouldn't see again for months, maybe even years. Sam was too sleepy and disoriented to even register what was going on. Teri could only continue to stare.

Jack stared back, the grin on his face about a mile wide.

"Jack, any particular reason you came back?" Teri finally asked, emboldened by the dazzlingly happy smile on his handsome mug.

He reached inside his coat and pulled out Bartholomew. "I didn't think Sam would be able to sleep through this storm without his buddy, Bart," he said. "And I guess I was right."

Sam immediately perked up. "Bartholomew!" he exclaimed, reaching for the stuffed bear. "So that's where you've been, hiding in Daddy's coat!"

Jack chuckled. "No, actually he's been hiding in Daddy's car." He gave the bear to Sam, then kissed him on the head and tousled his hair. Sam smiled sleepily.

"The bear was in your car?" Beau repeated, looking surprised. "How did it get there?"

"That's what I'd like to know," Jack said, quirking an eyebrow at Teri.

"Don't look at me," Teri quickly disclaimed with a nervous laugh. "I didn't do it!"

"I know you didn't do it," Jack admitted, shrugging out of his coat. "Trouble is, I can't figure out who did."

Teri watched him hang his coat on the coat tree, her eyes wide with wonder. "Are you staying?"

Jack crossed his arms in a nonchalant pose. "Yeah, for a while."

Beau was looking at Jack with a puzzled expression. Teri couldn't blame him. Jack seemed like a totally different person from the sober, unhappy man who'd left the house a little over two hours ago. "How long is a while, Jack?" he asked.

Jack glanced at his watch. "Oh, say…about a month. Long enough to help with the wedding and be your best man, Dad."

Beau's eyes brightened like stars and he smiled happily. "That's great, Jack. Just great!"

"A month!" Teri repeated excitedly. "But what about your assignment?"

"I'm calling my agent tonight to tell her I'm not ready for another long-term assignment. I'm taking some time off. Like you, Teri, I've needed a vacation for a long time. And when I'm ready to go back to work, I'm going to arrange it so my overseas assignments are few and far between." Jack walked over to Teri and gently lifted Sam out of her arms, snuggling the sleepy child and his bear against his chest. "It's time I stuck a little closer to home." Then he gave Teri a look that made her heart melt.

She couldn't believe what was happening. It seemed that Jack had suddenly realized what he'd been missing out on. And all because of... *Bartholomew?*

Teri had been so excited and intrigued by Jack's sudden reappearance and turnabout in attitude, she just now began to consider the mystery of how Sam's bear got in Jack's car. She couldn't imagine anyone in the household doing such a thing.

Then a light went on in Teri's brain, and she understood. There was no other explanation. She'd asked for a miracle and she'd gotten one. This was all Caroline's doing!

"Why don't you two take Sam on up to bed?" Beau suggested, nudging them toward the stairs. "If Ginger and Viv hear you out here, they'll be all over you like ticks on a dog. If you want some time alone together—" he gave Jack a significant look "—you'd better put the boy down, then freshen up... or whatever... before joining us for hot chocolate later." Beau leaned close to Jack and whispered, "The hot chocolate is optional, of course, if you find something else you'd rather do."

Teri and Jack couldn't misunderstand Beau's hints, and they didn't want to. They did exactly as he suggested, putting Sam to bed, watching him fall back to sleep the instant his head hit the pillow, then hurrying down the hall to Jack's bedroom.

Once behind the closed door, it took them exactly two seconds to find themselves in each other's arms. They kissed hungrily and happily.

After several minutes of bliss, Teri pulled back, laughing. "What happened, Jack? What's changed?"

"Let's just say *I've* changed," Jack said. "Or, at least, I'm trying to. I believe in miracles now, Teri, and that opens up all kinds of possibilities."

She looped her hands behind Jack's neck and smiled coyly. "Do you believe I really had an NDE?"

Jack tenderly studied her face and traced the curve of her cheek with his finger. "I don't know what happened to you that night, Teri. But I do know it changed your life—and mine—forever. The past few days with you have been wonderful. That first night when I lectured you about enjoying the small things and not making work your life, I'd been ignoring my own family for months at a time." He sighed. "It was just like you said. I *was* afraid. Afraid of loving someone, then losing them or failing them somehow. I'm a helluva good photojournalist, but wondering if I can cut it as a full-time father still gives me hives," he confessed ruefully.

"You're a wonderful father," Teri assured him. "And being around Sam all the time will only sharpen your skills."

He pulled her close and lightly nipped her ear, making a pleasant chill race down her spine. "Do you think I'd be a good husband?" he whispered.

Teri's eyes filled with happy tears as her heart swelled with love. "I think you'd be an excellent husband, as long as you married the right woman."

He pulled back and looked at her, his eyes glinting mischievously. "And the right woman is . . . ?"

"Yours truly, Teri the Terror...the new and improved model, of course."

Jack laughed. "Is that a yes?"

"As long as you don't think I'm too old to wear white for the wedding," she teased, "it's a definite yes."

As Jack pulled her to him and kissed her, Teri whispered in her heart, *Thanks for the miracle, Caroline.*

And a sweet voice with a Southern drawl whispered back, *Life is good, my dear. And Heaven can wait.*

THREE WEEKS LATER, Teri watched and smiled and sniffled from the sidelines as Ginger and Beau were married at Oak Meadows. Disregarding her sister's frequently repeated opinion, the bride wore white...and so did the groom. Teri couldn't remember witnessing a happier ceremony or watching a more radiant couple take their vows.

The house was full of Viv and Ginger's relatives on this joyous occasion, and Teri had never seen Sam so excited to be around so many of Aunty Viv's grandchildren from Idaho. He was one happy camper.

A month later, at Christmas, Teri took her own walk down the aisle, or rather down the stairs at Oak Meadows and into the drawing room where she'd first danced with Jack to the tune of "Love Me Tender."

For a few weeks before the wedding, Teri had gone back to Sugarbaker Realtors to tie up loose ends. She wasn't sorry to leave her career behind because she was already planning another one. She now worked at home, venting her creative urges by writing a motivational book entitled, *Heaven on Earth.* To her shock and delight, the book climbed to the top of the *New York Times* bestseller list after just two weeks in print.

Jack had his own share of success, too, even though he limited his work assignments to the home front. Teri was filled with pride when he received national recognition for his photographs of the rural South.

Nine months after they were married, Teri gave birth to a baby girl. She and Jack had agreed on the name months before; they called their daughter Joy.

*HARLEQUIN®*

**A M E R I C A N ◆ R O M A N C E®**

You asked for it...You got it! More MEN!

**MORE THAN MEN**

We're thrilled to bring you another special edition of the
popular MORE THAN MEN series.

Like those who have come before him, John Jarvis is
more than tall, dark and handsome. All of those men have
extraordinary powers that make them "more than men."
But whether they are able to grant you three wishes, or
live forever, make no mistake—their greatest, most
extraordinary power is of seduction.

So make a date with John Jarvis in...

> **#656 RED-HOT RANCHMAN**
> **by Victoria Pade**
> **November 1996**

## Maybe This Time...

Maybe this time...they'll get what they really wanted all those years ago. Whether it's the man who got away, a baby, or a new lease on life, these four women will get a second chance at a once-in-a-lifetime opportunity!

Four top-selling authors have come together to make you believe that in the world of American Romance anything is possible:

**#642 ONE HUSBAND TOO MANY**
Jacqueline Diamond
August

**#646 WHEN A MAN LOVES A WOMAN**
Bonnie K. Winn
September

**#650 HEAVEN CAN WAIT**
Emily Dalton
October

**#654 THE COMEBACK MOM**
Muriel Jensen
November

Look us up on-line at: http://www.romance.net

MTTG

# Merry Christmas, Baby!

A romantic collection filled with the magic of Christmas and the joy of children.

SUSAN WIGGS, Karen Young and Bobby Hutchinson bring you Christmas wishes, weddings and romance, in a charming trio of stories that will warm up your holiday season.

*MERRY CHRISTMAS, BABY!* also contains Harlequin's special gift to you—a set of FREE GIFT TAGS included in every book.

Brighten up your holiday season with *MERRY CHRISTMAS, BABY!*

Available in November at your favorite retail store.

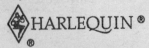

HARLEQUIN ®

MCB

# REBECCA

## 43 LIGHT STREET

# YORK

## FACE TO FACE

*Bestselling author Rebecca York returns to "43 Light Street"*
*for an original story of past secrets, deadly deceptions—and*
*the most intimate betrayal.*

She woke in a hospital—with amnesia…and with child.
According to her rescuer, whose striking face is the last
image she remembers, she's Justine Hollingsworth. But
nothing about her life seems to fit, except for the baby
inside her and Mike Lancer's arms around her. Consumed
by forbidden passion and racked by nameless fear, she
must discover if she is Justine…or the victim of some mind
game. Her life—and her unborn child's—depends on it….

Don't miss *Face To Face*—Available in October, wherever
Harlequin books are sold.

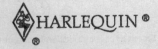

HARLEQUIN ®

43FTF

# 1997
## Reader's Engagement Book
## A calendar of important dates
## and anniversaries for readers to use!

Informative and entertaining—with notable
dates and trivia highlighted throughout the year.

Handy, convenient, pocketbook size to help you
keep track of your own personal important dates.

Added bonus—contains $5.00 worth of coupons
for upcoming Harlequin and Silhouette books.
This calendar more than pays for itself!

Available beginning in November at
your favorite retail outlet.

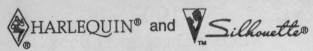

**HARLEQUIN®** and **Silhouette®**

## are proud to present...

### HERE COME THE GROOMS™

Four marriage-minded stories written by top Harlequin and Silhouette authors!

Next month, you'll find:

| | |
|---|---|
| *The Bridal Price* | by Barbara Boswell |
| *Annie in the Morning* | by Curtiss Ann Matlock |
| *September Morning* | by Diana Palmer |
| *Outback Nights* | by Emilie Richards |

**ADDED BONUS!** In every edition of *Here Come the Grooms* you'll find $5.00 worth of coupons good for Harlequin and Silhouette products.

On sale at your favorite Harlequin and Silhouette retail outlet.

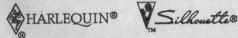 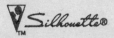

HCTG1096